FISHER OF MEN

PHOEBE ALEXANDER

*To all my lifestyle friends: May the fishing always be good in
your neck of the sea!*

PROLOGUE

The softness of the bed cushioned Leah's body as the shock of him throwing her down absorbed into the sheets. Her lungs struggled to fill with air under his weight when he took both of her wrists and pinned them above her head, nestling them in the silky amber-colored waves that fanned around her face.

He seemed infinitely pleased by her gasping and breathy moans. When a smile spread across his lips and the trademark dimples popped out under his scruffy stubble, she stropped thrashing. *He's enjoying this a little too much.*

"Why are you doing this to me?" Her green eyes were wide and meek as she searched his face for the truth.

"Because I want you to stop playing the innocent good girl, Leah," Cap demanded. "You and I both know there is a vixen in there lurking beneath that prim and proper exterior you show the world. That's the woman I want."

She felt exposed, though she was still clothed. *He hasn't actually figured out how to strip me down using just his mind yet. "Yet" being the operative word, of course.*

She fired back the first thing that came to mind: "What

makes you so sure that's who I am? Maybe I really am a good Christian girl."

"Because I feel the way your body responds when I kiss you...when I touch you. I smell your desire, Leah. You can't hide it."

He propped himself up on his elbows, freeing her wrists and diminishing the crushing weight against her breasts. He lowered his head so his breath fell against her neck while his teeth lightly grazed the skin over her collarbone.

Her body involuntarily stiffened, her pelvis shifting to meet his squarely. *Ugh. I guess he has a point.*

Her body raised its white flag of surrender as he yanked her camisole down with one finger, exposing two creamy mounds of flesh jutting up from an ivory lace bra. He decorated the space between her breasts with soft, wet kisses.

"God doesn't hate sex, you know." He peered down at her again from his perched elbows, his lips glistening from the artwork they'd created on her cleavage. "He invented sex, after all. He made us to feel pleasure. It's not a sin."

She let his words spiral through her mind. She'd always believed there was virtue in abstinence, in self-control and denying her desires. She'd always pitted Good Girl Leah against Bad Girl Leah, rewarding herself when good triumphed.

Cap's claim challenged every notion she had of sex. All the ambivalence, the confusion, the conflicting feelings she'd been struggling with since she met him all came down to this crux. *What if he's right? What if my Good Girl and Bad Girl selves can peacefully coexist?*

ONE

The music pulsated throughout her body. The sanctuary was dark, but the stage was awash in multi-colored lights cast from rigs on the ceiling. It was the kind of lighting used at rock concerts: spiraling teals and purples intermittently spiked with yellow-green dots. The lights shifted like a kaleidoscope turning in front of her eyes.

I can't believe I'm in church, she kept thinking. It seemed to be the only thought she could grab on to. Everything else in her mind was swirling wildly, moving too erratically to process, just like the crazy dancing lights.

The song ended, and the worship leader began a prayer. Leah bowed her head instinctively, but she was distracted, imagining what her mother would say about this display. Her parents were eager for her to find a church home in her new town.

The band segued into the next song with a driving beat and fast tempo. Leah's hips begin to sway to the rhythm before she could think to stop them. She felt the music in her soul, down deep where the Holy Spirit resided within her.

•••

Leah's weeks consisted of sixty-plus hours at The Pearl, the upscale resort where she worked. She started out as the front desk night manager, fresh from finishing her undergrad in Hotel Administration at Cornell, but only a year later, she snagged the assistant general manager position.

Her boss had retooled the job description and gave it a swanky new dual-purpose but ridiculous title: *Guest Experience Strategist and Staff Liaison Specialist.* She often summarized: "I make sure everyone is happy: guests and employees."

Her parents were still adjusting to the idea of their daughter working in the hospitality industry. Since her birth, they'd not foreseen any other future for Leah, the oldest of three, aside from being shipped off to Bible college and settling down with an aspiring minister, much like Mrs. Miller had done. Naturally, her parents had found the perfect way of doing things. Why wouldn't their daughter want to follow in their footsteps?

But Leah Miller was the small-town girl who ventures far from home and makes a name for herself in the big city. *Just another cliché,* she thought as she slid her conservative church-going pumps off and contemplated what to do with her one day off. She didn't feel especially motivated as she propped her feet up on her rattan ottoman. All she wanted to do was replay the events of the previous night when she'd been called into work unexpectedly...

She was the Go-To Girl at The Pearl, the manager who

would cheerfully spring into action whenever called to duty. One of the resort's bartenders was out taking care of her sick toddler, a bartender needed to work a large private party that had been booked months in advance.

"It's off-season in a resort town," her boss had reminded her. "We've got to impress this group so they'll continue to book here. We could have a lucrative long-term deal on our hands if they like it here!" His voice was animated and full of urgency.

"What kind of group is it?" Leah wondered what type of organization wanted to party in a ghost town. During the late fall and winter months when it was too cold for warm-weather beach activities, Ocean City hibernated.

Her boss, Barry Sampson, checked the record on his computer. "I'm not really sure. It just says Casey's Group. They reserved the ballroom, and we don't book that for less than a hundred guests. No catering contract, but they requested the full bar menu. It's going to be a busy night, too busy to rely on only two bartenders." She was sure dollar signs were dancing in front of his eyes.

"Okay." Leah had smiled into the phone, always eager to please her boss. "I guess I'll brush up on my bartending knowledge this afternoon then."

His audible sigh of relief whistled through the phone. "Atta girl!"

"It's no problem." *Besides, it's not like there's anything else going on in Ocean City in the middle of November. Otherwise, I'd be home alone surfing Netflix and stuffing my face with junk food.*

S he had climbed the steps to the back entrance of The Pearl, entering the administrative offices. There was a pile of mail and notes on her desk right in the center. Leah didn't spend a lot of time in her office. She was a hands-on manager, always making the rounds to the front desk, to housekeeping, to the kitchen, then out to the pool and then back through the lobby to mingle with the guests. She took her responsibility to keep everyone happy *very* seriously.

No time to look at that pile now. She glanced at her watch. It was 6 PM and the party started at 7. She needed to get over to the ballroom and see how the set-up was coming along.

She greeted the other two bartenders with a little wave. "Trish called off tonight," she explained. "So I guess you're stuck with me. I couldn't find anyone else to come in."

"It's all good." Steve, the senior bartender, was a tall, gaunt man with dark skin and kind eyes. "We'll have you doing moves from *Cocktail* before the end of the night!" he predicted, the words sliding smoothly out of his wide, toothy grin.

The other bartender, Gina, was a short, slight woman with a tan complexion and thin lips. Leah suspected she was around fifty years of age, though she was relatively new to bartending.

"Oh, look at her, staring at you like you've got two heads!" Gina shook her head at her colleague. "She's too young to remember that movie!" Her dyed-auburn hair with the slightest wisps of gray peeking out around her temples was whisked back into a severe bun.

Steve chuckled his deep, silky laugh. "Don't mind her," he told Leah, cocking his head toward his fellow bartender. "She always likes to remind everyone how old she is. I think it's kinda amusing, especially since I'm even older." He winked.

Leah's eyes grew wide. She would have never guessed Steve was older than Gina, not in a million years. She tied on a blue apron emblazoned with The Pearl's logo, pushed the double doors open into the back of the ballroom, and peeked inside.

The room looked festive and elegant. Ornate brass chandeliers hung from the vaulted ceiling with their pearly white glass lamps, the bulbs dimmed for ambiance. Twenty white tables were spread with fresh white linen tablecloths, anchored with round mirror tiles that held long white candles in gleaming silver candlesticks. Between each pair of candles were simple, tasteful floral centerpieces featuring white roses, blue carnations and greenery with little sprigs of faux pearls jutting out like baby's breath.

Leah scanned the perimeter of the room. Two sets of dark wooden doors on the side connected to the rest of the hotel, and on the short sides hung floor-to-ceiling navy blue velvet curtains. The bar area was near the entrance to the kitchen. Directly across the room, the D.J. would set up in front of the parquet dance floor that would soon pulsate with multi-colored lights and thumping music.

Leah imagined what the elegantly appointed room would look like in another hour, filled with at least a hundred people, *perhaps ladies in cocktail dresses and men in suits?* She wasn't sure what to expect from Casey's Group, but by quickly perusing the contract, she gathered it was a local charity organization.

The image bubble she'd created burst as the double doors from the hallway pushed open and a middle-aged woman with immaculately coiffed copper-colored hair and long red manicured fingernails sashayed across the paisley carpet on four-inch stiletto heels. She was a woman of girth, with broad shoulders and wide hips, and she appeared to be on a mission.

Captivating Leah with her look of fierce determination, she began addressing her long before she got within ten feet. "The night manager at the front desk told me his supervisor was bartending tonight? A Ms. Miller, I believe? Would you mind getting her for me?"

Leah smiled. She was used to guests underestimating her rank and mistaking her for a local college student at a weekend job.

"I'm Leah Miller, Guest Experience Strategist. I'm more than happy to assist you with whatever you need to make your stay at The Pearl extraordinary." It was her well-rehearsed, standard introduction, accompanied by her outstretched hand.

The copper-haired lady didn't seem taken aback, launching into a lengthy and spirited complaint involving the front desk staff not allowing early check-ins or late check-outs for her guests, then morphing into something about an eight-foot table that was supposed to be set up in the hallway, and finally a rant about the drink special.

Leah only understood about half of what the woman spouted, but the pleasant smile affixed to her face did not waver. "I'm sorry, I think I missed your name?" She extended her hand toward the lady, making a post-tirade attempt at cordiality.

"I'm so sorry." The lady sighed, grasping Leah's hand firmly. "I guess I'm a little stressed. This is our first time booking an event here, and you have different protocols than the last place we used. I'm Casey Fontaine."

"No apologies." Leah smiled warmly. "I will talk to the desk staff about the check-in issue. Now, about that table..."

She turned to one of the waiters who was wheeling a cart of leftover mirror tiles back to the storage closet. "Peter, please get an eight-foot table and tablecloth from storage and... How many chairs do you need, Ms. Fontaine?"

"I think four would do nicely," she replied. Peter was off and running no sooner than the words passed through Ms. Fontaine's lips.

"Let me grab Steve and Gina, our regular bartenders, to clear up the matter about the drink special," Leah offered. "Just a moment, please." Ms. Fontaine nodded graciously as Leah headed off for the kitchen, swiftly reappearing with her staff in tow.

Steve went over the drink specials with Ms. Fontaine, and within a few minutes, the worry lines faded from her face. "Thank you so much," she gushed, grasping Leah's hand firmly in both of hers. Despite her brusque, assertive personality and large stature, Ms. Fontaine's hands were soft and warm. "You've been a huge help, Leah."

"Is there anything else I can do for you?" Leah's face glowed with her guest's compliment. This was the part of her job she loved most: seeing her guests content and satisfied after receiving service beyond their expectations.

"I'm so glad you'll be behind the bar tonight. I will definitely come and find you if there are any other issues," Ms. Fontaine replied.

"Yes, please do!" Leah watched Ms. Fontaine and a few of her entourage exit the ballroom to the hallway.

Within the hour, guests began to arrive. Most entered the ballroom concealed in coats or wraps, and Leah was shocked to see most of the ladies were rather scantily clad underneath. Some wore corset tops with short black skirts, fishnets and towering high heels. Others donned curve-hugging low-cut dresses, out of which ample cleavage spilled. The men were more conservatively dressed, sporting dress pants and button down shirts or polos.

Leah had spotted a sign next to Casey's table in the hallway announcing the "Charity of the Month." They were collecting cans and nonperishable items for a local food bank, and the large gift-wrapped box was overflowing by the time the last of the guests arrived. But Leah had no clue what the provocative attire had to do with the food bank collection.

She was baffled as she scanned the dance floor. One gentleman was weaving his way across the dance floor, smacking and squeezing the backsides of different women, who didn't seem to protest in the slightest. And several women were kissing and groping each other as they danced.

What the heck kind of party is this?

She hustled back to the bar, where a trio consisting of two men and a woman approached. The forty-something-year-old woman was petite with long, curly dark hair brushing her exposed shoulders. She wore a tight-laced bustier that forced her ample bosom to strain against the smooth black leather. Her arms were interlocked with the two men on each side of her, one of whom was just a little taller than her with dark hair and a mustache.

The other man broke free from her clutch to pay for the drinks. He was tall, 6'2" or 6'3", with tousled, sun-kissed sandy-blond hair graying at the temples and matching silvery facial scruff outlining his full lips and chiseled jawline. He handed Leah a twenty-dollar bill for the eleven-dollar check and grinned enough to show a dimple through his short beard.

"Keep the change." He winked, his blue eyes revealing both a buzz and a hint of mischievousness.

"Thanks." Leah returned his smile, quickly making

change and stuffing it into the tip jar. She planned to let Steve and Gina split the contents at the end of the night.

"You're not really a bartender, are you?" he guessed, his eyes locking onto hers.

The dark-haired couple for whom he'd bought the drinks had already made their way back to the throng of guests congregating near the D.J.'s table. She watched the woman grind her pelvis against the backside of another woman on the dance floor until the scruffy man at the bar's piercing ocean-blue gaze drew her back into his realm.

Charisma emanated from him, a halo of good-natured warmth and acceptance. People gravitated toward men like him, shared their deepest secrets with them. Leah had felt the pull of this stock character's magnetic charm before. She knew what kind of power a man like that could have over women, even as a naïve twenty-seven-year-old with only a small catalog of romantic experience.

"Actually, no, I'm not." Her voice was pleasant enough, but she was struggling to stay professional. "I had to fill in tonight for a bartender who called out. I'm the Guest Experience Strategist."

"You don't say." When he smirked, his dimples became even more evident. "I, too, like to think of myself as a Guest Experience Strategist!" He flashed another wink as his lips spread into a grin, parting wide enough to show his pearly whites.

Leah suppressed a gasp as she scrambled for a response to his not-so-subtle innuendo. *Just who does this guy think he is, anyway?*

Testosterone oozed from his pores. *I'm sure liquid courage has something to do with his boldness.*

She had dealt with plenty of inebriated hotel guests in

her short career. The best strategy was to smile and nod, unless hotel rules were being violated, of course.

He straightened to his full height and extended his hand. "I'm Captain Chris Sheldon," he offered smoothly.

"Military?" Leah asked, her eyes bright, ignoring his outstretched palm. There was an Air Force base in Dover and a Navy base on the Eastern Shore of Virginia, so it wasn't unusual to have officers as guests at The Pearl.

He chuckled, flashing the dimples again. "No, no, I'm a charter fishing captain. My friends call me 'Cap.'" He pumped his arm up and down once as if to remind her he was waiting to make contact with her.

When she finally accepted his handshake, the warmth of his skin wrapped around her and sank into her pores. "It's nice to meet you, Captain Sheldon."

"The pleasure is all mine..." He paused with an expectant grin, waiting for her to reciprocate by sharing her name.

"Oh, sorry, I'm Leah, Leah Miller," she managed awkwardly.

"Leah," he repeated, his hand still wrapped around hers.

She wondered if he was ever going to let her hand go. Had someone forgotten to turn down the heat in the ballroom, or were her cheeks flushing from embarrassment? *Either way, this is almost painful!* She waited for him to loosen his grip on her, hoping it would cool her down.

"I bet you haven't ever bartended a party like this before." When he let her hand slowly slip from his, the warmth his touch had generated evaporated from her skin.

"I've never bartended at all," she admitted. "Not a party 'like this' or otherwise." *What in the world did he mean by that?* She tried to conceal her curiosity behind the forced business-like smile plastered to her face.

He laughed and stepped another foot closer to her, close enough that his elbow could rest on the bar while he leaned toward her. *Why isn't anyone else coming up for a drink?* she panicked, glancing around at the seemingly happy crowd and then toward the kitchen door to see if either Steve or Gina was returning from break.

"You don't know what kind of party this is, then?" he wagered, his eyes glued back on hers.

She was beginning to feel flustered and in need of rescue. She hadn't planned on having any in-depth conversations with party guests unless they were about how the hotel could make their stay more enjoyable. This was beyond the scope of her job. *It's none of my business what kind of party this is, even if the guests do seem a little different than expected.* She let the plastered smile hold her lips in place as she very slowly shook her head and raised her eyebrows.

Captain Sheldon laughed again. "It's a swinger party, Leah. We're swingers."

TWO

That Sunday afternoon the details of the prior night's party still buzzed in her head, and Leah was finding it difficult to relax on her day off. She heard Captain Sheldon's voice echoing through her mind as she zoomed through all the cable channels, unable to land on any program compelling enough to pull her attention away from her thoughts.

Her observations about Casey's Group immediately made sense to her after his admission. Everything clicked: the provocative attire, the kissing and groping, the exchanging of partners on the dance floor. But still: swingers? It seemed like a mythical construct to her, like Santa Claus or Bigfoot.

To each their own, I suppose.

The guests looked happy, and Casey Fontaine was beyond pleased with the outcome of the event. The Pearl had done a great deal of business that night. The bartenders poured drinks well past midnight, and nearly all the rooms had been booked. Leah's boss would be pleased, and that was what mattered most.

So that's that. I'm going to chalk it up as a win!

After that final judgment, she took her puppy, Glory, for a walk and filled her mind with thoughts of her family, the morning church service and its over-the-top spectacle, and all the files on her desk eagerly awaiting her return to work. Despite her careful attention to all of those important matters, that Cap character from the party kept triggering little flashbacks. Those ocean-blue eyes and dimples were simply unforgettable.

●◦●

L eah worked so much over the weekend, she barely felt like she'd had a weekend at all. It started slowly enough, but then suddenly it was Sunday night, which concluded with a brisk stroll around the complex as the sun set in crimson majesty over the still, purple waters of the bay.

Now bright Monday morning sunshine soaked into her bones as she made her way across the lobby toward the elevator that would take her up to her boss's second-floor office. Getting called into the boss's office used to fill Leah with a sense of dread, but Barry Sampson never had anything but words of praise for his star manager.

She felt lucky to have what most would consider a "cool" boss. He was level-headed, personable, under-standing and always took the time to tell her she was doing a great job. He was a bit of a jokester, though, and constantly admonishing Leah to lighten up.

Her green eyes wide and bright, she took a seat in the chair on the other side of the desk. "You wanted to see me?"

"I got an email from Casey Fontaine this morning raving about the outstanding service she received at her group's private party on Saturday night. She mentioned you personally. And she was so thrilled that she decided to book the ballroom for their group's Christmas party next month! She asked if she could come in and meet with you tomorrow to go over the details. Apparently, she was pretty impressed with you, Miss Miller!" Barry grinned broadly, his ruddy cheeks glowing and his gray eyes creased with happiness.

"Oh, I'm so glad she was pleased," Leah replied evenly.

She had been contemplating whether she should mention the nature of Casey's Group to Barry. *He'd probably think it's funny, not to mention inconsequential. So I guess I shouldn't let the cat out of the bag unless there's a problem.*

From what she'd seen on Saturday night, Casey's Group was relatively easy to manage, if not a touch on the exuberant side. Then again, most groups under the influence of alcohol tended toward rowdiness. Other than kissing and groping, Leah hadn't noticed anything problematic.

When the meeting was over, it was already noon. Ordinarily, she walked three blocks back to her apartment to take Glory out for a walk during her lunch break. But the day was postcard perfect, and now that Daylight Savings Time had ended, the sun was setting so early. She didn't want to miss another opportunity to walk along the deserted boardwalk with her eager puppy in tow.

Leah informed her assistant of her plans and proceeded out the back doors of The Pearl where her Jeep was parked far away in the outer echelons of the lot. She drove the three blocks to her apartment complex and ran upstairs to retrieve Glory.

The brown-eyed beagle's tail began thumping against the foyer's tiled floor as soon as she heard her owner's key turn in the lock. Leah commanded her to sit while she pulled the pink leash off the hook near the front door. It was taking the pup every ounce of restraint she could muster to keep her paws on the floor. She gave the furry creature a treat to reward her patience, scooped her up and carried her back down to the Jeep.

She drove down Coastal Highway from 60th street all the way to the inlet. Glory's ears flapped in the wind as she hung her little head out the cracked window on the passenger's side. "I know, girl, it'd be much more fun with the top down. Just wait until the summer! You're gonna love it!"

She had gotten Glory at the end of the summer, and the eight-week-old pup was so little at the time that Leah had was afraid to drive around with the top down for fear she'd blow out.

Glory had blossomed into a healthy and inquisitive four-and-a-half-month-old with enough energy for a whole litter of puppies. Leah hated that she didn't get to take Glory outdoors as much as she'd like. The beagle was relegated to her crate for several hours a day, and never was a dog happier to see her owner than Glory when Leah returned home from work.

She was half-tempted to sneak Glory in the back door of the hotel and keep her in the office, but she was too afraid she'd make a mess or bark and disturb guests, though she was sure Barry would get a kick out of her. He had two basset hounds of his own.

"I'm so glad you have that dog with you now," Leah's mother told her every time they spoke on the phone since Glory's adoption. "I think it's so much safer than you being in your apartment alone or walking all around town all by yourself."

"Geez, Mom, I'm in a tiny little resort town, not the

Bronx," Leah had laughed, looking into Glory's huge brown eyes and wondering how likely it was her little body would spring into protective action should the need arise. *She looks about as menacing as a...as a cute puppy, that's what.*

She fastened the pink leash onto Glory's matching pink rhinestone collar and led the dog out onto the sidewalk. It was eerie to see only a few cars scattered along the streets around the inlet. In the summertime, visitors might drive around for an hour looking for a place to park.

The breeze had picked up and was blowing Glory's ears back, but she headed nevertheless bravely into the strong gust, dragging Leah behind her. It was amazing how much pull sixteen pounds of beagle had, and the closer to the water she got, the stronger the pull became.

As Leah looked both ways to cross the street, despite the lack of traffic, a shop on the corner she'd never noticed before caught her eye. It was a weathered two-story building with dark-stained wood siding and a faded red tin roof. A huge yellow sign with black block lettering announced "Bait and Tackle," and a neon sign in the window blazed blue and green with the words "Charter Fishing."

An image of Captain Chris Sheldon from Saturday night's party instantly flashed behind her eyes. *I'm sure there are lots of charter fishing captains in Ocean City.*

She tried to shake off the question of whether she had stumbled into his natural habitat. Even though Glory was fervently straining toward the beach, Leah crossed the street in the direction of the shop instead, her curiosity pulling her as if she had it on the leash instead of the dog.

The shop was closed—unsurprising since it was November and no one was on the boardwalk. The windows looked dark, but she peered inside, searching for a clue to convince herself this was not Captain Sheldon's shop. She saw nothing that would confirm or deny her suspicion.

Then she stepped around to the side of the building where a wooden staircase ascended to the second story. A metal mailbox clung to the weathered siding with black letters across the face spelling out S-H-E-L-D-O-N.

THREE

After her long lunch outing, Leah holed herself up in her office to tackle the towering stack of paperwork. She'd taken a picture of her little pup attacking a wave and then another of her tiny paw prints in the sand.

I wish I could just stay out here all afternoon. Barry would be disappointed if she didn't take care of the pile of work that awaited her.

She was just about to start a pot of coffee in the staff lounge when her cell phone buzzed on the desk. It was her best friend from college, Aimee, who had finished the hospitality program at Cornell alongside Leah. Aimee had every intention of climbing the corporate ladder in some swanky hotel but had instead gotten married and was now just about ready to pop out her first baby.

Leah leapt for the phone just in case there was some sort of birth news, even though Aimee was still several weeks out from her delivery date.

"Before you even ask, yes, I'm still pregnant!" Aimee made no attempt to disguise her naturally snarky tone.

Leah laughed, envisioning her best friend, small and olive-skinned with a glossy black bob and a perfectly round baby bump. "I know better than to bug you about that!" Her friend had always had a short fuse, perhaps the Italian in her coming out.

Aimee launched into an impassioned rant involving an attempt to assemble the baby's crib, but she and her husband were dismayed to learn that half the hardware was missing. "We had no choice but to trek all the way back to the store and ream out the manager for selling us a crib that had been returned and clearly not checked for all its parts!"

Being trained in the hospitality industry made both women intolerant of poor customer service. Leah could only imagine the earful that the store manager got.

Angry pregnant lady with a degree from Cornell's hospitality program? That is one smart but crazy hormonal bitch! Leah mused.

"So, you got a brand-new crib, right?" Leah guessed.

Her phone glued to her ear, she'd ventured out of her office, down the hallway and out the back doors. She walked around the parking lot and through the beautifully landscaped grounds until she was bayside, soaking up what was left of the day's Vitamin D supply. The sun was sinking toward the horizon, reaching up to catch the golden orb with crimson arms.

"I sure did, as well as a fifty-dollar gift card for our hassle. I threw in that we had to fight traffic and stand in line and that all the stress was giving me contractions!" Aimee bragged.

"That's too funny!" Leah giggled, knowing how gifted her friend was in the dramatic arts. "So I'm still planning to come up to help out for a while after the baby's born."

There was a pause on the other end.

"What?" Leah asked, confused. "I thought we'd agreed about this."

"Leah, it's going to be Christmastime shortly before the baby is born. I don't want you to use your vacation time to come help me. Your parents would be so angry if it prevented you from going home! You should really go see them for Christmas."

"I'm staying here in OC for Christmas," Leah explained. "Coming up to Philly for a few days to help you with the baby isn't the same as journeying across the country to Nebraska. Besides, you're my excuse for not going home!"

"But you haven't been home since June," Aimee argued. "I know your mom has to be freaking out by now. They've never gone this long without seeing you, not even when we were in school!"

Leah hated being told what to do. She had thought a lot about making a trip home for the holidays, but every time she imagined it, she was filled with a sense of dread. She simply did not feel like she belonged in Wahoo, Nebraska, anymore. She had outgrown that place.

The town seemed like a collection of scenes from Norman Rockwell paintings: charming in a saccharine 1950s way. It was so wholesome. it might rot your teeth out.

Since moving to Ocean City, Maryland, her eyes had been opened to things she never knew existed. Like Casey's Group—and after meeting Chris Sheldon and then stalking his place of business, she couldn't seem to get him off her mind.

Sure, Leah had heard of swinging. But to actually meet a swinger...let alone a whole room full of them? For them to exist and be real people? It was beyond her imagination.

And to think, those attending Casey's party looked like

ordinary people. They were articulate, professional, career-minded people, not crazy drug-using hedonists who thought of nothing but sex. It was just one of many misconceptions about people and life that seemed glaringly apparent after spending so much time away from Wahoo. The world wasn't split into the proverbial black-and-white dichotomy of good versus evil like her father preached from the pulpit of Wahoo Christian Church.

"I appreciate your concern, Aimee, but my parents will be just fine without me, and my mom is not freaking out at all. You know my brother Andrew just got engaged, right? She's so over the moon with that news that I've kind of slipped off her radar the past few months. And that's fine with me. I want to settle in here."

Aimee immediately perked up, a tiny gasp of glee slipping through her lips. "You mean find a man and get married?"

Leah laughed. "Maybe. Or perhaps I'll just take over The Pearl and become filthy rich someday!"

She relished the way the ocean breeze blew the layers of her strawberry blonde hair into her face. "You know, I really do love living here. I can't believe I was landlocked in Nebraska for most of my life. I didn't even know what I was missing."

"True," Aimee reasoned, "but you're in a resort town where people are always coming and going. There aren't any men who actually live there full-time to sweep you off your feet. And besides, you're so busy with work, even if there were eligible bachelors, you wouldn't be in the right place to meet them, not the local ones anyway."

Leah sighed. "I know." This problem had not escaped her notice, and she'd contemplated several methods of meeting local men, but at the end of the day, she was so caught up with The Pearl and Glory that she rarely had the energy to venture beyond her comfort zone.

"Case in point," Aimee continued, "what did you do last weekend? I bet you didn't do one thing that put you in a position to meet an interesting, available local man."

"Well..." Leah stalled as she mentally reviewed the past few days. "I bartended for a local charity group's private party on Saturday night. I met a couple of interesting people."

"Interesting how?" Aimee took the bait.

"Because they were swingers!" She had been dying to tell someone.

There was another pause as Aimee was thrown off guard. "Swingers? What the hell?"

Leah laughed out loud. "I know; it's crazy, isn't it? I did sort of get hit on by this one guy though."

"I bet you did!" Aimee joined in the giggling. "Oh my god, swingers? You really are living a wild and crazy life, aren't you?"

"Don't worry, I kept it strictly professional," Leah assured her friend. "Me and a swinger? Can you imagine? That's completely ridiculous, isn't it?"

"Well," Aimee advised her, "I don't recommend shacking up with a swinger, but maybe you ought to think about not being quite so professional *all* the time...you know, let your hair down a little. You tend to be pretty serious, and that might put men off a bit. They might think you're too intense."

In her younger years, that criticism would have put Leah on the defensive. But she knew Aimee had a point; her feedback came from a place of care and concern. "You're probably right. But I also believe God will bring the right man to me when He thinks I'm ready."

Aimee, a non-practicing Catholic, clearly didn't have the energy to argue theology with her friend, so she just sighed. Leah knew what that signaled: it was time to wrap up the conversation. "I'm still going to visit you after the baby comes," she brought the discussion full circle. "Just try and stop me."

"Okay, okay, well, hope you have a good week. Let me know if you come across any interesting, non-swinger men, alright?" Aimee conceded.

"Sure thing. And you take care of that little bun in your oven!" And with that, Leah ended the call and headed back into The Pearl.

FOUR

The next morning, Leah walked with Glory over to the beach to catch the sunrise over the Atlantic. The crisp salt air blew across the waves, sending tiny water droplets into the air as the surf crashed on the sand. Glory splashed in and out of the constantly reaching and receding foam-crested waters.

My apartment is going to reek like wet dog tonight, but at least she's having fun, Leah mused.

Far off on the horizon, a fishing boat made her think of Captain Chris Sheldon, his dimples, silver-streaked beard and ocean-blue eyes glowing in contrast to his tan, weathered skin. She let herself wonder if he was married or single, how old he was, if he was from the area, what led him to pursue swinging, and all sorts of questions to which she was not truly sure she wanted answers.

It's been so long since I looked at a man and saw anything more than a father, a brother, a boss, or a guest at The Pearl...

She dragged Glory back toward her apartment as the

little dog protested by pulling back toward the surf. *Maybe it means I've healed. Finally.*

Leah shook away the chill that crept up her spine, a chill spawned by the idea of falling in love. After the last time, she vowed never to let it happen again. *Having one's heart ripped out and stomped upon should be a once-in-a-lifetime experience.*

But there was something in Chris Sheldon's smile and mannerisms that reeled her in so swiftly, so unconsciously, an unsuspecting fish taking the bait. His charm and magnetism were too alluring to be resisted.

The last time she fell victim, the fisherman was a selfish, narcissistic jerk disguised as an ambitious graduate student. *Surely once a man has some years on him,* Leah thought, considering Mr. Sheldon had to be at least forty years of age, *surely he learns to think about someone other than himself.*

Surely.

❖ ❖ ❖

Leah stared at the book her mother sent in the mail, a collection of daily devotionals for women. The cover was pink with the silhouette of a woman walking along a shoreline. *No doubt Mom saw this and thought of me on the beach.*

Mom would probably have a heart attack if she knew I hadn't cracked open my Bible outside of church for months.

A silvery blade of guilt stabbed Leah in the heart. *But I do pray,* she offered up as a consolation. *I pray all the time.*

As she halfheartedly flipped through the book, several references to being a godly wife and mother leapt off the pages at her. A lump formed in her throat. It was just another reminder that her parents measured success on a different scale than the rest of the world.

What if God's plan for me isn't marriage and motherhood?

She flashed back to a youth group missions trip to an orphanage in Mexico the summer before she left for college. She held motherless babies, rocking them in hand-hewn rocking chairs, their little chests pressed against her shoulder, downy heads resting in the crook of her neck as they drifted off into sweet slumber.

No matter how hard she tried to envision one of those tiny bodies coming from her own womb or to imagine soothing an infant's wails at her own breast, it was a vision she was unable to grasp. And now, at twenty-seven, despite her biological clock ticking away, it seemed even less tangible than at eighteen.

She had never told her mother she lacked maternal aspirations. It would have broken the poor woman's heart.

After Leah graduated from high school, her mother made the abrupt conversion from expecting her daughter to keep her legs tightly closed to incessantly reminding her that she dreamed of grandchildren. The irony of this sudden change was not lost on Leah.

After a steady diet of *abstinence, abstinence, abstinence* for eighteen years, now she was getting seven hearty courses of *procreate, procreate, procreate. Within the confines of marriage, of course!*

Leah had diligently maintained her virginity throughout high school, not that she had much of a choice. With her parents breathing down her neck twenty-four-seven and the entire church congregation watching her every move with hawk-like precision, how could she possibly have gotten away with fornication?

A conversation raced back to her memory:

"So, Leah, I was talking to Nancy Jones today, you know, the lady in the produce department down at the supermarket, and she said she saw you and Nick Anderson holding hands behind the bleachers at Friday's football game. Is he your boyfriend?" her mother had asked her one day.

Leah's face had flushed at her mother's accusation. Holding hands was not the only thing she and Nick Anderson had done behind the bleachers. He had also slipped his clammy but eager hands up her sweater. His trembling finger had tentatively brushed her nipple, sending a shock of electricity through her body so hot it kept her warm for hours afterward, despite the frigid chill of the dark, fall night. She was only fourteen, and it was the first time a boy had touched her.

She learned a lesson, though, that night: the bleachers had eyes. And big mouths. And after a couple more creepy incidents she was able to extrapolate this lesson to the entire town of Wahoo.

Not that a couple of boys didn't try to persuade Leah to push her limits.

"I heard that preachers' daughters are the biggest sluts in town," the new boy at school, Kyle Jacobs, had taunted her.

Prom night her junior year, her willpower was truly put to the test. Her date, Mark Elliott, was a handsome, if not slightly nerdy senior with his own car and a full ride to a small private liberal arts college where he planned to study music. He was the type of kid who was quiet in a group setting, but when he and Leah were alone, they enjoyed all manner of fascinating conversations.

A few weeks prior to prom, he took Leah parking on the

other side of a cornfield, far off the paved road where anyone might see them. Her parents thought she was at the late movie. The couple scrambled into his back seat with their lusty breaths steaming up all the windows of his 1990 Ford Tempo.

As he pressed his weight against her body, she felt his erection stabbing into her bare thigh even through his khaki pants. He'd pulled her skirt up and, balancing with one knee on the seat and one foot on the floorboard, he inched his long, thin finger under the fabric of her panties where it met the crevice of her thigh.

She was so shocked, she bolted upright, hitting her head on the car door. The back of her head was instantly throbbing, but the impact had the effect of knocking the sense back into her.

"Not now," she whispered, her voice hiding in the depths of her throat. "Let's wait till prom."

When prom night arrived, he clearly hadn't forgotten her promise. This time in the back of his Tempo he stripped her down to just her bra and panties and rendered himself completely naked. And this time when he lowered himself onto her body, it was his rock hard manhood pressed directly against her trembling flesh, no material separating them, save for the flimsy triangle of her thin cotton panties.

"I want you so bad, Leah," he'd breathed into her ear, the hot words searing into her like flaming embers.

Her body responded to the deepness of his voice, which rose from a place of desperation, of urgency and need. Her pelvis pushed up against him, her hips trying to resist the desire to move so her trembling sex could press against his hardness.

His teeth grazed the tender flesh where her neck met her shoulder. Her hips no longer under her control, she involuntarily shifted to reposition him. If not for her chastity-saving panties, the tip of his cock would be perfectly in line with her lips.

She ground against him, the pressure building behind that dampened cotton triangle covering her virginal sex. He thrust into the fabric barrier, grasping her pert breasts in his hands as his mouth worked its way across her collarbone. Lingering along the edge of explosion, Leah thought about those moments she'd explored her own body, the slippery wetness and the swollen nub that sent torrents of pleasure throughout her.

Her body tensed and released, setting off spasms between her legs. She was sure Mark felt it because suddenly his body shuddered against her. In tandem with a groan rising from deep within his chest, the evidence of his own climax soaked into her panties and trickled down her thigh.

She remembered thinking on the way home that night: *that didn't count, right? He didn't penetrate me, so I'm still a virgin, right?*

During her freshman year of college, she finally succumbed to her lust. Her rationalization? She was in love and planned to marry fellow Cornell student William Garrison. Their first time was a fumbling, awkward mess, as he was similarly inexperienced.

It'll get better, she consoled herself.

And it did for a while, but there was a distinct plateau. *This is why everyone disses "married sex" all the time. Right?* She wished she had a girlfriend she could talk to about such matters. And that's when she met Aimee.

Aimee was blunt and matter-of-fact in a way Leah had never experienced in her small Midwestern town where tact ruled and euphemisms were tossed about like New

Years' resolutions. Leah had been taught to spare feelings, to sugar-coat, to conceal her true thoughts to protect others.

Aimee hailed from Philadelphia, the product of a brash Italian family and an entirely different upbringing. It was a miracle the two women could not only tolerate each other but grew to love and appreciate each other's differences as well.

Leah remembered one of the first promises Aimee made to her when they were paired together for a group project: "I may not tell you what you want to hear, but I will always be honest."

It was a revelation to Leah. Complete honesty and transparency enabled a trust she had never been able to achieve in a relationship, platonic or romantic. And it was actually the contrast between her relationship with Aimee and her relationship with Will that gradually opened Leah's eyes to the splinters that would tear the couple apart.

Not surprisingly, it was Aimee who was there to catch Leah when she was reeling from heartbreak. She told Leah to go out and live, to throw caution to the wind and get that man and the damage he'd done out of her system.

Leah went on a binge. Not a drug or alcohol binge, but a sex binge. Frat parties, random hook-ups with guys she met online, double dates with Aimee as her wingwoman that ended up in some dank apartment off campus or even back in her dorm room. Anything to dull the pain that Will inflicted and make her forget the way he treated her. She didn't even know all of their names. They were just disembodied penises with the sole purpose of filling the void he left, both literally and figuratively.

But then Leah went home for Christmas break.

She sat in her father's church and listened to him preach about the loving God who offered her redemption and eternal salvation. All she had to do was repent. It was the same message she'd heard since birth, but it resonated with her in a way it never had before. So repent she did, and she felt a peace and a clarity she hadn't ever felt before.

When Leah returned to campus in January, Aimee immediately sensed the change in her friend. "Hey, you gotta do what you feel is right," Aimee had offered her support.

Leah didn't often reflect on the year she'd let her faith fall to the wayside. She felt she acted selfish, immature and out-of-control. She accepted the forgiveness she'd prayed for and moved on. It was a chapter of her life laid to rest, and she preferred not to revisit it.

For the rest of her undergraduate career, she refused to date and instead threw herself wholeheartedly into her studies. Shortly before graduation, she met Todd Phillips—he was smart, ambitious, confident, and loving. And he was a believer. *This is the man God sent for me,* she was certain.

But there was never the physical connection she hoped for.

In a year of dating, they barely made it past holding hands and kissing. Todd explained that he was courting her, which he insisted was ordained by God. Perhaps her disconnect with him was due to the promise she'd made after her relationship with Will failed, the promise she'd never let her heart get trashed again. Leah wanted assurance that Todd would stir her passions someday. He was so good and so right, she faithfully believed God led her to him—he was her soulmate.

But little did she know that Todd was harboring a secret that would destroy their relationship along with Leah's trust in men.

FIVE

Leah heard her beagle whimpering from her crate as she locked the door to her apartment and headed down to her Jeep. She was already running late because she'd had to clean up a mess Glory made in the hallway. Casey Fontaine was coming promptly at 9 AM, and she did not want to be late. Ms. Fontaine did not seem like the type of woman one should trifle with.

Casey was impeccably dressed in a navy pin-striped single-breasted suit, the buttons done up to accentuate her hourglass figure and camouflage the girth of her midsection. Under the suit jacket peeked a satin camisole matching her scarlet patent leather kitten heels adorned with delicate bows.

She sat right outside Leah's office with another woman beside her, a statuesque platinum blonde with heavily-made up eyes, tan skin and pale frosted lips. She wore a denim skirt, brown cowboy boots and a ribbed purple sweater that stretched over her ample bosom.

Leah wondered what Casey did for a living and if the

purple-sweater lady worked for her. *Maybe she's her assistant?*

"Good morning, Ms. Miller!" Ms. Fontaine gushed with a sugary-sweet smile. "This is my friend, Rhonda Sillery. She's on the admin team for our charity group and helps me with event planning."

The platinum blonde offered up a sideways smirk and extended her hand.

Leah shook it, noticing Ms. Sillery's grip was a little firmer than expected. She plastered on her professional smile and ushered the pair into her office, where they took seats across from her desk. "I'm sorry I'm a little late. My puppy made a mess right as I was getting ready to leave!"

Casey erupted with a crystalline laugh. "Oh, don't apologize. We're a little early, I believe. The early bird catches the worm; isn't that right, Rhonda?" She turned to the blonde, who squealed with amusement at what must have been an inside joke.

Leah pulled out her file for Casey's group. "What can I do for you today, Ms. Fontaine?"

"Oh, please call me Casey. Ms. Fontaine is way too formal for the type of group I'm heading up. I assume I can trust you to be discreet about my group and its members?" Her perfectly arched copper-colored eyebrows rose expectantly.

Leah smiled sincerely and nodded, Chris Sheldon's declaration about the group's purpose ringing in her ear. "I have nothing but the utmost respect for you and your group's privacy, Casey, I assure you."

"You have a very trustworthy face, Ms. Miller. I can tell your parents raised you right," Ms. Fontaine proclaimed. "In any case, as you may have noticed from our last party, our group raises money and donations for various charities, but at our core, we're advocates for an alternative lifestyle of a...sexual nature." Leah had expected her to whisper the "S" word, but in fact, she seemed to pronounce it more boldly. "I want to make sure that's not an issue for the hotel or the management because, to be honest, we had some issues at our last venue."

"As long as your guests respect the rules of the hotel and the rights of our other guests, I can't imagine it being a problem at all," Leah replied.

"We were on our best behavior last month," Rhonda finally chimed in. "What we'd like is a little...um...leeway in the ballroom, since it's private."

Leah struggled to keep her cheeks from flushing. She had inadvertently conjured up the graphic image of a full-out orgy, a writhing pile of bodies in the middle of the ballroom floor. Captain Chris Sheldon was right in the thick of it. She cleared her throat to try to erase the mental picture.

"What exactly do you mean by 'leeway'?"

"How do you feel about nudity?" Casey fired back as if she was expecting Leah's inquiry and had a counter-question locked and loaded.

"In the private ballroom?" Leah was stalling so she could maneuver through her options and discern what Barry would have her say. She wished she felt authoritative enough to give Ms. Fontaine a definitive yes or no, but the truth was that it needed to be discussed with her boss. She shook her head out of disappointment in herself, but realized instantly her reaction came across as negative to the two women.

Rhonda uncrossed her legs and then re-crossed them, alternating the leg on top. "I thought you said she was cool," she snickered under her breath toward Casey.

"I said she was young." Casey laughed, still smiling,

even though Leah's face was blank and her shoulders had dropped.

"I'm not saying no," Leah jumped to her own defense. "I just need to discuss it with Mr. Sampson, my boss. He's a pretty reasonable man. He's out today; otherwise, I'd call him in right now. Maybe you could give me a list of specific behaviors you'd like to have approved? I just don't think we have any precedent for this. I hope you understand."

"Oh, of course!" she exclaimed graciously, stretching her ring-clad fingers back against each other. "I didn't expect you to say 'just have at it; clothing is optional.' I know you have the monumental task of keeping everyone happy: our group, guests, staff, the managers. You seem like a very diplomatic and capable young woman, Ms. Miller, and I know you will try your best to make sure everyone's desires are granted." The word "desires" slipped out with a possibly unintended sultry tone, as if she were used to using that term in other contexts.

Well, I suppose I'll have to tell Barry about the purpose of the group after all, Leah realized as Casey and Rhonda wrapped up the meeting. They'd gone on to discuss the ballroom and lobby décor, the discounted room rate for Casey's group members, and the menu and drink specials. The date was set for the Christmas party—only two weeks away.

As the two ladies stood up to leave, Casey looked Leah up and down from her shoulder-length strawberry blonde waves to her black pump-covered toes. "Do you rent or own, Ms. Miller?" she asked, fishing in her pocketbook until she pulled out a business card.

"Oh, I have a little apartment a couple of blocks away," Leah replied, surprised at the forwardness, not to mention randomness, of the question.

Casey Fontaine gently placed the glossy card into

Leah's outstretched hand. She turned it over to reveal a glamorous photo of Casey with her hair elegantly coiffed as it had been the night of the party and a thick layer of retro-looking makeup. She looked like she'd stepped out of a 1950s pin-up calendar. "Casey Fontaine, specializing in commercial and residential real estate," the card announced.

"If you ever feel like house hunting," she offered in her smooth, melodic voice. "You know, your puppy would probably love to have a nice backyard to run around in!" She winked for emphasis.

"Oh, I have no doubt of that," Leah agreed. "Maybe in the spring."

Casey nodded approvingly and shook her hand, then turned to her friend. Rhonda caught the prompt and grasped Leah's hand. "It was nice to meet you," she said, but her words had a slight stench of insincerity wafting off them.

Or maybe that's just her perfume, Leah thought with a snide laugh as she watched the two women exit her office. *That was totally something Aimee would say. Speaking of whom...*

She dug out her cell phone to get some pointers from her best friend about how to broach the topic of Casey's Group with Barry.

● ●

Leah wasn't able to go home to take Glory outside at noon because she'd been waylaid dealing with a staff issue. There was a bit of a squabble between the front desk manager and one of the clerks that required Leah to step in and arbitrate. She was glad she was able to get everyone calmed down, but she was worried about her pup's poor bladder exploding in her crate while she waited.

Once things seemed back to normal at the office, Leah decided to pick up Glory and drive down to the inlet for a couple of hours to enjoy the afternoon sunshine. She'd stay late to make up the time later in the evening.

Glory was barking with joy as soon as her owner's key turned in the lock. The speed at which her little tail wagged was mind-boggling, and she was so wiggly, Leah could hardly get her hooked to her leash and back out the door. She took Glory around the side of the building, where she barely bothered to sniff before releasing the contents of her bladder on a grassy area just a foot or two from the sidewalk.

"I bet you feel better now, little girl, don't you?" Instead of answering, Glory bolted to the Jeep, dragging Leah behind her. Leah got them both situated before taking off for the boardwalk.

She parked in roughly the same spot as she had during their last venture to the southern edge of town. This time she didn't play stalker. Captain Chris Sheldon was the furthest thing from her mind as Glory eagerly pulled her in the direction of the water.

When Leah's black leather slingback pumps sank into the sand just off the boardwalk, she chided herself for not remembering to bring a different pair of shoes. *I think it's too cold to take them off, but what the hell?* Leah told Glory to sit while she slid the heels off and hooked them both under the finger of her free hand.

The thin stockings didn't begin to shield her soles from the bone-chilling shock as the sand enveloped her feet. She decided to jog to keep the blood circulating to her toes.

Glory was all for that idea and accelerated a little faster than Leah expected, taking her by surprise. When the puppy jerked hard on the leash, Leah tumbled to her knees just as a foamy wave washed up on the shore to soak her skirt.

At least it's not white! She tried to laugh off the situation even as the chill seeped into her flesh. She scrambled to her feet, glancing around to make sure no one was watching.

Much to her dismay, there was a tall man with a very friendly and intrigued-looking chocolate Lab springing toward them. Leah couldn't tell if the other dog was more interested in her or in Glory, but before she could ponder the situation any further, the chocolate Lab was inches away from Glory, sniffing her rear end.

Leah glanced up to see if the owner was going to exercise any control over the beast, who was obviously much larger and more aggressive than Glory. When he was only a foot away, the man pushed his mirrored sunglasses up onto his blond-streaked hair and locked eyes with Leah as he began to apologize.

Is that who I think it is? If I'm going to fall on the beach, it really must *be as humiliating as possible.*

"Oh, hey, Captain Sheldon... Leah Miller from The Pearl." She stood up as gracefully as she could, brushing sand off her legs as she went, and pulled Glory's leash to force the pup back to her side. Then she realized she'd dropped her shoes in the fall, and they were washing out in the surf.

"Oh, crap! My shoes!" she shrieked. *So much for graceful.*

Captain Sheldon jerked his Lab's leash and ordered, "Go get those shoes!" as he pointed to them bobbing in the waves.

As if the dog perfectly understood English, he charged into the water and returned in mere seconds with the pair of shoes clutched in his jaws. The captain laughed and patted the wet dog on the head. "Good boy!" he exclaimed, turning to Leah with the heels outstretched toward her. "Guess they don't call them retrievers for nothin', huh?"

Leah laughed, but it came out of her mouth as a high-pitched squeak instead of the elegant, melodic ringing she'd tried to channel à la Casey Fontaine. Glory was going completely nuts trying to chase Captain Sheldon's dog, who had run off down the beach, basking in the freedom his owner had just granted him. He seemed to be claiming his prize for fetching Leah's shoes, and Glory was insanely jealous.

"What's your dog's name?" She hoped to replace his memory of her squeaky cackle with something less mortifying.

"It's 'Keeper.' You know, like 'this fish is a keeper'?" He grinned, and the dimples she'd remembered over and over again since their initial meeting were coaxed out of hiding.

Leah chuckled, a bit more relaxed this time, her throat feeling less constricted. "I figured as much. My beagle is named Glory."

"'Glory'? That's an unusual name for a dog," he observed. "Although I guess 'Keeper' isn't an everyday sorta name either, is it?"

"She was born on the Fourth of July. So...like the flag? 'Old Glory'?" Leah explained with a smile. Glory tried to jump up on Leah's legs, getting even more sand on her wet skirt in the process.

"Love it," Captain Sheldon assured her, the dimples still in view. Keeper had made the rounds up to the boardwalk and back down to the surf and was returning to them now, as if to further rub it in Glory's face that he was untethered and she was not.

"Oh, let them play a little!" he encouraged her.

She didn't want to let go. Glory was still a puppy, and she wasn't sure what she'd do with her first taste of freedom, so she compromised by letting her leash out several yards. The beagle instantly followed Keeper back into the waves.

For a moment Leah and the captain stood watching their dogs splash and play in the surf as they got acquainted. *Why is it so easy for dogs and so awkward for humans? Maybe we'd have an easier time if we started by sniffing each other's behinds!*

Captain Sheldon stared down the deserted beach, checking to see if anyone was around who could overhear their conversation. "So I guess we have another party coming up at The Pearl," he broke the silence.

"That's my understanding," Leah said vaguely, not wanting to reveal that she had spoken with Casey Fontaine earlier. She did not underestimate the importance of discretion.

"You gonna tend bar again?" His bright blue eyes glimmered in the late afternoon sun. Leah thought she detected a hint of hopefulness in them but wasn't sure.

"I hope I won't be subjecting anyone to my less-than-skilled bartending this time, although I do believe I will be on the premises that evening," Leah predicted, seamlessly slipping into work mode.

He stared at her for a moment as if trying to negotiate his next move. The way his eyes bore into her revealed he couldn't have cared less about her professional obligations.

I think this is what they call eye-fucking?

"Do you want to grab some coffee or something?" he finally asked.

Leah's spine stiffened as she realized her suspicions were completely on the money—he really was hitting on her. In less than thirty seconds, she ran all sorts of scenarios through her head, a feat she had perfected in the course of her job.

She often had to decide very quickly how to respond to a guest or staff member in a way that upheld the policies of The Pearl but also provided the greatest satisfaction to the people involved. *But this is not work, and my job is not to make him happy.* She was glad she had delineated the boundaries because something about those dimples, those eyes, and the way his strong hands affectionately stroked Keeper's wet fur made her wonder what it would be like to please him.

"I've really got to get Glory home and then get back to work," Leah apologized through a sincere smile.

His dimples went back into hiding. "Ah, okay, some other time then?"

"Sure," she agreed, but in that Midwestern way of saying what the other person wanted to hear.

I really shouldn't get involved with this man. Seems like it would be a huge mistake; you know, separation of work and pleasure, plus he's a swinger and...need I go on?

"Great!" he exclaimed, considering her response an issued raincheck. "Have a good afternoon at work, and I'll see you at the Christmas party." He reached out to touch her on the arm, then added, "If not before."

His fingers felt warm and dry even though he had just been petting his dog's cold wet fur. And it felt like he was touching a much larger surface area than just two tiny inches on her forearm. Even when he pulled away, she still felt the impression of his fingers burning into her flesh.

"See you later, Captain Sheldon," she returned to her business-like tone.

"Please," he returned his fingers to the same spot, "call me Cap."

SIX

The sanctuary was crowded. Were there really that many more people in attendance or was because the Christmas decorations had shrunk the empty space?

Christmastime already? Where did the fall go?

Even with three Christmas trees aglow and the nativity set on the altar, Leah was having a hard time getting into the Christmas spirit. When the pianist began to plunk out a jazzy, contemporary rendition of "Angels We Have Heard On High," it all seemed forced and fake to Leah.

Maybe I'm just going to be a Grinch this year.

She was still thinking about the conversation she'd had with her mother the day before. Despite what she'd told Aimee about her mother being too distracted by her brother's engagement to miss her for the holidays, Mrs. Miller laid a thick, sticky guilt trip on Leah. "It just won't be the same without my baby girl here!"

"I know, Mom, but I don't have that many days off, and besides, I feel like I should go to Philly to help Aimee out with the baby. She really wants me there." Leah felt bad about lying to her mother, but wouldn't her mother let her off the hook if she thought she was taking care of someone else in lieu of visiting?

"Well, do you think you can come home later in the winter? Maybe in February or March? You can help us with the wedding plans."

"Sure, Mom, I'll see what I can do." It pacified the woman for the time being.

Leah shook the memory of the conversation out of her mind and closed her eyes, trying to prepare herself for worship. She sat with her legs primly crossed, her skirt pulled down conservatively over her thighs and covering part of her knee. She had noticed one member of the worship team's black velvet dress fell a good three or four inches above the knee. Her mother would have been outraged.

What is my problem today? I am clearly not feeling this worship thing.

Her church was down near the inlet, and in seconds, her mind was wandering over to Captain Sheldon's shop. *I can't imagine what he does on Sunday mornings. I'm sure it's not church.*

She envisioned him sprawled in bed, tangled in the covers with Keeper curled up at his feet. *But is there anyone else in bed beside him?*

Ever since she'd run into him on the beach a few days before, her interest in him was renewed. *He asked me out, but I said no. That was my gut reaction, to say no. But why? Would it really be wrong to go out with him?*

But still, her curiosity was piqued. *What was it like...being a swinger? How do people become swingers?*

How in the world am I daring to have these thoughts in church?

She glanced around at the worshipful faces of the congregation. She would have bet money none of them were thinking of swinging.

She tried to erase thoughts of Cap from her mind, but he was just a symbol of a bigger problem. She was lonely and wished she had someone outside of work to spend time with. *Maybe it's time to think about an online dating site?*

●●●

"**I** did a totally crazy thing!" Leah gushed into her phone. She was trying to cook dinner and keep Glory out of the trash that desperately needed to be taken out.

"What's that?" Aimee inquired. "I hope it's something wild and crazy and totally out of character for you, girl, because I'm so big and knocked up right now, I can't even get out of my chair, let alone go on any adventures."

"Yeah, and once the baby comes, your adventures are going to consist of cleaning spit-up and changing stinky diapers," Leah teased her friend.

"I know, I know, but just think about how damn cute of a baby I'm baking in there. I'm sure all the icky parts will be well worth it."

She decided to cut to the chase: "Okay, so here's the deal: I made a profile on an online dating site."

Her friend's initial reaction was a shrill cackle of disbelief. "I guess you've reached the point of desperation!" Aimee poked fun at her, possibly thinking it was just a joke.

The silence on the other end answered that question.

"Oh, sweetie, I'm just being silly. No one wants you to find a man more than I do!" There was a pause. "Well, except maybe your mom." When Leah remained silent,

Aimee's tone softened like caramel under heat. "So....tell me about the site you joined."

Leah knew it was ridiculous to be upset by Aimee's ribbing, but she was embarrassed and more than a little anxious about her choice. "It's just a free site," she said with a catch in her throat, like her larynx was lassoed by a rope of phlegm.

Am I really this desperate? A couple of hours ago, it all made perfect sense.

Changing the subject seemed like a good idea. "You know, I ran into that swinger guy the other day on the beach."

Maybe I shouldn't have joined. I feel like such an idiot! She buried her face in her hands as she awaited her friend's reaction to this new revelation.

"Oh yeah?" Aimee simply asked, no judgment this time.

"Yeah, he has a cute chocolate Lab named Keeper, who went into the water to fetch my shoes that I'd dropped. He asked me for coffee..."

"The dog?" Aimee laughed.

"No, silly, the guy!" Leah was giggling now too. "His name is Chris, but he goes by Cap."

"Cap? What the hell kind of name is that?"

"He's a fishing boat captain," Leah explained. "Anyway, I said no. But I wanted to say yes..." She couldn't believe she was admitting this. "Kinda..."

Aimee was the silent one this time, mulling over the ramifications of her best friend agreeing to coffee with a swinger. "Eh," came her final ruling, "coffee's no big deal. You should have gone. You're so out of practice talking to men—except for at work. It'd probably be good for you to practice."

Leah's heart raced a bit. She'd never expected to receive

Aimee's blessing. "You act like I've been tucked away in an all-female commune or something! Do you really think I'm that out of touch with the dating world?"

"I'm sure you do a great job communicating at work," Aimee assured her. "But it always took you a while to get warmed up back when we were in college. And by warmed up, I mean drunk. Since I'm assuming you're not drinking anymore..."

As much as she hated reflecting on her year of debauchery, she knew Aimee was right. *They don't call it "liquid courage" for nothin'.*

"I wasn't drunk," she defended herself. "I just needed a couple of drinks to loosen up."

"Right. But still...when was the last time you had a drink? Hell, when was the last time *I* had a drink?"

Leah reflected for a moment. "Um, I think I had a daiquiri when I came up to visit you right before I got Glory... Does that sound right?"

"Seriously, Leah, you need to cut yourself some slack. You haven't had a drink since the summer; you haven't had sex in like three years. Girl, you are wound so tight, it's amazing you haven't exploded yet! I don't know how you do it...all this deprivation. It's all I can do to abstain from alcohol for the baby, but at least I'm still getting laid regularly."

"I know, I know," Leah conceded.

In some ways, when she'd started at The Pearl, she felt like she'd made a bargain with God, still trying to atone for the sins of her college days. *If I just walk the straight and narrow, God will bless me.* Wasn't that what her father always preached?

"So what do you recommend?" Parts of her were reluctant to fix something that wasn't broken. *I'm not broken. I'm just lonely.*

"I'm glad you joined that dating site. I hope you meet some nice guys, and hopefully even Mr. Right, but honestly it wouldn't hurt you to date around and just go out and have fun. You're not going to be in your twenties forever, you know."

"Yeah, maybe I should just head down to Seacrets this weekend and get wasted," Leah suggested sarcastically.

Seacrets was a huge nightclub that attracted a decent-sized crowd even during the off-season but was downright gridlocked with both locals and tourists during the summer months. It was a well-known spot for "hooking up."

"Atta girl," Aimee replied. "Have a few drinks for me too!"

Leah knew she was kidding, that Aimee did not, in fact, condone her best friend going out to a club by herself, getting wasted and going home with some random stranger. She sensed Aimee had grown bored with the conversation and was ready to talk about her aching back, swollen feet and Braxton Hicks contractions for a while.

Later, after Leah had gotten the dinner dishes cleared and the bag of trash removed without too much damage from Glory's ever-curious snout, her phone buzzed with a notification that she'd received her first message on the dating site.

● ◦ ◦

The conversation Leah had with Aimee the night before was still ringing in her head as she drove the short distance to work in the morning. The few emails she'd gotten on the dating site were not promising. She couldn't stomach poor grammar and spelling, and many of the prospective dates' photos consisted mostly of them posing with dead animals: deer they'd shot or fish they'd caught. *Yuck.* Though she did wonder if any of those fish had been caught on Cap's boat.

She went to Barry's office first thing to discuss Casey's group and her request for leniency about nudity and "displays of affection" in the ballroom. All weekend, she'd been mulling over how to approach her boss—"displays of affection" seemed to be the most tasteful option.

"How was your weekend?" Barry asked as she entered. The huge grin on his face instantly revealed the impact of the short vacation he'd just returned from.

"You look great, Barry; you must have had a relaxing trip!" Leah beamed. *A relaxed and happy boss is a good boss.*

"Oh, it's amazing what a few days in Florida can do for you in the middle of the winter," he gloated. "I played golf, sat on the beach, and flirted with ladies in all the finest establishments. Made me wonder why I don't get a job down there so I can enjoy myself all year round!"

"Well," Leah played devil's advocate, "here we have that atmosphere in the summer, and it's ridiculously busy. Don't you think it's nice to have the off season so we can recuperate? Where would you go to get away from it all?"

"Oh, look at you being all rational and logical," Barry teased her. "So, what's up? Problems while I was away?"

Leah straightened her shoulders and took a deep breath. "No problems whatsoever, I just wanted to touch base with you about Casey Fontaine and her group that rents out the ballroom for their charity events."

She took a seat in the cushy, upholstered chair next to her boss's desk. "I met with Casey on Friday, and she was very pleased with The Pearl. She had a request, though, and

I didn't feel comfortable giving her a firm answer until I'd discussed the matter with you."

"Okay, what kind of request?" Barry's brows rose with curiosity. His skin was glowing from the Florida sunshine, and Leah thought he looked five or ten years younger than before his vacation.

"Well," Leah began, "I'm not sure how much you know about Casey's group. It's a charity group, yes, but they also practice an alternative lifestyle."

Now she had captured Barry's undivided attention. He was leaning forward, his elbows on his desk, his mind visibly spinning with various interpretations of Leah's words. "Um...okay...alternative how?"

Leah tried to explain without any tone of judgment: "They're swingers."

She thought Barry might spit his coffee clear across the office. "What?!" he sputtered with evident surprise. She was sure he was blushing, but he was so tan, it was difficult to tell if the color was from the sun or embarrassment. "Well, isn't that interesting?"

Leah managed to stay calm and collected. She had known for so long now, the element of shock had completely vanished. Now it was just a reality that needed to be dealt with.

Could The Pearl accommodate the group's wishes without alienating their other patrons? That was really the question at stake.

"They seem like a very close group, and Ms. Fontaine seems committed to making sure we maintain a good relationship. They're just asking for a little leniency..."

"What do you mean by 'leniency'?" Barry asked. She'd never seen his eyes so wide.

"Well, they have the ballroom rented, and they want to

be able to do some contests and other things that might require partial nudity or public displays of...um...affection. They just want to make sure the parameters are agreed upon beforehand. Ms. Fontaine is extremely conscientious and respectful of The Pearl and our other guests," Leah explained.

She was trying to maintain a neutral stance so she could get Barry's unbiased reaction, but she couldn't help revealing her pro-Casey's Group slant. And no one was more surprised by that slant than Leah herself.

"So, what are your thoughts on the matter?" Barry was also trying to display his best poker face.

"Since the group is contained in the room, and all the doors are shut, in other words, there's a great deal of privacy, I think we should grant their request...within reason, of course. If we aren't able to meet their needs, they'll pull out from The Pearl, and some other hotel will earn their business. From what I understand, that is what happened with their last contract." Leah tried to drill down to the heart of the matter, the heart being money, a concept near and dear to her boss's heart.

"That seems like a legitimate concern," Barry agreed. "I would hate to lose their business. If the group members really enjoy The Pearl, it could spawn more business; the group could grow, and word will get out. I think it's very important that we do whatever is in our power to please the group."

After a few more moments of contemplation, his fingers interlaced on the surface of his desk. "How about if you tell her we will accept nudity from the waist up and PDAs are okay, but no sexual acts. And only in the ballroom, not in the hallways or other public areas of the hotel."

Leah typed a few quick notes on the tablet she carried

with her to meetings. "That sounds reasonable," she stated, folding the cover back over the electronic device.

Barry's vacation grin returned. "I have to say I'm a little intrigued about what some of these contests might entail!" He laughed and gulped down the rest of his coffee, jovially slamming the mug down on his wooden desk. "You just never know what you're going to run into in this business, do you?"

Leah had to admit she'd seen a lot of unusual things in her time in the industry: the good, the bad, the ugly, the funny, the sad. *Maybe I'll have enough material to write a book someday*, she considered as she headed back to her office to call Casey Fontaine. She had a feeling Casey would be pleased with what she had to relay.

SEVEN

Leah was restless in her bed that night, thinking about the dating site. She was starting to wonder why she had even bothered.

If I get one more email saying nothing but "hi how r u," without even the decency of proper capitalization and punctuation, I might scream.

Tension gripped the muscles in her neck like the talons of a hawk gripping its prey. Her body stiffened, but she took a deep breath, trying in vain to relax. Glory was snoring in the next room, having fallen asleep on the sofa.

Leah had gone back to work late in the evening to finish up some paperwork. When she left, she decided to stroll through the lobby to check on the front desk night staff. After being assured all was well, she made her way out the marble-tiled entrance of The Pearl and cut back through the gardens and the patio adjacent to the pool area on her way to the parking lot.

In the thick shadows, she saw two entwined silhouettes. It was a pair of lovers embracing, moving gently in the pale moonlight, eclipsing each other so it was impossible to discern where one body began and the other ended. She paused behind a tree to watch them.

In the darkness, she couldn't tell if the couple was young or old, beautiful or ugly, even whether they were male or female. She was paralyzed in the shadow of the tree, holding her breath and straining to hear any sounds. She could have sworn she heard a sigh as she moved closer.

Her newfound proximity revealed a woman's arched back, white throat exposed to the cool night, offering tender flesh to her lover's hungry mouth. The man held the woman by her waist, his hand gripping the small of her back and pulling her into him. Their mouths met, unifying their shadows again.

This time when the woman pulled away, she fumbled with the buttons of her blouse, exposing her round breasts that matched her white throat in color. The man bent his head, his hands still around her waist, lifting her toward him so he could taste her. Her moan echoed through the still air, and Leah imagined his teeth had raked against her nipple.

Now in bed alone, Leah remembered the image, the shades of moon-drenched gray and the parts her mind had colorized as they were held up to the light of her imagination. The moans, gasps, and whimpers her mind recorded played as a soundtrack underscoring the memories, setting off a dull ache that radiated throughout her body.

Her thighs quivered as she moved her hand between them. It had been so long since she'd been touched like the woman in the garden. It had even been quite a long time since she had touched herself. Thus, her body was caught off-guard as slim, nimble digits parted the soft flesh between her legs, finding it wet and wanting.

Leah sighed at her own touch as she fantasized about being caught up in a passionate rapture, devoured like a last meal in the arms of a lover. She longed to feel those strong hands encircling her own waist, to feel the hardness of her lover's teeth as they bit into her breast.

She gasped as her index finger slid all the way inside, feeling the walls of her pussy wrap around her like an embrace. It had been too long.

Leah rubbed her fingers against her swollen clitoris as her other hand found her breast. She squeezed her nipple between her fingertips, eliciting a jolt on the verge between pain and pleasure, a line of electricity that flowed from the hand on her breast directly to the other that massaged her sex.

Pressing her eyelids shut and throwing her head back against the pillow, she returned to her fantasy of being the woman in the moonlit garden. Her thighs began to tense, and her breaths began to quicken as the pressure mounted toward its peak.

The shadowy figure of the male lover morphed under the influence of her imagination. She pictured him hovering above her, poised with his erect cock throbbing against her lower abdomen. "I want you, Leah," he grunted, pushing his hips into her and shifting until his crown rested directly at the top of her lips.

The voice, she had heard it before; it sounded so familiar. Her thighs trembled beneath him as she pressed her backside into the bed to grant him access.

She opened her eyes to see if he was looking at her, and they were the deep blue of the ocean. As he slowly sank to her depths, she exploded, her walls squeezing the two fingers that had been moving inside her.

As the waves dissipated, she realized the lover in her fantasy was none other than Captain Chris Sheldon.

EIGHT

The December wind whipped through Leah's hair and bit into her cheeks. She stuffed her hands in her pockets and wished she'd chosen warmer pants for Glory's morning walk. It was still dark outside; the dawn had not yet crept up on the ocean. She loved the way the horizon blushed as the sun started its chariot ride across the clouds. That thin crimson line separating the water from the sky was like a little miracle every morning: the promise her slate was clean and everything would start anew.

After making coffee, Leah awakened her slumbering laptop, the screen illuminated with her last destination: the dating site. She audibly groaned at the idea of viewing more unappealing profiles but was nonetheless intrigued by the little pink "4" indicating she had four new messages waiting.

It was the second message that caught her eye. The sender's profile photo was a stunning amber and fuchsia sunset crowning a silhouetted fishing pier. She clicked on the message to read: "Lost any shoes in the ocean lately?"

accompanied by a winking emoji.

Her heart began to thud against her ribcage as she clicked on the user name, "OCKeeper," to view his profile. The second picture featured him with his chocolate Lab perched beside him on a porch swing, fishing rods and tackle boxes in the foreground. She skimmed his stats:

Age: 42
Height: 6'3"
Body Type: Athletic
Sign: Aquarius
Occupation: Business owner
Education: Bachelor's Degree
Children: Has children, might want more
Pets: Has dog(s)/has cat(s)

Leah read his "about me" section closely:

Laidback gentleman. Nature lover. Loves to cook. Looking for a partner in crime, someone to enjoy the sunrises and sunsets with, someone to go out on the boat with or come home to at the end of the day.

He listed books, movies, music and food he enjoyed. But what truly caught her eye were the six things he claimed he couldn't live without:

My daughters
My dog
Water in all forms
Liberty
Touch
Passion

Leah was shocked to see the last three—they were abstract, not what she expected. Clearly the simple fisherman was more complex than she'd given him credit for. His responses were downright cerebral compared to other profiles she'd read, where the top items tended to be things like *cell phone, internet, my truck, music, beer.*

She replied to his message: "No, all of my shoes seem to be accounted for, thank goodness. So... I'm sort of surprised to see you on this site. You seemed to have plenty of admirers at the party last month."

● ✶ ●

Leah's day was in full swing, and she'd already forgotten about the response she sent Cap on the dating site. She was quite adept at separating her work and personal life, although lately there had not been much to separate. She was deeply engrossed in a spreadsheet that detailed hours for the housekeeping staff when her office phone buzzed.

"You have someone here to see you, a Chris Sheldon," her assistant's high-pitched squeaky voice eked out.

Her cheeks flushed instantly. *Oh, why did I send him that message?! It's really true that people will say all sorts of things on the internet that they'd never be brave enough to say in person, isn't it?*

Realizing regret was unable to take back her semi-snarky words, she inhaled deeply. It was a feeble attempt to calm herself down, but only seemed to inflame her anxiousness.

"Send him in," she replied to her assistant.

She saw the dimples before anything else. "Well, hello there, Miss Miller," his smooth but tangy voice projected into her space. He spoke with an Eastern Shore accent like many locals, which was something like a cross between a British and a southern accent, if there could possibly be such a thing. It was subtle, only pronounced on a word or two. With a wide grin, he extended a small brown paper bag toward her, his pearly whites visibly emerging between his lips.

"What's this?" she asked, her eyebrows elevated. She couldn't imagine what on earth he'd be giving her and was nearly afraid to look.

"They're doggie treats!" He beamed. "For Glory. A local shop around the corner from me on the boardwalk makes them. She was testing a new recipe and wanted me to pass them out, get some feedback. And, well, you're one person I know with a dog."

Leah was a little shocked that he'd come sixty-some blocks north just to give her a bag full of dog biscuits. "Wow, that's really kind of you, Cap. I'm sure Glory will appreciate them." She wasn't sure what else to say. His thoughtfulness nearly stung after the sarcastic note she'd sent him earlier in the day.

He was still beaming and nodding. There must have been something else, a further reason for his visit. His dimples were so deep and fixed, it was as though they were permanent indents in his cheeks.

"Did you get my message?" she finally asked, prepared to hear an earful of defensiveness.

His eyes did a little bug-out with surprise. She nearly giggled as it was the first time she'd seen him caught off guard. "Oh, on the site..."

Nope, now the dimples are gone, just as I feared. And so is the grin. "I hope I didn't offend you," Leah apologized, seeing his lips had curled into a frown. "I was really just teasing."

"I had forgotten all about the message to be honest. I only read it briefly on my way here. And, actually, Leah," he said, his voice deep and creased with seriousness, "I would love an opportunity to sit down with you and explain all of that stuff."

"All what stuff?" Leah played innocent. She wanted to know if he'd drop the S word again so freely, especially now that he was sober.

He cleared his throat and lowered his voice to about half-volume. "You know, the swinging stuff. I think we should talk about it." His expression was hopeful, but his tone betrayed his suspicion that she would not agree.

She decided to hold him in suspense a little longer. "That dating site is...wow!" she changed the subject. "I knew there was a dearth of eligible bachelors in the area, but I had no idea the pickings were really this slim."

"I see," he replied neutrally. He ran his fingers through his perpetually wind-tousled hair. He was wearing faded jeans, thick work boots and a flannel jacket with the sleeves rolled up to show his strong, well-defined forearms.

She never thought she'd be the kind of girl who went for the über-masculine type, but she undeniably felt something tingling within her body as she basked in his presence. At 5'9" she was a tall woman, and she was far from petite in build. She'd always dated slim men around the same height as her. Looking up from her desk at Cap with his hulking, 6'3" frame, she imagined how soft and feminine she might feel in his arms.

She helplessly stared, unable to divert her gaze, all the while wondering what he thought when he looked at her. Her body stiffened with resolve. "So, I guess I should take you up on that offer for coffee, then?"

His eyes had not wavered from hers; they still had missile lock on her thick-lashed green orbs. "Coffee," he said emphatically, one dimple peeping through his beard, "no."

She shook her head, confused by what had just happened. *Did he just say no to me?*

She cycled through a hundred questions in the split second it took him to explain: "Not coffee. I'm thinking dinner. Come to dinner with me."

Her lips spread into a smile, the breadth of which she could not seem to control. "Dinner? Sure, okay, I can do that."

"Tonight?" Cap pressed.

He is so darn persuasive with those dimples and sincere-looking blue eyes. God help me. "Okay," she agreed, against her better judgment.

"I'll pick you up. Seven o'clock." It was a statement, not a question.

"You can pick me up at seven here, yes."

His cool assertiveness forcibly gave way to a huge grin. His face was awash with victory as a single word passed through his parted lips: "Perfect."

NINE

Leah could not remember spending so much energy agonizing over her wardrobe options since she had her first interview at The Pearl. "I want something sexy but not sleazy," she explained to Aimee on the phone as she ransacked her closet searching for the perfect outfit.

"Sleazy?!" Aimee laughed. "Girl, I'm quite sure you don't own one thing anyone would consider sleazy! Can't you just grab a nice black pencil skirt and a sweater that shows a little bit of cleavage and get on with the date?"

Leah was creating a huge pile of rejected clothes on her bedroom floor, the type of unnecessary mess she loathed making.

She threw down the skirt and went to grab Glory's leash from the hook beside the front door. "Come on, girl," she seethed, "get on with it!"

"What's your deal?" Aimee chastised her. "Look, I'm sure you're nervous, but you're not going to have a good time if you get yourself all worked up into a tizzy about what you wear and about your dog. He doesn't care about any of that.

Just wear whatever, go out, have a drink or two, have a good time and BE YOURSELF!"

"Tizzy?" Leah laughed. "What are you, like a grandmother or something? I haven't heard that word since I was a little girl!"

"Oh good, you're laughing; that's a positive sign." She breathed a fake sigh of relief. "Okay, text me a picture when you get dressed and then call me tomorrow, 'cause I want to know *everything*, got it?"

"Yes, Grandma," Leah teased and hung up the phone as she took Glory back down the stairs and into the grass in front of her apartment building to do her business.

She did a once-over in the full-length mirror in the hallway: deep red t-strap heels, a simple straight black skirt that fell just to her knee, and a jade-colored sweater that made her gold-flecked green eyes look greener than ever and revealed the slightest shadow of cleavage between her breasts. Her strawberry blonde hair was behaving nicely, falling in loose waves around her shoulders, and a simple diamond pendant sparkled at her collarbone.

You know, I don't look half bad! She snapped a picture for Aimee.

She texted back: "Go get 'em, Tiger!"

•••

Leah stood at the front desk chatting with the night manager Eric while she waited for Cap to arrive. She was a little leery of her staff seeing her leave the building with a man, but... *I'm an adult, right? I'm allowed to have friends*, she justified the decision to herself.

At seven on the nose, she saw Cap's broad-shouldered figure enter the glass doors of The Pearl. He had ditched the flannel and work boots and now donned a pair of well-fitting dark-washed jeans and a simple black button-down shirt with thin blue and white pinstripes. He had trimmed his facial scruff to just enough to give his face a silvery-textured sheen.

Once they pulled out of the parking lot in his huge navy blue extended-cab truck, he let out a deep sigh. "Now I can finally tell you how beautiful you look tonight and not get you in trouble at work."

Leah reached deep into her throat for her voice. "Thank you." When her cheeks turned scarlet, she was glad the lighting was dim in the cab of the truck. "And you look very handsome yourself."

She breathed in and out, centering herself and urging her body to calm down, but she noticed her fingers were trembling slightly in the dark.

"So we're going to this great little place at the marina in West OC. Of course, it's much better when it's summer, and you can sit outside on the water, but it will still be pretty nice, I promise," he said as they made their way toward the inlet and over the bridge.

Cap parked the truck, and Leah carefully climbed down, putting one heeled foot on the ground while she swung her other off the seat and desperately fought to maintain her balance.

"Oh, sorry," she apologized with a little nervous giggle. "I didn't realize you were coming to help me!"

"I'm glad you have long legs. I've discovered that most ladies can't handle it." When he winked at her, she wondered if that was actually a veiled reference to something else.

She followed him inside the restaurant, and it was like a scene straight out of *Cheers*, only instead of a collective roar of "Norm!", it was "Cap!" He gave the hostess a peck on the cheek and whispered something in her ear.

Leah stood with all her weight on one foot, trying to project confidence despite feeling like she was on display. *I wonder how often he brings dates here?*

A dozen or so pairs of eyes bore into her as she followed Cap and the hostess down a hallway and then an aisle that led to a room with huge glass windows on three sides. They were seated at a corner table with a perfect view of the purple dusk hovering over the glassy ripples and the marina lights reflecting from their silver towers.

Cap pulled out the chair for her, and she eased herself into it. She tightly gripped the menu as if it would help keep her focused and under control. The waitress was polite but touchy-feely with her date, and Leah couldn't help but wonder if that familiarity was from knowing him intimately.

I think that's the main problem with dating a swinger. I can't help but think he's had every woman in town, and if he hasn't, then he probably wants to.

She tried to rid herself of that negativity—it would put a serious damper on her enjoyment of the evening, but she was feeling quite challenged. *What would Aimee tell me to do? That's right, she'd tell me to order a drink, relax and have fun. And I'm supposed to have a drink for her anyway.*

"So, Miss Leah Miller..." Cap opened his menu and peered up at her over its pages with his engaging eyes. In the flickering candlelight, they appeared dark but inviting, like if she looked deeply enough, she might unlock all of their secrets.

"Yes?" Her voice was like silk.

"What's your poison, babe? You don't strike me as a beer drinker. Wine?"

"Wine is fine." Leah snickered at her unintentional rhyme. "I like fruity, girly drinks too."

"I bet you do. Like a Crush probably..." his voice trailed off as his eyes delved back into her, searching for the keys to unlock her own mysteries.

She stared at him blankly, unsure if "crush" was a reference to her tingly, blush-worthy feelings for him, the ones she knew she was incapable of hiding from him. Some men were completely oblivious to the interests of the fairer sex. Captain Chris Sheldon was not one of those men.

"Oh, it's a drink," he explained, recognizing her bewilderment. "It's an OC Crush, an orange drink with vodka. You'll love it, I promise. Or I could get you a nice glass of wine instead."

Oh, right. It's a local favorite. See, I'm a lousy bartender. Should've known that one.

"Either is fine." She took a deep breath and willed herself to relax. To find that part of her that used to be adept at flirting. "Either is fine...or both."

She bit her bottom lip and leaned forward just enough to flash a clear view of her pale, ivory breasts jutting out from her black push-up bra. "You know, I'll probably be more...conversational...when I have a little alcohol in me."

"Probably?" He laughed. "Clearly, you trust me not to take advantage of you if you want both."

"Haven't you ever wanted your cake and eat it too?"

"All the time," he replied in a soft, deep voice. "All the time."

•••

There was never a lull in the conversation. Leah would be hearing bits and pieces of it echo throughout her mind for days and possibly weeks following their evening together. Despite her preconceptions, Chris Sheldon was a gentleman: an intelligent, educated, sophisticated gentleman. He was certainly not what she was expecting from an Ocean City native who grew up the son of a charter fisherman.

He was a savvy entrepreneur, always looking to diversify his business and for new commercial ventures to explore. He owned a stake in a seasonal bar/restaurant on the boardwalk and told Leah that, with Casey Fontaine's help, he was hunting for a warehouse to start a new enterprise. He shared that he had two grown daughters, Emma and Ashton, both of whom had grown up and moved away. No grandchildren—yet.

For her turn, Leah revealed that she was the oldest of three children, the daughter of a minister and music teacher who still lived in her tiny hometown of Wahoo, Nebraska. She mentioned her time at Cornell, her best friend Aimee who was about to give birth, and even – briefly and without much detail – her wild year of torrid promiscuity.

"We went to church growing up too," Cap shared. "My mother still goes every week, as a matter of fact." He looked into the distance for a moment, as if scanning his memory for images of his former church-going self. "Just 'cause I don't go doesn't mean I don't have beliefs."

Leah nodded. She understood. She had heard that so many times before. "So what about the swinging stuff?"

"I'm a single man," Cap explained. "Now that may change at some point, and then I suppose I would have to take into account what my partner wanted, although I'd be lying if I didn't admit I hope she'd want to do it together. But, for right now, I don't think there's anything wrong with me having fun. And I think God has better things to worry about than who I'm hanging out with."

As much as he'd promised to fully elaborate on his life-style, that was all he said on the matter. After three hours together, he offered to get her back home at a reasonable hour since she had to get up and go to work in the morning.

"So I guess you get to sleep in every day during the off-season?" she assumed as he walked her to the door of her apartment building.

"Gotta love the off-season," he admitted with his bellowing chuckle. "Now, come this summer, I'll be getting up at 5 or 6 AM every day, weekends included, for the morning charter. I need to bank up my sleep now."

She was poised to go up to her apartment, the keys digging into the palm of her hand. But Cap stood firmly planted, leaning against the wall of the building, his eyes glued to her intently. She smiled, unsure of where things were supposed to go from here.

Do I kiss him on the cheek? Do I wait for him to say goodbye? Do I just put my key in the lock?

"Leah," he whispered, stroking his finger down her cheek. It felt rough against her smooth skin. "I really enjoyed your company tonight."

She tried not to let the butterflies in her stomach reach her throat and steal her words. "And I yours."

"I would really like to see you again." His finger still rested against her cheek, but now his face had inched closer to hers, and she could feel his breath falling on her skin.

"I think that could be arranged," she answered, voice satin-smooth, the butterflies still at bay.

Then there were no more words; she felt his mouth on

hers. So fast, like a heartbeat, it was pressed against her, warm and gentle, with just the right amount of moisture. The softness of his lips sank into hers, and after a moment, his tongue parted her mouth. Then he tenderly grasped her face in his weathered palms as he continued to kiss her, pulling her so close to him that their bodies melded together from lips to thighs.

After what was a flash and eternity all at once, she reluctantly broke free and climbed the stairs to her apartment, allowing herself one last glance back at Cap and his dimples smiling up at her. Deep kisses could often feel too wet, too invasive, or too intimate, especially when shared with a virtual stranger. But there was nothing "too" about Cap's kiss. It was just exactly perfect.

TEN

That kiss was permanently etched on Leah's memory. While folding laundry, the feeling of his lips against hers came back to her with a vengeance, stirring a feeling in her core so long forgotten she scarcely recognized it. When she took Glory for her morning walk, it pressed against her insistently. And then as she climbed up the back entrance to The Pearl to start her work day, again it haunted her.

She felt dizzy, bombarded by erratic sensations: jumbled fragments of conversation, the smell of wine on their breaths, and the blue-tinged tendrils of candlelight from the table at the marina restaurant where they'd dined.

The memories were suspended in her mind like silky rose petals washed away during a rain shower, floating in a puddle yards away from their origin. Despite her best intentions to be herself and stay in the moment, she couldn't help but feel like the woman with Cap the night before was someone other than the Leah Miller she'd been for the past five years.

When Aimee called to review the date, Leah hesitated

to answer her phone. *How could I possibly articulate all these crazy thoughts I'm having?* But she knew her friend's curiosity would plague her all day if she didn't say something, anything to quell her thirst for juicy details. She would keep calling and calling until she got the answers she craved.

Naturally the sole word from Aimee was a very inquisitive: "SO???"

"Oh, Aimee, it was amazing!" Leah exhaled the words before she could grasp control of her tongue. She had been dying to let out that sigh, and it wasn't as if she could go gushing to Barry or the morning front desk staff or the head of housekeeping about her night out with the local boat captain.

Aimee seemed a bit dumbfounded as evident in her long pause before finally reacting: "Wow...really?"

Leah straightened her back in her leather desk chair and crossed one leg over the other, attempting to regain her composure. "Actually...yes," she found her pragmatic tone, "it was a nice change of pace to go out with someone who is mature and comfortable with who he is. He's really very sharp, well-educated, believe it or not, and worldly and—"

"So he's not just a dumb hick fisherman from the backwoods of Delmarva?" Aimee interrupted.

Leah gasped a second before a giggle set in. "Oh, come on, seriously, do you think I'd be interested in some random redneck? I could have found that in Nebraska!"

They both laughed. Hailing from the big city, Aimee had a pretty stereotypical impression of anyone from a rural area, despite everything Leah had done to try to dispel those stereotypes.

"So...what about the swinging thing?" she changed directions.

"Well," Leah began, "he didn't say that much about it really, just that he was single and enjoying himself and would obviously reconsider his lifestyle should he ever find himself in a relationship."

"Ah, good answer, very diplomatic," Aimee said approvingly. "But he didn't share any other details about it? How he got started with it? Nothing like that?"

Leah shrugged. "No, not really, but I didn't pry either. Maybe next time?"

"So there'll be a next time?" Her friend's pitch rose with excitement.

"I think so," Leah answered, trying to sound like the mature twenty-seven-year-old she was and not like a boy-crazy teenage girl. "He did say he'd like to see me again...and...he kissed me goodnight."

"Oh!" Aimee squealed. "How was it?!" She sounded as if she was perched on the edge of her seat, as much as a very pregnant woman could be without losing her balance, anyway.

"Perfect," Leah replied evenly. "Absolutely perfect."

● ● ●

Barry breezed into Leah's office at precisely ten o'clock, his large hand wrapped around a navy blue mug of coffee bearing The Pearl's logo. "Everything's set for Casey's Group this weekend, right?" he asked as though he already knew the answer.

She glanced up from her computer screen, instantly wishing she was less discombobulated. "Is that coffee for me?" she joked, stalling while she fumbled for the right file folder from the stack on her desk.

"You look tired," he observed with a smirk and raised eyebrow. "Everything okay?"

"Oh, of course!" She forced her lips to perk into a smile and fought the urge to rub her eyes, vigorously thumbing through the papers in the folder instead. "Do you want to take a look at these drink specials? I think everything else is coming along nicely."

He took the sheet of paper from her hand and skimmed it. "Looks great to me, as always." He searched her eyes again as if trying to figure out what was different about her. "Do you want me to get you some coffee? You just seem a little... I don't know... I hope you're not coming down with something."

Geez, I go out one night during the week, and the whole world can tell, Leah chided herself. *Is it really because I look tired, or am I just so distracted thinking about him that it's written all over my face?*

She dismissed his offer with a sparkly laugh and a wave of her fingers through the air. "Don't be silly. I would never expect my boss to get me coffee!"

"Well, an ordinary boss would never offer," Barry retorted. "Good thing you have the World's Best Boss!" He gestured with the mug extended toward her before realizing it was The Pearl logo mug and not his "World's Best Boss" mug that she'd given him the year before as a joke since he perpetually claimed the title.

Leah laughed. "Don't worry about a thing, Barry. Everything is set for Saturday night."

It's a good thing I feel competent and accomplished at my job, because I sure as heck feel like a fish out of water with this dating thing.

As Barry left her office, Leah's phone buzzed with a text from Aimee:

> Aimee: So are you going to sleep with this Cap guy or what?

> Leah: OMG, seriously? What kind of question is that?

> Aimee: A pretty damn legitimate one, that's what.

> Leah: *eyeroll emoji* How did we get to be friends again?

> Aimee: Because I'm irresistibly lovable. BTW you really need to get laid.

Leah fought the urge to send back something snarky, but then...

> Aimee: Hasn't it been more than two years now?

Leah remembered a couple of times she went out with co-workers from The Pearl when she first started her job. It was the beginning of the summer, and she was in an unfamiliar town where she hardly knew anyone. The locals had dragged her out to Macky's or Fager's or some bar that wasn't Seacrets but was close by, promising her she'd feel a lot less stressed if she just enjoyed a few drinks and let loose.

She had warned her colleagues that the last time she "let loose," it had been a disaster, which wasn't entirely true but it worked for an excuse. However, her new friends were undeterred and insisted she go out with them. The result was an encounter with local law enforcement...

After myriad frozen concoctions, she woke up the next morning in the bed of a stranger. The young, good-looking, well-muscled man in bed next to her was an Ocean City seasonal police officer who also had a little too much to drink on his night off. He promised he'd text her later, but he never did.

And that was the last casual encounter Leah had experienced. She dated a couple of men the first two years she lived in Ocean City, but those relationships suffered due to her heavy workload at The Pearl.

She thought about all the men she'd dated, attempting to explain why her dating life had been such a miserable failure. She could divide her former beaus into two clear-cut categories: the player and the too-sweet guy she could never make herself fall for. Thinking back to the kiss she shared with Cap the night before, she was pretty sure which category he belonged in.

It had been almost three years since a man had kissed her, touched her, been inside her. She reached for her phone.

> Leah: IDK if I'll sleep with Cap. I very well may.

When she thought about last night's kiss, she wasn't sure she would be able to resist any further advances...

● ● ●

Leah was waiting to hear back from Aimee about which dress she should wear to the party on Saturday night. There was a sleek black number that showed some skin above her knee but had a high neck, a deep crimson dress with a plunging neckline and a floaty skirt, and a silky hunter-green dress with ruching around the middle that also showed a fair amount of décolletage.

"So are you going to the party as a guest, as Cap's date?

Or are you going for work?" Aimee had asked for clari-fication.

"I'm still going to be there in an official work capacity, but I won't be bartending this time, thank goodness. My job is mostly to make sure everyone stays happy, and also because Cap says I should mingle and see what their parties are all about. He thinks I'll be pleasantly surprised," Leah explained.

"Gotcha. Well...does that mean you've been talking to him since your date?"

It had been two days since her date with Cap, and she had not heard from him other than a text to say he'd had a good time, which he'd sent later that night after their kiss. Leah was trying to hold out and wait for him to contact her again, but she was starting to lose patience.

"No...not since that night. Maybe he just assumes we'll talk on Saturday at the party? He knows I'm going to be there."

"Yeah," Aimee agreed with her theory. "That could be. Well, let me take a look at the dresses again, and I'll let you know."

That was the night before. Now Leah was back at work and starting to feel fidgety and restless.

She lifted her long arms high above her head and felt the muscles and tendons stretch in her shoulders and down her ribcage as she peered out her window that overlooked the parking lot. She squinted when she thought she saw a navy blue extended-cab truck with big tires pulling in, but upon further inspection, she was sure it was one of the county street department vehicles instead. Disappointment rushed over her before she could stop it.

She studied the sky with its thick layers of gray clouds. Even though she couldn't see clear to the ocean, she knew the waves were topped with choppy white crests rhythmically slamming against the dull beige sand.

Looks like rain or snow. More disappointment. She had briefly considered running home to grab Glory and driving down to the boardwalk. *Never know who you might run into down there...*

Winter was a double-edged sword on the Eastern Shore of Maryland. The break from the hustle and bustle of the other three seasons was welcomed and much-needed, but the bitter cold dampness blowing off the water seeped into one's bones.

"I still need to go take Glory out." Just as she slipped both of her feet back inside her heels and stood up on wobbly, half-asleep legs, she heard a sharp little assertive knock at the door.

Before she could say "Come in," the door handle turned, and gripping the other side was a large, weathered hand, followed by a pair of deep-set blue eyes and a strong square jaw capped off with two youthful dimples.

Judging from his reaction to her standing there in the middle of her office, Leah must have looked shocked: shocked to see him there entirely, or shocked he would just waltz in unannounced, but shocked nonetheless.

His face filled with chagrin, the dimples fading into oblivion. "Oh," he blurted, "guess I caught you at a bad time? I can come back later if you prefer." By the last phrase, he'd settled back into his smooth Eastern Shore drawl.

"No, no." Her face brightened with the blood rushing to her cheeks. "I was just getting ready to go take Glory out. I always try to do that at lunchtime."

"I see." He turned around to look at the door, which he'd shut behind him when he entered. He grinned and slid toward her. In moments, his faded jeans were brushing against her well-tailored wool skirt.

Without another word, his arm wrapped around her waist as he pulled her closer. Now her breasts smashed against his chest, and she smelled cologne and salt air rising off him. Her eyes involuntarily closed, anticipating that his lips would soon be on hers, but instead, she felt an unexpected jolt as the wetness of his mouth triggered a nerve in her neck, just below her ear.

When she jumped, he pulled her even tighter in his embrace. Her body melted in submission to his touch as his other hand directed her chin toward his face. Their lips finally met just as they had when they'd last said goodbye. And it was every bit as perfect.

"Come have lunch with me." He pulled back just as her eyes began to open. She felt his whisper falling on her cheek and breathlessly agreed.

This time he took her north to 94th street, to a little restaurant/bar he said was owned by a friend of his. Once again, the knowing looks upon seeing their friend with a young woman, hearty backslapping and "Hey, where ya been hiding yourself this winter, Cap?" ensued.

Someone inquired as to why he hadn't yet embarked upon his annual trip to the Florida Keys, to which he responded, "That's after Christmas. Why, you wanna go?" By the time they'd reached their table near the back of the restaurant, Cap had about a half dozen comrades planning to stow away on his boat during his upcoming voyage south.

Leah was no stranger to the feeling of being recognized everywhere she went in a small town. Back in Wahoo, everyone knew she was Pastor Miller's daughter. Instead of asking her about fishing trips or where she'd been hanging out, she heard things like, "Tell your father that was a great sermon last Sunday!" or "Does Pastor Miller know his daughter is out past ten o'clock?"

The anonymity she'd cloaked herself in since moving east was a comfortable garb, although Barry assured her that with her new title, increased contact with guests, and elevated prominence in the affairs of The Pearl, she'd soon become recognized out and about in Ocean City.

What about Cap's friends? she wondered. *Do these people know he's a swinger? Are they swingers too?*

Why would any of these men care if their forty-two-year-old pal was out sampling a wide variety of fruit? Wouldn't they just cheer him on? Stupid double standard.

"You okay?" Cap pushed the second menu toward her. "You seem sort of distracted today."

Her throat clenched as if it refused to allow sound to come up through her larynx. She shook it off and forced the words to squeak out, "Um, sure, I'm fine. No worries." She smiled but noticed he still looked skeptical. "Okay, so I admit I'm a little nervous about tomorrow night..."

He let her admission hang in the air between them for a second, long enough for the waitress to take their order. Leah's cheeks flushed, and she wondered if he would ignore her trepidation or address it head-on.

Finally, he said, "I was nervous my first time too."

Great, that doesn't really put me at ease. She managed to smile gracefully in spite of her mind somersaulting over all the possibilities. But those thoughts lost out to the one pushing its way to the forefront: how much she wished lunch was over and they were alone again, his lips pressed against hers.

She got her wish about an hour later. Cap accompanied her while she led Glory down the steps and into the backyard behind her building, telling her about the fishing trip he had planned for January and how there wasn't a "snow-ball's chance in hell" that any of those half-dozen guys shouting at him from the bar were actually going with him.

"So, who *is* going with you?" she asked, powerful curiosity forcing her hand. She got a vision of him surrounded by a harem of tan-skinned, long-legged, bikini-clad goddesses, all vying for a chance at sleeping in his bed.

"You, I hope," was all he said, and it was then that Glory decided to do her business just a few feet from them.

"Nice," Leah grunted under her breath, directed at her dog, not at Cap. She wanted to ask him what he could possibly mean by that, if he was being facetious, but the mood had already shifted. She tugged Glory up the stairs, her black pumps clicking with every step. Cap followed right on her heels, seemingly surprised that she could go so fast in heels.

She returned Glory to her crate, feeling frustrated. For once, she wanted to forget about her responsibilities and be whisked away to that euphoric state she'd felt the two times she'd been in Cap's arms. He was waiting for her on her sofa, sitting with one leg crossed over the other. His arm was stretched across the back of the furniture, and he looked relaxed, not the least bit nervous like she was.

She had only had one man in this apartment who wasn't related to her, and that was nearly three years ago. Between the novelty of having male company, the poor timing of her dog, and wondering if she would be missed at work during her extended lunch break, she was flustered and on edge.

He patted the sofa cushion next to him, the one that would allow her to lean against his outstretched arm. He was so open, so inviting, the dimples winking at her as she approached him.

She sat, turning slightly toward him, and just as she

began to get comfortable, he surprised her by grabbing her wrist and jerking her toward him so her long legs had no choice but to straddle his hips. She was so startled by the maneuver that she immediately acquiesced, her rear end sinking down and coming to rest on his thighs. It all happened in one swift motion, her being pulled on top of him and his mouth devouring her as if he hadn't just eaten lunch.

In seconds, he was pulling the charcoal gray sweater over her head and unfastening her bra with one hand, discarding both on the sofa beside them. Now her bare breasts were pressed against his flannel shirt as his hands stroked up and down her half-naked body until he pushed her back slightly, giving him room to cup her soft, creamy white breasts in his huge, weathered hands. He lifted each to his mouth in succession, planting a soft, wet kiss on both of her erect pink nipples.

She sighed, partially with pleasure and partially with reticence. *How can I let him do this when I barely know him?* her conscience was crying out, trying to drown out the sound of her pounding heartbeat, which was thundering away in her ribcage like an entire herd of wild horses.

His eyes opened and locked onto hers, silently asking her permission to continue. She knew exactly what he was asking, and she felt his swelling manhood straining toward her through the denim. As if her mind had temporarily been held hostage by her growing desire and then suddenly released, she stiffened and slid her legs to the floor.

Duty called. Plus Glory was whining in her cage. "I really need to get back to work, Cap," she explained, her regret evident.

She watched the dimples come back as he pretended to be perfectly alright with stopping there. "I hope I didn't offend you," he said, oozing charm. "I just... God, Leah. I'm so sorry. It's just...I want you. Couldn't help myself just now."

Leah hooked her bra then slid it back around so she could slip her arms through the straps and conceal her breasts again. "It's okay, just not the best timing," she replied to his not-very-sorry apology. "Some other time?"

"I know you'll be working tomorrow night," Cap said as he watched her dress. "But when you're done with work, if you want to come back to my place after the party, that would be...nice." It felt like it took him a beat or two to decide on the word "nice" from among more salacious alternatives.

Leah tried to imagine going back to his place after walking around a swinging party all night. *I guess I've done stranger things before. A long time ago, of course.*

She promised him she'd think about it and then walked him to the door, leaving him with a hot imprint of her lips burning against his cheek.

Maybe Aimee is right; maybe I do just need to get laid.

She looked at her phone to see what she'd missed during lunch, and sure enough, Aimee had texted:

> Aimee: Wear the green one. It's sexy, matches your eyes, and won't be too unprofessional. Plus it looks like it's easy to take off.

ELEVEN

Leah couldn't remember ever feeling so nervous about hosting an event, not even during her internship in college where she had a ton of pressure riding on her to make everything perfect. *It's just another party,* she kept telling herself as she did her hair, applied makeup and slid on the green dress that Aimee had chosen for the evening.

As she was getting ready to step out, her phone lit up with an incoming call from her parents' number. The contact photo was of her childhood home, a *Brady Bunch*-esque two-story with brown siding and very symmetrical blue-shuttered windows. Her first instinct was to answer because otherwise her mother would keep calling all night long, and, well, taking a call from her mother while "chaperoning" a swinger party just didn't seem right.

"Hi, Mom." She hoped she could make the call snappy.

"Leah Elizabeth Miller, I haven't heard from you in over a week! You didn't return my last phone call. I left a message!" Mrs. Miller's shrill voice pierced through her daughter's eardrum.

The shrillness shot down to the pit of her stomach where it tumbled around with the remains of her dinner. "I know, Mom, I'm sorry. I've had a really crazy week."

"Too crazy to talk to your mother," she sighed. "I sent off a Christmas package to you today. I just wanted you to keep an eye out. You know how long packages take to arrive from Nebraska. It's like they're traveling to another continent or something!"

"I know," Leah commiserated. "Crossing the Chesapeake Bay is almost like crossing the Atlantic. I need to get busy mailing home some stuff for all of you too, so thanks for reminding me."

"I still wish you'd come home to visit. We're having a lovely candlelight Christmas Eve service this year! Patty Bryson is singing with her two daughters. Do you remember Patty and her daughters, Rachel and Anna?"

"Of course, Mom." It was amazing how sometimes her mother acted as if every memory Leah ever made in Wahoo had been magically erased when she moved away.

"Well, your father has some really nice stuff planned, and we would love to have you here for it," she urged, her voice tinged with that guilt-inducing tone that mothers specialize in.

"I wish I could," Leah lied between her teeth, "but Barry needs me here, plus Aimee will be calling me any day to tell me she's in labor!"

"Is there a man who might be keeping you there for the holidays?" Mrs. Miller queried, her voice hopeful.

"Oh, Mom, don't be ridiculous. It's just work and Aimee, I promise." *And that's not a lie—because who knows what Cap is doing for the holidays.* "Okay, I'm sorry to cut you short, but I have to go into work tonight to manage a catered event."

"I see," her mother responded, not disguising her disappointment. "Can you call me tomorrow after church, then?"

"Sure, Mom, no problem," she vowed while sliding her feet into four-inch stiletto heels. *If my mom only knew...* Leah wondered how quickly her parents would disown her if she were ever to become involved in the "lifestyle," as Casey Fontaine and Cap called it.

The lobby of The Pearl looked like a winter wonderland. Leah had supervised some of her staff wrapping each branch of the trees in white lights as well as the columns that delineated the rotunda between the front desk and the grand staircase to the second floor. The lights wrapped around the columns were swathed in iridescent tulle, which created an ethereal, fairy-like effect. Everything was soft and glowing, and despite the stilettos clicking against the marble tiles, she felt like she was floating on air as she made her way down the hall toward the ballroom.

The ballroom was just as elegantly appointed as the lobby with pine boughs gracing every table along with pearlescent glass orbs aglow with candlelight. More Christmas trees were arranged in little bunches around the perimeter of the room, their lights twinkling like faraway stars.

She froze when she caught a glimpse of Cap out of the corner of her eye. She nearly wobbled out of her heels, so powerful was his draw. *Why is my body so out of control when he is near?*

Regaining her balance, she realized he was walking toward her after helping the D.J. wheel in his equipment and park it near the table at the end of the room. Leah watched his long, self-assured gait and the smile that spread wide across his face as he made his approach.

"Well, good evening, Ms. Miller!" His salutation oozed from his lips like honey.

She extended her hand, hoping he would shake it platonically, but instead he planted a soft kiss right below her knuckles. When she pulled her hand away, she could feel the slight moisture he'd left behind and couldn't help but remember what his lips felt like pressed against her neck in that curve leading to her shoulder.

This is going to be a long night. She smiled cordially at him and then distracted herself by glancing over to watch the servers preparing the trays of salad and bread to be delivered to each round, crisp linen-covered table.

"I know you're busy," he offered, the sly smile still producing a dimple. "I'll come and find you later, once things get underway." His promise was accompanied by a wink.

She looked at him gratefully and nodded with her business-like smile. *He is a gentleman, after all.* She briefly thought about how, after a few drinks, she might wish he were less so.

But that's his hook...(damn it, another fishing reference)... He knows all about charm and class when it's required, and when it's not...he's a man who gets what he wants. And that is precisely why he's so dangerous...and exciting...all at once.

Leah went about accomplishing all of her tasks, stopping into the kitchen to chat with the chef, making sure the head of the waitstaff was ready for service, checking in with the bartenders, and asking the front desk staff if there had been any issues with check-ins.

Everything appeared to be running optimally until Leah nearly bumped into Casey Fontaine. She was blazing in a fiery red sequined evening gown clinging to her ample curves, a brown mink stole hanging from her shoulders. Her hair and makeup looked professionally applied. She was the epitome of glamor.

"Oh, Ms. Fontaine, you look breathtaking!" Leah gushed just as Casey leapt toward her, enveloping her in a tight hug. Leah's lungs felt squished as she was overwhelmed by how strong the older woman's thick limbs were. She politely patted Ms. Fontaine's back as she tried to resist squirming away.

Casey was the one who broke the embrace, but she kept ahold of Leah's right hand so she could twirl her around like a ballerina. "You are positively exquisite!" she decreed. "That forest green is simply stunning on you!"

Ms. Fontaine looked around The Pearl, from the staircase, past the rotunda to the rest of the lobby stretching before them. "And this place...oh, Leah, you and your staff have really outdone yourselves. The Pearl has always been lovely, but it is downright enchanting tonight. I feel like I've stepped into a dream, the most beautiful of dreams!"

Leah was beaming. She was rightfully proud of her staff and their work, but she had been the one to bring it all together, and knowing she had exceeded Ms. Fontaine's wildest expectations was the best reward she could ever hope for.

"I'm so glad you like it," she replied humbly. She noticed Casey's friend Rhonda had joined her. Her face looked pinched and her body stiff, as if she wasn't comfortable with the display of affection she'd just witnessed between her friend and Leah. She looked like a protective watchdog, her lips nearly curled into a snarl.

"Hello, Rhonda, nice to see you again," Leah offered warmly, extending her hand.

"Doesn't everything look amazing?" Casey sang, her golden voice flecked with joy.

Rhonda forced a smirk. "Yeah, it looks great. Thanks, Leah." She gave Leah's hand a perfunctory shake.

That woman does not like me, Leah observed, but she shrugged it off as she headed back toward the ballroom.

She allowed her mind to wander back to Cap. *Seeing him with another woman—that will be the true test if I'm okay with this whole thing. Although he did say that for the right woman...he would consider putting all this behind him.*

I wonder if I could ever be that woman? Am I too young for him? Too inexperienced?

She shook the questions out of her mind, unsure if she really wanted the answers.

She found Cap chatting with Trish, the bartender for whom she had filled in during the last party. Trish was a single mom in her early thirties with shoulder-length curly brown hair and warm brown eyes. She was friendly and had a way of connecting with guests that made her a good bartender.

Leah stood several feet back and observed Trish's response to Cap's flashing dimples and gleaming ocean-blue eyes. *She has no idea I'm dating that man,* Leah thought. *I wonder if she has any clue what type of party this is.*

She forced herself to stop staring and went to check in with the kitchen again. Casey had been worried about a multi-course plated dinner when ordinarily she provided hors d'oeuvres and a bar menu.

"I know it seems paradoxical," she'd confessed to Leah during their prior meeting, "but my group members really are creatures of habit. They don't like changes in venues or menus or whatever their expectations have been set for. Convincing them that The Pearl was going to be great after the debacle at the last place was quite the challenge."

It did seem odd to Leah for a lifestyle dedicated to

sampling a variety of "foods," but then again, she was discovering there were a whole lot of other discrepancies between her limited knowledge of swingers and the reality of them.

She looked around the room at the ladies in their formal gowns and gentlemen donning sharp suits and even a few tuxedos. Leah was mildly surprised to see the group on their best behavior after Casey received permission for more adult activities and exposure in the ballroom.

As the night wore on, the ballroom became more and more deserted. The D.J. appeared bored under his spinning kaleidoscope of lights. The bartenders looked tired as they leaned against their stations, prompting Leah to dismiss them around midnight.

"But what if someone else wants a drink?" Gina protested.

"I'll take care of them," Leah promised.

Only four guests remained in the huge ballroom: one couple was slow-dancing on the parquet floor with their bodies tightly conjoined, and the other was in the dark recesses of the corner between the wall of windows and the D.J. table. Leah could tell they were caressing each other and kissing, probably believing they were concealed behind a trio of Christmas trees.

I wonder where Cap went? She was proud it had been over an hour since she'd last thought of him.

Before she could dwell on him further, Casey ambled into the ballroom. She wore a huge grin on her face, her hair was slightly disheveled, and she carried her heels in one hand by their straps. Her mink stole was absent as well as most of her lipstick; only a crimson ring outlining her lips remained. She stumbled toward Leah, evidently still buzzing from earlier alcohol consumption or perhaps an intoxicating romp in one of the hotel rooms.

Probably both, Leah thought with a laugh.

"This is simply the most marvelous party I have ever hosted," Casey gushed, her words only slightly slurred.

"Oh, I'm thrilled!" Leah replied. "Everyone went home pretty early though, didn't they?"

Casey erupted in glittery laughter. "Oh, no, my dear, quite the contrary. I think most people went upstairs to play." She winked. "Did you book all the rooms in our block?"

Leah nodded. "We even had to add some rooms earlier in the week."

"That is the sign of a successful swinger party!" Casey proclaimed, raising the glass she carried in her other hand victoriously.

"I'd toast to that if I had my own drink." Leah eyed the remaining burgundy liquid swirling in the crystal stemware, praying it didn't slosh out onto the carpet.

"Well, they're cleaning things up in here, and I know the ballroom has to be shut down by one anyway. Why don't you come up to my room and have a drink?"

It was more of an expectation than an invitation, Leah ascertained.

She nodded, and Casey set her wine glass down on the bar top. She grabbed Leah affectionately by the hand to lead her toward the elevators. Once on board, she pushed the button for the fourth floor, then quickly realized she really meant five for the top floor. She laughed at her mistake and then tugged Leah so close to her that Leah's hunter-green silk ruching touched the red sequins of Casey's bodice.

"I'm so glad I met you, Miss Leah Miller. You are just

the best little hostess, a woman after my own heart. I hope you don't mind if I give you a hug!"

Hey, at least she asked first, Leah noted before nodding briefly and being wrapped in Casey's tight embrace, just like she had at the beginning of the night.

When the elevator doors finally slid open, Casey released Leah and pulled her down the hallway toward the suite at the end. Leah knew the room well. It comprised the entire west end of the fifth floor and offered a breathtaking view of Assawoman Bay.

The thick navy blue drapes were all pushed to one side of the floor-to-ceiling windows revealing the bay several stories beneath them. The hazy moonlight fell in dappled ripples across the inky water, and the lights from houses on the banks dotted the shore like fireflies against a summer night sky.

Only a single lamp illuminated the bar area of the suite; the rest of the space was dark. Casey slid over to the lighted area and opened the door of the mini fridge. Leah heard some glasses clinking together and then liquid being poured. She arrived at the bar area just in time for Casey to push a drink into her hand.

She took a sip and felt it burn down her throat. It was much stronger and more corrosive than anything she was accustomed to drinking. She took another sip with the conflicting interests of not offending her hostess and avoiding intoxication.

I really need to make it home in one piece. And I really expected Cap to hunt me down to invite me back to his place.

It didn't take long for the thought of him to creep back into her mind. *What if he's downstairs looking for me?*

She thanked Casey for the drink and for helping make the party a success and graciously excused herself. Casey was standing by the windows looking out across the bay when the younger woman exited the room.

Leah made her way down the long hallway of the fifth floor when she heard deep moans and a shrill scream pierce the tranquility of the night. She quickly traced the sound to a room about halfway down the hall from the elevators and observed the door to the room was ajar.

Leah pushed the door open just enough to give herself a full view of the room. Her knees were trembling as the forms dispersed throughout the space came into focus. Rhonda, the statuesque bleach-blonde, reclined in the plush armchair between the windows and the king-sized bed. Looking closer, Leah realized she was sitting on the lap of a compact nude man with a hairy chest and thick dark hair, the man whom Cap bought drinks for the night she first met him.

Sure enough, the petite woman with the long curly dark hair on the bed was his wife. Between her legs perched a muscular man with deep russet skin and a shiny, bald head, slurping and licking her sex as if he were devouring ambrosia. The muscles in his back rippled as he worked his mouth and tongue on her clit and labia.

Another man, pasty-white with a bit of a beer gut, knelt as he fed his cock to the woman with one hand, the other massaging her small breasts that jutted out the top of a scarlet satin corset. And, finally, there was one more man to make it four, taking pictures from the side of the bed closer to the window. Leah's heart seized when she realized it was Cap.

Sensing motion, Leah glanced over to see what Rhonda was doing. She had repositioned herself on her knees on the floor in front of the window, grasping the mustached man's erect cock on one side of her while Cap moved into place on the other side and plunged his stiff cock into her mouth. She switched back and forth between the two men, who peered down at her approvingly, deep moans forming on their lips.

The sight of Rhonda pleasuring two men just feet away stirred passions within Leah that she had long suppressed. She looked back toward the bed and watched the dark-haired lady, whom she quickly learned was named Pam because the man she was sucking kept saying her name, buck against the lips of the man between her legs.

"That's it, baby," the muscular dark-skinned man growled. "Come for me, baby." She watched Pam deep-throat the man kneeling by her face while she thrashed in wild ecstasy, the climax seizing control of her body. She tried to pull back from the cock in her mouth so she could catch her breath, but the beer-bellied man gripped her face and forced her to take all of him down her throat, rendering her incapable of producing sound.

Rhonda positioned herself in a 69 with the short, hairy man, literally riding his mustache while Cap slid his cock into her from behind. Leah watched Cap drill away at her pussy, his thick, tan hands gripping her hips while her mouth bobbed up and down on the other man's shaft. Her screams of pleasure were intermittently muffled when her mouth was stuffed full of cock.

On the other bed, Pam recovered from her orgasm and quickly announced, "I'll take what she's having!"

The brunette fumbled with the clasps to her corset, finally releasing her breasts and tossing the article of clothing halfway across the room in one swift motion. The pasty beer-bellied man stretched out on the bed so Pam could mount him in the 69 position, straddling his face and lowering her soaking wet pussy to his lips while she also wrapped her lips around his cock.

The other man, apparently named Jason, rolled a condom onto his thick black cock and took his position behind Pam, working himself slowly into her dripping hole. He fucked her slowly and steadily so she didn't have to sacrifice her focus on the cock in her face.

"There is *nothing* better than being fucked while I have a nice hard, thick cock to lick and suck!" she managed to exclaim to approving groans from her male companions as well as Rhonda, who was still by the window in a matching configuration.

Leah continued to watch through the crack in the door. She felt like she was suspended in an alternate reality, the scene playing out before her so foreign that she could scarcely grasp it. It was beyond her wildest, kinkiest fantasy. She had never even thought to imagine herself having two partners, let alone being one participant in a group of six consenting adults.

This is like live porn. Not that I have ever even watched porn, but I guess it goes down like this? She just couldn't wrap her head around it.

Eventually Jason was spent and went to clean up. Pam climbed off the other man, whose name Leah now learned was Tony, and lay down on her back so he could move into position to fuck her.

Jason came back to the bed and lay down beside her. She stroked her fingers down Jason's thigh and around his balls while Tony pulled her legs up and pushed them back almost to her ears so he could bury himself balls-deep inside her. She nearly cried out from the intensity as Jason leaned over to take one of her nipples into his mouth. Leah observed that his once-spent cock was already beginning to stiffen again as he suckled at her breast.

Rhonda had meanwhile moved beside Pam on the bed,

where the mustached man began fucking her again and Cap stood at the edge of the bed feeding her his cock. Then everyone changed positions yet again. Jason assumed the position between Rhonda's thighs so he could bury his face in her freshly fucked pussy.

Cap began fucking Pam, while her husband now stood beside the bed feeding Rhonda his cock. Her eyes burned with desire, her mouth open and her lips begging him to feed her his load.

He pulled his cock out of her mouth and stroked until it erupted in three long spurts, covering Rhonda's face and mouth. He bent to lick the thick white semen off Rhonda's chin, then allowed her to suck it off his tongue. When Rhonda turned to Pam, their lips entangled as they shared the semen, swirling it on their tongues.

"Fuck! That is *so hot!*" Tony grunted as his face contorted, his own orgasm gripping his entire body. He convulsed, letting a loud groan rip from his throat, and eventually collapsed on the bed next to Rhonda.

Jason then assumed Cap's place, sliding his cock into Pam and wasting no time relentlessly drilling into her juicy cunt. Pam's small white hands buried themselves in Jason's fleshy brown ass cheeks, helping him achieve maximum depth inside her.

Cap looked past the bed and toward the door, where his eyes locked onto Leah's. Her entire body went numb as soon as it sank in that he recognized her.

She hadn't had time to process her feelings about his involvement in the scene unfolding before her. Everything was happening so fast, she felt dizzy and drunk as if she'd downed five drinks in Casey's suite instead of one. Her head and heart were both pounding in unison as Cap began to make his way toward her.

I'm not ready for this. It was the one clear thought that finally pierced through the muck. *I'm just not ready.*

Cap's naked body approached Leah, silhouetted against the moonlight streaming in from the windows on the far side of the room. Before he reached her, she slipped out of sight, closing the door behind her. She was halfway down the hall when she heard the door open and Cap's distressed voice calling after her, "Leah, wait! Leah!" But he couldn't chase her down since he hadn't redressed.

By the time she reached the elevators, the echo of his voice had faded into the stagnant air of the hallway. Nausea stirred in the pit of her stomach, threatening to force its contents up her throat. She swallowed hard, refusing to let herself react physically to what she'd just seen. *The emotional reaction is bad enough.*

On the elevator ride down to the lobby, she erased Cap's number from her phone.

"Wait, you mean like an orgy?" Aimee gasped. Her best friend's rampant curiosity was so strong, it threatened to reach through the phone and grab Leah around the neck to choke out the answers she craved.

Leah was doing her best to stay calm. She'd been up all night pacing between her living room, kitchen and bedroom, and at last she was more weary than agitated. Glory was on high alert, attuned to her owner's mental anguish and standing guard near the sliding glass door to the little balcony where Leah kept a grill and her beach paraphernalia.

She'd finally turned off her phone around 3 AM. A Maryland number repeatedly called, and she was positive it was Cap. She couldn't think of anything to say to him, and if she was being honest, she was angrier at herself than him, anyway.

It's not like I didn't know he was a swinger. What did I think he was going to do at a swinger party? Keep it in his pants all night?

When she turned her phone back on again at 8 AM there were three texts waiting from Aimee demanding an account of the previous night.

She described to her friend the beautifully decorated lobby and ballroom with their twinkling evergreen trees, pine boughs and tulle-wrapped columns. She launched into great detail about all the lovely gowns and the handsome men in their tuxes and how everything was truly magical up until the moment she realized the man she was interested in was impaling two other women's various orifices with his dick.

"Yeah, I guess you'd call it an orgy," she admitted. "There were two women and four men. One woman, Pam, was part of a couple. Her husband – never caught his name – was the one with the mustache. Then there was Casey's friend Rhonda, the blonde I suspect hates me. And then there were two other men, Tony and Jason. Tony was this sort of doughy-looking white guy, and Jason was a younger, very ripped Black man. And, of course, there was Cap."

"So how long do you think you were standing there watching?" Aimee asked.

"I don't know, probably a good fifteen or twenty minutes...maybe longer. It's all so hazy now." She tried to remember what compelled her to stay so long. *Because it was like a train wreck?*

Aimee sighed into the phone, which sounded a little like a hiss. It wasn't often that she was at a loss for words, but she was clearly struggling to find the right ones to console her friend. "I wonder why you watched for so long... Did it turn you on?"

Ugh, I was afraid she would go there. Was I waiting to be invited to join in?

After the elevator arrived in the lobby, Leah had gone to

use the staff restroom near her office. She was shocked to discover that her panties were soaking wet. Despite her personal convictions, her body had responded on a visceral level to the scene in the hotel room. There was nothing she could say or do to deny she was aroused by what she witnessed.

"Truthfully, yes, a little." It was now her turn to sigh. "Is that bad?"

"I think you're just a little confused by it all," Aimee offered. "And I think that's perfectly understandable. You've practically reclaimed your virginity in the last few years, and instead of easing back into the proverbial baby pool of sexual activity, you're jumping headfirst into the shark-infested ocean!"

"Well, that's a very colorful way to put it," Leah agreed, impressed as usual by her best friend's flair for the dramatic. "I'm just not sure what to do now. I can't really be mad at Cap. He didn't do anything wrong."

"Why don't you just talk to him?" her friend suggested. "Talking never hurt anyone, right?"

"Talking is what got me into this mess. If I hadn't talked to him, then I would have never known he had so many layers. I would have never wanted to unravel his mysteries. I wouldn't have gotten sucked in by his charm and those damn dimples."

"Damn dimples," Aimee agreed.

But Leah knew it was futile to completely ignore him. It was a small town, and he knew where to find her.

●　●

L eah noticed, quite a bit too late, that she missed church that morning. She was planning to lie down and close her eyes for twenty minutes before scrambling to make the 10:30 service, but she quickly slipped into a comatose state until 1 PM, when the phone ringing assaulted her peaceful slumber. It was her mother again.

"How was church this morning, sweetheart?" Ms. Miller chirped into the phone at approximately four million decibels.

The pain radiating from a point behind Leah's right eye was staggering. She saw spots dancing on the white curtains in her bedroom, a sure sign a migraine was about to erupt. Nausea and intolerance to light would soon follow.

"I didn't go today," she confessed, not even able to muster the energy to lie.

Mrs. Miller wasted no time reaching into her maternal speech arsenal for her patented tone of disappointment. "Why not, honey? What's wrong with you?"

"I worked late last night, and I have a migraine today," Leah explained. "I am just sitting in my apartment in the dark hoping Glory won't make a mess on the floor before I feel up to taking her out."

Her mother's disappointment hastily gave way to empathy: thick, gooey empathy. Mrs. Miller only had two modes for responding to her children's illnesses: denial (as in "Take two Tylenol and a hot bath; you'll be fine.") and extreme nurturing mode, and clearly the latter was the response *du jour*.

"Oh, darling, you have just been working yourself way too hard lately. You don't ever take any time off; you're there at night and on the weekends all the time. You have absolutely no social life outside of church. It's just not right that you're stressing yourself out so much. No wonder you have migraines! You need to go tell that boss of yours that you need more time off—that way you can come home for Christmas."

Leah held the phone several inches away from her ear while her mother completed her diatribe. It was far easier to acquiesce than argue at that point. "Sure, Mom, I'll tell my boss what you said and let you know, okay?"

"Go take a nap, sweetheart. You'll feel better when you wake up, and then you can take Glory for a walk in the fresh air. It's already been so cold out west this weekend. Winter has definitely arrived in Nebraska."

Leah did feel somewhat fortunate that the temperatures in coastal Maryland were holding in the mid-fifties, even though there was a fierce breeze blowing in off the bay, and flat layers of clouds stacked against the horizon, threatening rain. "Okay, Mom, thanks. Tell Dad I said hi."

"Sure will, honey. I love you," she sang in her chirpy voice.

"I love you too, Mom."

Leah hung up the phone and sighed, which made Glory perk up her ears and come into the room to investigate. Satisfied that nothing fun was going on without her, she turned herself in a circle twice and then lay down so her hindquarters were curled against Leah's back. And there the pair slept for the next two hours until Leah's slumber was interrupted once more, not by a phone call this time but by a knock on the door.

Her head felt considerably better as she rolled off the bed and to her feet, but she realized she was a little dizzy and disoriented from not eating all day. She expected to see a pair of blue eyes and dimples when she opened the door, and her suspicions were immediately confirmed. Except there was a pair of deep brown eyes, a wet nose, and a furiously wagging tail as well.

"You wouldn't answer my phone calls," Cap explained in an apologetic voice as he let himself inside Leah's apartment.

She took a step back away from the door to grant him passage, surrendering her control over the situation. Glory immediately went from dead sleep to high alert mode in roughly a nanosecond, leaping off the bed and bounding into the foyer, her toenails clicking loudly on the tile. The two dogs spent the next sixty seconds sniffing each other's rear ends while their owners formulated speeches in their respective heads.

Cap went first once he was seated on the wicker loveseat in the living room. Leah returned from the kitchen with two glasses of iced tea and took a seat in the matching chair on the diagonal from him.

"I wanted the chance to spend some time with you last night," he began. "I was just finishing up with my friends, and then I was going to come downstairs to find you."

His explanation annoyed her to such a great degree that she retorted: "Finishing up *with* your friends or finishing *doing* your friends?" She was shocked she'd let something so catty come out of her mouth to someone she barely knew.

His one-dimpled smirk revealed he found some humor in her accusation, but he swallowed hard and tried to maintain his seriousness. "I'm sorry if you weren't ready to see that yet. I didn't intend to get involved in anything last night, but Rhonda practically dragged me into the room. I wish you would have come inside to watch and maybe join in, if you felt comfortable... It would have been hot to have another woman there." Now both of his dimples were on display.

Leah shook her head. She hadn't decided how she wanted to handle this situation: express her moral outrage? Brush it off? Forgive and forget? She hoped to have more time to think before having to choose.

"Can you just give me a moment?" She stood up to excuse herself. "I'll be right back."

She scurried down the hall to the bathroom and slipped inside, locking the door behind her. The tiny six-by-eight-foot space enveloped her like a cocoon of safety.

She looked in the mirror over the sink, leaning in so close, she could see all the pores on her nose, the few stray eyebrows that needed to be plucked, and the smattering of golden freckles across her cheeks from her childhood that had never faded. She pushed several strands of her thick strawberry blonde hair behind her ear and blinked a few times to distribute the tears that had formed in the corners of her eyelids.

What the heck am I doing here? What is that man doing in my apartment?

She instinctively sank to her knees on the shaggy seafoam green rug, feeling its twisted fibers dig into the flesh of her shins and prayed for guidance. A tear slid down her cheek that she quickly flicked away as she raised herself to a standing position. Then she went back to face Cap.

"Everything okay?" he asked, concern in his eyes. He'd taken his baseball cap off and set it on the rattan glass-topped coffee table. Keeper, already tired of Glory's puppy shenanigans, had retired lazily at his owner's work boot-clad feet.

Leah nodded. "First, I want to say I'm sorry if I overreacted last night. You were with your friends at a swinger party, and you had every right to do what you do at those types of parties. I shouldn't have been so... I don't know..."

She reached into her heart to pull out some words, hoping God had placed some there for her to grab hold of.

Cap stared at her sincerely while scooting himself to the very end of the loveseat till he was close enough to place his weathered hands on top of hers. His nails were clean and well-groomed, and the hair on his knuckles was nearly white-blond, it was so bleached out by the sun. She noticed how warm and strong and capable his hands felt on top of hers, and how small and dainty hers were by comparison.

"Just say what's on your mind, Leah. Don't sugarcoat it for me. Let it all out." His word "out" had a glaring Eastern Shore pronunciation. She almost got hung up on that one word, "out," and how there could be more than one way to say those three simple letters pushed together.

She pulled her hands from under his and took a sip of her tea, buying herself a little more time to collect that basket of words she'd been fishing for. "Alright, fair enough," she finally conceded. "I'm going to be honest with you."

His eyes widened, and the edges of his lips curled into a smile, but not enough to reveal the dimples. He crossed one boot so his ankle rested on his knee and leaned back with his arms outstretched across the back of the loveseat. She had captured his undivided attention.

"When I first started watching what was going on in that room, I wasn't really thinking of it as you. I felt like I was watching a movie, a porno, or whatever, just faceless bodies, strangers pleasuring each other. And it was so fascinating to watch the movements, to see how different configurations arose, to hear the sounds of ecstasy filling the room. And I thought, 'Wow, this is beautiful, all these people working together to make love.' Truthfully..." she winced at admitting it, "I was getting sort of aroused by the whole thing."

He shifted slightly, taking in her words like a long swig of ice water on the hottest day of the year. His smile had flourished, and his cheeks had taken on just a tiny flush of color. Leah couldn't help but notice when he shifted that a bulge had developed between his legs. She immediately forced herself to look away.

"And then what did you think?" he asked, anticipating that something changed her perception.

"Then I started thinking about you and me...and how badly I wanted you the other day. And how badly I still want you now, and knowing that you were...with these other two ladies and not me, and... What does it all mean to you, anyway?"

His eyes held hers as she continued, "I'm not sure I can ever be part of your world, let alone understand it. Maybe because I was brought up to believe in one woman and one man till death do they part, or maybe because I'm just naïve or close-minded or whatever. I don't know if I'm really okay with it, after all, even though I really wanted to be." She finished her explanation as his boot dropped back to the floor, bringing both of his feet next to Keeper again.

He took a breath. "First of all, I never expected you to be part of that world, Leah. I hope you believe that. Would I enjoy it? Oh sure, most definitely, I'm not gonna lie to you. But I'm not interested in you for purely sexual reasons, and that's also the God's honest truth."

"You're not?" A beat of silence slipped by. "Well, then what, friendship?" She knew she was baiting him.

He smirked. "I think maybe you've conflated sex with love your whole life. I'm pretty sure that's the problem."

"What do you mean by that?"

"Well, you're spouting off that Judeo-Christian one man and one woman bullshit, and I want you to think about that for a second. You know, back in Bible times, people got married when they were like fourteen and died when they were forty. Women were property and had no rights. Men had harems of wives and concubines. How is that one man and one woman? How is that anything like what we do today?"

"That's the Old Testament," she retorted, matching his volume, "not the New Testament."

Cap sighed. "Here's how it is for me," he changed tactics, "sex is a physical thing. It's on the surface, see? It's body parts coming together. Like when I put my hands on top of yours a minute ago, I might have interlaced my fingers with yours, and we would have been connected, right? Sex is the same thing, but with genitals."

Leah was on the edge of her seat waiting to see where this would go. Her gold-flecked eyes urged him on, and she was grateful Glory was occupied with a bone in the corner while Keeper dozed. She didn't want to miss a minute of this; she was on the verge of getting the answers she desperately needed.

"Sex is a physical thing, okay? And then we layer emotions on top of it. It could be passion or lust or friendship or...or it could be love. It's a physical act that *may or may not* express a whole bunch of emotions, and love is only one of them. Does that make sense?" He leaned forward, his elbows resting on his faded denim-covered knees.

Leah's mind raced through Bible verses, reconciling every biblical reference to sex she could think of with Cap's explanation. The whole subject was murky. She had to sift through 2000 years of biblical, theological, and doctrinal commentaries on what was probably the most primal of all human impulses after eating, drinking and breathing—countless layers of sin, shame, and eternal damnation all piled up and aiming to control sexual desire. Her headache was definitely back in full swing.

Pardon the pun.

"I know it's probably a lot different from what you've been taught," he said with a reassuring smile. "I don't want to push you or pressure you. I just wanted to help you understand that this is something I do for fun. I've made wonderful friends in the lifestyle, and we like to do things to make each other feel good. That's really all there is to it. There's no agenda. No obligation. No expectations. Just fun."

He paused for a moment and leaned closer to her, taking her hands into his again. "How do you fit into it? Well, I don't know right yet. Maybe we're destined to just be friends...or maybe there's more there. I don't think we know each other well enough to determine that yet."

Leah nodded; it was the one thing he'd said that she could wholeheartedly agree with. Everything else seemed a hopeless jumble at the moment. Despite her prayer and despite their discussion, she still felt like climbing into his lap like she did the other day and having his strong arms wrapped around her.

She wouldn't, of course. She couldn't. But she wanted to.

He was still holding her hands but now sat up, perfectly straight-backed, poised to stand. "Alright, I'm sorry I just invited myself over like this. I'm normally much more of a gentleman. I just hated to think you were upset and didn't want to talk to me, and I didn't want to lose you...as a friend or whatever other potential there may be." He squeezed her hands into his affectionately. "Are you still mad?"

She shook her head and smiled. He hadn't meant any harm; she was sure of that. "I'm sorry I'm such a mess. I guess I still have a lot of stuff to figure out," she admitted.

"You're what, twenty-seven?" he confirmed.

She nodded sheepishly, uncomfortable having her age compared to his. She'd done the math already several times, and every time she freaked herself out a little bit more.

"Yeah, I'm pretty sure I have fishing gear older than you are," he teased her. "There's no rush. Tell ya what, why don't we just try the friendship thing for now, and we'll see how it goes, okay?"

She couldn't help but feel a momentary pang of disappointment. But the angel sitting on her right shoulder told her it was for the best.

THIRTEEN

Leah didn't feel like sharing the details of her conversation with Cap that evening with Aimee, who had called about an hour after Cap left. Long distance friends had to rely on each other to admit when something was wrong. Aimee couldn't look into Leah's eyes and see it written all over her face. In any case, she didn't answer the phone.

Thankfully, Leah's Monday work day passed quickly. Barry wanted the lowdown on Casey's event and was thrilled to hear it went off without a hitch. The next event on their calendar was a Valentine's party. Casey said she'd come in soon to make the arrangements.

She was grateful Glory was waiting anxiously for her at home. A combination of loneliness and restlessness had settled over her like a thick swath of clouds, and seeing her puppy's wagging tail and knowing she wanted nothing more than love and affection kept Leah's heart from aching. She clipped Glory's pink leash onto her collar and led her downstairs to the small side yard.

It was 6 PM, and the stars were already out in great

number, clustered around a sideways crescent moon that looked like a perfect smile hanging in the darkening heavens.

No wonder it's so dark so early; it's nearly the winter solstice. She recognized Orion's belt with its bright triad of stars glimmering as the constellation rose in the sky.

I used to love looking at the moon and stars through the telescope when I was little.

Her dad would take Leah and her brothers out into the field across from their house and set up his antique telescope that had been handed down through three generations of Millers. The four of them would take turns peering through the tiny lens. Mr. Miller would always end their stargazing by reminding his children that God created the stars and the moon on the fourth day in the creation story told in Genesis.

Even though Leah knew she was standing beneath the same endless, starry sky as her family back in Wahoo, they all seemed so far away these days. When she was little, she could have never imagined living across the country from them. But here she was.

Maybe I should try to go to Nebraska for Christmas after all.

She rolled the idea of going home back and forth in her mind. She couldn't make it in time for the actual holiday because she'd already promised the two evening front desk managers she would work Christmas Eve so they could be home with their families.

I could leave on the twenty-sixth, though. She debated whether or not she wanted to browse for plane tickets online when she got back inside.

But what about Aimee?

Her best friend's due date was December twenty-eighth, and although it was unlikely she would deliver early, Leah hated to chance missing the birth. Aimee would tell her to go enjoy her family; the baby would still be there when she returned. But Leah felt conflicted nevertheless.

A warmer thought distracted her when she allowed herself to wonder what Cap did for Christmas. Did he see his daughters? He had never said anything about his ex-wife; she just knew they had been divorced for several years.

She hadn't heard from Cap since their discussion the night before. *It's for the best. I'm sure we'll cross paths again soon.*

That night after she determined airfare was a little pricey to justify making a last-minute trip to Nebraska, she decided to log back into the dating site. It had been several days since she'd last checked her messages, and it seemed as though the men of the Delmarva Peninsula had already begun to lose interest in her. As usual, there were no viable options.

She fell asleep and was swiftly swept up into a dream about a trip to Africa. It was one of those dreams that felt incredibly vivid and realistic, down to the smells and tastes. She and Glory were on a safari, and she could nearly feel the bumps of the terrain under the tires of the SUV as it made its way through the savanna.

In the dream, she looked at Glory, patted her little head and exclaimed, "This is the most amazing trip ever!"

She saw lions and elephants and giraffes, but what she couldn't see was who was sitting next to her. He had his hand on top of hers, that was the only thing she was sure of. And when she woke up, her hand still felt warm.

● ● ●

The next two weeks flew by as Christmas approached. Leah spoke with Aimee every day on the phone as her due date approached. "I can just see my water breaking at Christmas dinner!" she joked. She described the huge Italian feast her mother-in-law would make and how all of her husband's sisters and aunts were so loud that no one would probably even hear her moaning in agony with labor pains. "They'll find me doubled over in one of the bedrooms upstairs," she predicted with a dramatic sigh.

"Oh, don't be silly," Leah admonished her. "I'm sure everyone will be watching you like a hawk to see if all that tasty, spicy food starts your labor. And you'll probably hear all these old wives' tales for everything from how to get your labor started to how to soothe contractions to how you need to check on the baby every ten seconds when she's asleep!"

"Are you sure you want to work tonight?" Aimee pressed. "Maybe you should come up here, and we can just go out for Chinese or something?"

"I wish I could," Leah admitted. "It's going to be pretty quiet at The Pearl tonight, but I figured I'd crank up the Christmas tunes in the lobby, and I made some fudge to share with everyone. Now if I could only take in some wine, we'd really be celebrating Christmas Eve in style!"

"You're such a good boss, sweetie," Aimee complimented her. "I hope your staff knows how truly lucky they are."

"Awww, thank you!" Leah beamed. "So, are you feeling okay? Any more contractions?"

"Actually, I've been feeling awesome today! More energy than I've had in weeks. I scrubbed down the bathrooms and dusted and ran the vacuum all over the house. Can't really complain too much, especially since my stomach is roughly the size of another planet!" Aimee laughed.

"I hope I get to see you before you deliver," Leah replied, "because there is no way this stomach of yours can be anywhere near as huge as you describe it all the time." She'd also heard her friend liken her belly to Buddha, Texas, a whale and Santa's bag of gifts. Aimee never seemed to run out of hilarious and outrageous analogies, but Leah had a feeling her expectant friend was sporting a perfectly normal-sized baby bump.

"Well, looks like it won't be till next week at the earliest," Aimee lamented. "At my appointment a few days ago, my cervix was still thick and locked up tight."

"There's a mental image I really don't want sticking around!" Leah giggled.

"Haha, well, get used to it, dollface, 'cause once this baby is born, I'm going to be elaborating on all sorts of TMI stuff: sore nipples, diaper contents, episiotomies, and god knows what else. From what I understand, motherhood is not for the faint of heart. Just think: if you're along for the ride this time, nothing will shock you when it's your turn!" Aimee teased her.

"Oh, no need for that. I'm never having kids," Leah retorted. She had been thinking about it more than ever. *I don't think my aspirations for motherhood extend much farther than my fur baby Glory.*

She wished Aimee a merry Christmas and let her go so she could get ready for the traditional holiday dinner at her in-laws' house. As she set her phone down on the kitchen counter, she couldn't help marveling at what it must be like to be in her best friend's shoes.

Imagine knowing this is the last Christmas it will be just her and her husband. Next Christmas they'll have an almost-one-year-old. It's exciting and scary all at once!

She knew Aimee had dreamed of being a mother since she was a little girl playing with baby dolls. But as much as she tried, Leah couldn't imagine having a baby growing inside her, nor a tiny bundle wrapped up in her arms.

She shook off those thoughts as she put Glory in her crate with a new toy that held a treat the puppy would have to work to retrieve. "Merry Christmas, sweet girl!" Leah kissed her furry-faced little pup on the forehead. Glory was so intrigued with the puzzle toy that she hardly whined when Leah locked the door behind her and headed down to her Jeep.

She drove to The Pearl, finding it too chilly to walk in her dress pants and heels.

Leah logged herself into the front desk computer and dismissed the departing manager. She put three containers of fudge in the back room and invited everyone within earshot to spread the word that it was available. She'd used her grandmother Yoder's recipe, who, being an immigrant from Switzerland, certainly knew a thing or two about chocolate.

Accolades began to pour in from a few housekeepers and a security guard who passed through the employee lounge en route to their stations. "Mmmm...melts in your mouth!" Derrick the security guard exclaimed, licking his lips.

She settled down at the computer and glanced at her watch. *Four o'clock. This night is going to crawl, I'm afraid.* Before she began to feel sorry for herself, her phone buzzed with a text.

She assumed it would be Aimee, telling her a funny

story about Christmas dinner with the in-laws. But it was Cap. She hadn't heard from him in a few days.

Cap: Take you to dinner tonight?

Leah: Can't tonight. I'm working the desk till midnight :(

Cap: What?! I thought you were the boss!

Leah: I am the boss, but a very generous one, hence the working so others don't have to thing, she explained.

Cap: Wow, lucky employees. Alright, Merry Christmas and have a good night.

Leah: Merry Christmas to you too, Cap!

She couldn't help her disappointment when the conversation died there. Not only was she bored and would have enjoyed a texting buddy for the evening, but she also regretted this whole "friendship first" arrangement she agreed to.

I wish I hadn't overreacted at the party. But what are you supposed to do when you see something...something that crazy?

She still couldn't get the image of the six bodies out of her mind, all writhing on the bed in their various positions, the women's mouths and pussies full of throbbing cocks. There was a part of her still titillated by those graphic memories. There was a part of her that kept putting herself on the bed in place of Rhonda or Pam. But she doubted she could ever work up the courage to let herself experience anything that wild.

He sure gave up talking to me pretty quickly. I wonder what he ended up doing tonight.

She couldn't imagine Cap spending Christmas Eve alone. *He'll be hanging out with his fishing buddies, or maybe there's another single woman from Casey's Group who doesn't have anything (anyone?) else to do tonight.*

A few hours later, her shift was ending, and she was getting ready to log out of the computer system. She was updating the overnight manager about what happened during her shift (*which is pretty much a big fat nothing*) when those dimples she had pictured just hours before appeared in front of her in living color.

She was so startled about her vision coming to life, she nearly stumbled backwards into the night manager Bob, who caught her just before she sent them both flying to the floor.

Cap seemed highly amused by her reaction. "Nice to see you too!" he exclaimed, apparently channeling Santa himself.

"What are you doing here?" Leah replied breathlessly, regaining her balance and backing a comfortable distance away from Bob, who looked intrigued by what he was witnessing between her and Cap.

"I have Christmas dinner on the stove for you," Cap said with a wink.

Leah's eyes expanded to twice their normal size. She took a deep breath and turned to Bob, silently urging him to go check out the fudge in the employee lounge. Fortunately, he got the message and disappeared within seconds.

Great, Cap just made it sound like I live with him or something, Leah thought, desperately hoping Bob wasn't the gossipy type.

"So are you coming or what?" he asked, a boyish grin spread between the two legendary dimples.

I guess he didn't find some lonely single swinger to spend the night with after all. What the hell, right? I mean, it's Christmas.

"Can I stop by home and get Glory first?"

"I'd have it no other way," Cap replied chivalrously. He took a little mock bow and ushered her out the door. "Parked around back?"

Leah nodded just as the scowling wind whipped around and bit into her cheeks. She instantly regretted her decision not to wear her wool winter coat, opting instead for a soft cashmere cardigan. Her hair was flying all around her face as Cap pulled her body close to his, his arm draped over her shoulder. He was dressed for the elements in a thick Carhartt jacket.

His warmth enveloped her, soaking into her bones and abruptly vanishing just as he steered her to her Jeep, which was, of course, frozen. She fired it up as she watched him climb into his behemoth navy blue truck.

He rolled down the window. "I guess I'll follow you back to your place to get Glory, and then you can follow me to my place?"

She felt weird telling him she already knew where he lived. "You're down a block from the boardwalk, right?" she verified, trying to seem a little nonchalant and not-at-all-stalkerish.

He nodded. "That's right. You can park on the street in front of the shop if you know where it's at."

Leah shivered as much from nervousness as from cold as she put her Jeep in gear and drove the three short blocks to her apartment complex. She could tell Glory had been asleep but was trying to muster up the energy to welcome her owner home in full-on happy beagle style.

Leah grabbed a bag with food and small dishes for Glory and led the puppy downstairs and out into the frozen grass to empty her bladder. She coaxed the dog into the Jeep and went flying down Coastal Highway toward Cap's shop.

FOURTEEN

Cap was waiting on the porch. She recognized the swing immediately from his picture on the dating site. There were some beat-up tackle boxes and old rods leaned against the dark siding. The neon signs in the window were switched off, and only a faint glow emanated from inside the building.

"My apartment's around back," he explained, taking her by the hand that wasn't holding Glory's leash. "It's pretty small, and it's gonna be cramped with the two dogs up there, but you know, it's just me usually, so I don't need much space."

She wondered what happened when his daughters came to visit, but she didn't ask.

Keeper was standing guard at the door, and Leah could hear him whining all the way up the stairs. She was trying to focus on that and not the smell of years of accumulated fish odors that oozed from the walls and floors in the stair-well. *I'll get used to it...probably...*she convinced herself as she switched over to mouth breathing.

"Sorry about the smell," Cap apologized as he pushed the unlocked door open. "I don't even notice it anymore, but I see the way your nose is wrinkling up."

"It's okay," Leah assured him. "I'm starting to get used to it already."

She scanned the perimeter of the small space. They'd entered through the kitchen, which was galley-style with a bar and two stools on the far end between the kitchen and the living room. A cat dismounted from her window perch and slunk past them, trying to escape Glory's notice, but it was too late. Glory bounded after her and nearly sent Leah sprawling to the floor, much like the time she'd met Cap on the beach and lost her shoes in the surf.

"That's Marlina," Cap introduced her. "Like marlin the fish, but with an A at the end."

"All your pets have fishing-related names. I get it." Leah smiled. "Very creative."

"Why do I get the feeling you're making fun of me?" Cap shot back with a grin, his dimples revealing he wasn't in the least bit upset.

The malodorous fish smell was replaced with a spicy scent coming from a huge pot on the stove. Cap gently moved Leah to the side so he had access to the oven, from which he pulled a steaming hot loaf of French bread.

"So what's for dinner?" Leah's stomach was rumbling. She'd sampled a couple pieces of fudge during her shift but hadn't eaten a real meal.

"Homemade gumbo," Cap announced, his pride filling the room alongside the delicious aroma.

"Wow, impressive." Leah smirked, finding every movement he made to be interesting and revealing. *So he cooks too—that's really sexy.* She admired the way his thick, tan hand barely fit inside the oven mitt.

"You ain't seen nothing yet, baby!" He winked at her as he lifted the lid to give the gumbo a stir with a wooden spoon.

Twenty minutes later, the pair was perched on his loveseat next to the Christmas tree in the small living room area. The tree was real and, along with the spicy gumbo smell, Leah now had a steady stream of fresh pine filtering through her sinuses. Fortunately, that meant the fish smell from the staircase had completely vanished from her memory.

The tree twinkled with multicolored lights, along with those long, bubbling, retro-style lights she remembered from back in the '80s. The dogs had adjourned to Cap's bed, and Leah could hear them both snoozing, their bellies full of Christmas treats. The cat brushed up against Leah's leg once or twice before retiring to the afghan-covered velvet armchair across the room.

There was a sense of coziness and warmth that Leah had never been able to create in her own apartment. Maybe it was the Christmas tree or the throw rugs that covered the worn wood floors, maybe it was the dim lighting or the peaceful whirring of sleeping animals. She wasn't sure, but the homey comfort of it sank into her.

Cap was effervescent as he shared stories about adventures on the high seas, trying to get charter trips in despite impending storms. She shared some horror stories from college practicums and a little about what would be going down in the Miller household on Christmas Eve.

"My mother has this completely cheesy tradition she started when we were little kids," Leah explained. "She collected a dozen or so tiny brass bells tied with red and green ribbons. She keeps them on a very pretty, antique cut-glass tray and passes them out at the end of Christmas Eve dinner, which is always spiral-cut ham, scalloped potatoes, green beans and homemade yeast rolls, by the way. We each have to take a bell, and she makes us ring it while we sing 'Jingle Bells.'"

She laughed as the memory filled her mind so vividly that she almost felt like a little girl again. "Oh, we outgrew it years and years ago, and my brothers always roll their eyes when they see the bells come out on that tray, but we still do it to humor her. It'd kill her if we didn't play along. I know she's dying to share the tradition with grandchildren someday."

"Your parents sound like real nice folks," Cap observed. "Sounds like you had a fun, happy childhood."

Cap shifted so one knee was angled against the couch cushion and now brushed against her thigh. His hand moved closer to hers too, only millimeters from touching her.

"They are," Leah agreed, "in a narrow-minded, *if you're not a Christian, you're going to hell* kind of way." She laughed it off. "You know, other than that, they're super nice!"

"Well, I'm a Christian," Cap said, puffing out his chest. "Think they'd like me?"

Leah giggled and tried to picture taking Cap to her parents' house, introducing him as her boyfriend. It was a stretch, but she could pretty clearly predict their reaction to her bringing home a much older man, one who was divorced with daughters just a few years younger than her. They would *not* be pleased.

"You didn't get that, did you?" He watched her nose wrinkle at the thoughts spinning through her mind.

"Oh, about being a Christian?" She caught herself from her daydream, reeling herself back to his living room.

"Yeah, it was a joke. 'Christian' is my name, you know," he offered like a Christmas present all done up in shiny packaging and frilly bows.

"Oh!" she exclaimed. "I assumed your name was Christopher... That's...uh..." She scrambled to grasp how she should feel about him being "a Christian." "That's pretty ironic!"

"Leah is a biblical name, isn't it?" he asked.

She nodded. "From the book of Genesis... You've heard of Jacob and Esau? After Jacob tricked his twin Esau out of his inheritance, he went away to find a wife and fell in love with the beautiful Rachel. Her father made him work seven years to earn her hand in marriage. On their wedding day, when he lifted the veil expecting to see Rachel, it was her older and uglier sister Leah instead. Their father made Jacob work seven more years to earn Rachel's hand in marriage. Pretty sad, huh? Leah was the consolation prize."

"Wow...I have never heard that one before, and I thought I'd heard it all in Sunday School growing up." He took her hand into his, and she felt his warmth wrapping around her. "It's hard to think of you as a consolation prize..."

Her cheeks flushed slightly at his compliment, but she accepted it graciously. "Although Leah was not beautiful, she was loyal and gave birth to six sons, including Judah, the line Jesus came from. So Jesus was a direct descendent of my namesake. Pretty cool, huh?"

"I think I'd rather have that honor than beauty. Besides, physical beauty fades, right?" His eyes had missile lock on hers. "But you're lucky to have the whole package: brains, beauty, personality... You're no consolation...just a prize."

She held her breath for a moment. *Did those words really come out of his mouth?*

But she knew she hadn't misheard when his finger stroked down her cheek. She instinctively closed her eyes—she knew what came next. His lips smoldered against hers as she tasted some of the spices from their dinner burning into her tender flesh.

She hadn't opened her eyes yet when he pulled away. He spread a soft fleece blanket on the floor under the Christmas tree. In moments, he was lying on his side, beckoning her with his eyes and dimples to join him.

She lay facing him with her head resting against his massive biceps. He pulled her so close that her nose nestled in the tuft of his thick, silvery chest hair that peeked out from the top of his shirt. Her nostrils filled with the scent of his cologne, musky and wild. Cap's arm wrapped around her, and he lifted her shirt a few inches so his fingers could trail up and down the bare skin on the small of her back and the top of her ass.

She wanted to speak, to ask him if he'd changed his mind about friendship, to say that she had...but the words wouldn't form on her lips.

He lifted her chin to him again and whispered, "Is this okay?"

She could barely squeak the word "yes" out of her mouth, but her nod and the way her body melted into his gave away her answer perfectly. He covered her lips with his, and then words were unnecessary again.

Her body responded to his as it was designed to do, with no conscious thought or direction. *It's completely uncontrollable.* She exhaled a soft sigh at the chills racing down her spine.

This is what I've wanted him to do to me since the first time I saw him, and I'm not resisting. I'm complying, submit-

ting...a moth drawn to the flame. It's Christmas Eve, and I drank wine and let myself be seduced by the pretty bubbling lights reflecting in his eyes... And those damn dimples... And...it's okay, it's okay...

The Christmas lights cast their colorful glow onto his skin as he unbuttoned his shirt. Her back arched as he lowered himself on top of her, and she shifted her hips so he could slide her pants and panties down, leaving her unencumbered beneath him.

He was so gentle—all the kinetic energy in his strong, broad shoulders and hulking chest and arm muscles locked away as he touched her with the lightest brush imaginable. His fingertips just barely grazed her nipples once he released her breasts from their lace underwire cage. That disciplined restraint transferred to his mouth as his tongue darted out to lightly flick the hardened buds resting on top of her ribcage, and then even further south as he tasted her other hardened bud.

He drank her in, leisurely lapping the nectar off her succulent petals. She had never been so thoroughly and thrillingly consumed, as if she was the most delicate, extravagant dessert ever created.

His mission was clearly to force her to surrender to her climax, but she didn't want that. She vaguely remembered that feeling...that delicious feeling of a hard cock easing its way into her folds, sliding in so teasingly slow that she would tremble with desire until it reached her depths. Her craving for that feeling came over her—so strong, so overwhelming—she pulled Cap up across her body until she was tasting her juices on his lips.

"I want you now," she managed, her lungs compressed under his weight. "I want you inside me."

"Are you sure?" he asked breathlessly, as if he couldn't move another muscle until she convinced him it was the one thing in all the world of which she was absolutely certain.

He pressed against her thigh, throbbing, pulsating with the same desire she felt vibrating out from her core. But he remained the very picture of restraint, of self-control, balancing himself on top of her so she could still easily breathe. He positioned his rock-hard cock far enough away that he wouldn't be tempted to plunge it into her before she was ready.

When was she last poised like this, straddling the threshold of ecstasy? She had felt it before, years before. *This yearning, this longing...yes...I have felt it before, but not like this. Not so all-consuming. Not this powerful.*

"Yes, yes, please," she qualified, lifting her hips and pressing against him, hoping to catch the tip of his cock between her slit. "I'm sure."

He turned and fumbled for something in a basket near the tree, then she realized he was slipping on a condom. Torn between relief and impatience, her whole body clenched with need. He cradled her head in one hand, lifting her face to his until their lips met again. His other hand guided his cock inside her. She was not expecting the girth or the length, and she felt it stretching her inch by inch.

Cap sighed as she finally gave way to him. "Oh, god...Leah..."

Hearing her name pass through his lips sent a jolt from her brain straight down her spine and into her core. He began to slowly thrust in and out, pacing himself, his patience and self-control both exasperating and mind-boggling. It wouldn't take much to carry her over the edge; her own self-control had already been thrown out the window. She wrapped her legs around his, attempting to take him even deeper inside, pushing up to meet every grind.

"Cap...oh..." she pushed out, more breath than voice. "You feel amazing..."

She had nearly forgotten what it felt like to orgasm so intensely, so serendipitously, controlled by external forces and not by her own hand. The delicious crescendo foreshadowed the ecstasy, but the crashing waves of pleasure still washed over her unexpectedly. She cried out as she trembled and shuddered beneath him, and he held her closer yet, expertly steering himself through the swelling tide of her climax.

Lovemaking with Cap was not a ten- or fifteen-minute adventure, as it had been with past partners. It was a marathon, not a sprint. An hour and a half later, after she had been pulled on top of him, thrown over the side of the sofa, and then tugged down onto his lap as he sat on the loveseat, he finally announced in a deep, growling moan, "I'm going to come now, okay?"

She looked at him incredulously, her face caked with a mixture of sweat, makeup, and tears from the intensity of what seemed like hundreds of orgasms that had rocked through her body that evening. Every ounce of moisture and energy had been drained from her. She had never, ever in her life felt more satiated and full. She couldn't even respond to his question. Completely speechless, she could only manage a weary nod.

He began moving her up and down on his shaft after she lost the ability to lift her hips more than an inch. A look of concentration gripped his face as he buried his cock inside her. His hands digging into her hips, he began to bounce her faster and faster on top of his steel cock. Her breasts were jiggling so fast with his relentless pursuit of release, they were nearly vibrating.

Just when she thought she couldn't take any more, a jolt surged through him. His cock grew impossibly hard and then there was the sound: a primal howl that Leah immediately feared would wake the dogs. His thighs began to shake underneath her, and his face twisted before going completely slack, as if he'd gone from agony to ecstasy in a heartbeat.

"Fuck," he whispered, "oh, baby..."

His cock twitched inside her as his orgasm dissipated. He pulled her head down so it rested on his chest and wrapped his arms around her. "Baby, that was amazing," he breathed into her ear.

Despite his alleged long list of lovers, he genuinely seemed in awe. She felt his heart pounding against her temple as his body struggled to find equilibrium. Sweat dripped from his face onto her hair.

"Are you okay?" he finally asked.

"Yes," Leah answered, no louder than a whisper. "I...I've never been fucked like that before..."

She lifted her head just in time to see the dimples reappear. He smiled at her, still too weak to formulate a complex sentence. "I wasn't expecting it either...but I just kept wanting more and more of you."

She didn't have time to respond before he suggested that they retire to his bedroom. Glory and Keeper reluctantly repositioned themselves at the foot of the bed as Cap pulled back the quilt and sheet, ushering her in. The bed was crisp and cold, but his body next to her was warm and moist, still sweaty from their romp.

He pulled her into his arms again until her head lay on

his chest. "I think you've worn me out, sugar." He kissed her on top of her head.

"Likewise," she whispered. "Merry Christmas."

"Best Christmas ever," he qualified, and then in a few fleeting moments, they both surrendered to sleep, visions of sugarplums dancing in their heads.

Leah awoke to her phone buzzing on the nightstand next to Cap's bed. She scrambled for it just as Glory reacted to the sound with a piercing staccato bark. Cap didn't stir as Leah squeaked out a hoarse "Hello?"

"On my way to the hospital!" Aimee announced, seemingly through clenched teeth.

"Wow, really?" Leah was suddenly very, very awake. Glory hopped onto the bed next to her owner as if patiently waiting for instructions.

Cap rolled over onto his side and was still snoozing away, the plaid flannel sheets bunched at his waist. Leah observed the way the moonlight streaming between the blinds carved out the impressions and hollows of his back. She imagined those muscles being built from years and years of pulling ropes, reeling in huge fish and hoisting them into the boat.

She'd never been with an older man before, nor one who made his living doing physical labor. Years of work had shaped and molded Captain Chris Sheldon in a very distinct and perceptible way; he was hewn by his craft.

"Yeah, I'm at five minutes apart. Tony's driving as fast as he can. Thank God there's not much traffic on Christmas morning so it's not bad."

"How far is it to the hospital?" Leah tried to keep her excitement from amping her voice up several decibels.

"Usually twenty to thirty minutes. We've got about four more miles, I think. Looks like I'm going to have a Christmas baby! Isn't that exciting?" Her friend's pain had subsided long enough for her to sound happy and anxious to meet her new little one.

"Well, then, I'm on my way!" Leah's brain spun with the plans it needed to enact, starting with finding her clothes. Then she realized she'd have to call Bob and see if there was any way he could cover her shift at The Pearl's front desk.

"You can come later if you want. Go back to sleep for a few hours maybe? What are you going to do with Glory?" Aimee's breath was starting to quicken by the end of her last question.

"I'm not at home, actually... I'm going to have to run home and get Glory's things. Can I drop her off at your house before I come to the hospital?" Leah asked, not sure if her friend would be able to answer due to the low growl beginning to escalate on the other end of the phone.

Cap sat up in the bed and grabbed Leah's hand. "Are you okay? What's going on?" he demanded gruffly.

"What?!" Aimee shrieked as soon as the waves of pain began to subside. "What do you mean you're not home at 4 AM? Who is that talking? Who are you with?" Then she let out a huge loud groan that rang in Leah's ears.

"Don't worry about it," Leah answered. "I'll be there in a little bit. Just breathe, sweetie! I know you'll do great!"

"What was that about?" Cap asked.

Leah laid her phone back down on the nightstand with trembling fingers. The adrenaline was coursing through her body like it did when there was a problem at work and she had to spring into action.

"My best friend just went into labor!" Her voice was fueled by excited nerves. She pulled back the sheets and found the cold floor with her bare feet. She had already forgotten she was completely nude and suddenly felt exposed, even in the dim moonlight. "I've gotta get to Philly."

"What about Glory?"

Leah had already stumbled into the living room, scanning the floor for the clothes she'd worn the night before. She located her bra and slung it around her ribcage, fastened and slid it into place. She stepped into her pants, then slipped her shirt on, fumbling with the tiny buttons as she hurried.

She didn't notice Cap had entered the room, the sheets wrapped around him like a toga. "Do you want to leave Glory here?" he asked, which startled Leah so badly she almost tripped over her heels as she struggled to get them on her feet.

She was trembling from cold, from nerves, and from the reality of what had happened the night before, which was slowly but surely sinking into each of her wakening brain cells.

"I really don't mind," Cap pressed. "How long will you be gone?"

"Uh, I don't know, a few days at least." She slid her arms

into the cashmere cardigan she'd worn in lieu of a proper coat. "If I can get someone to cover for me at work."

I thought I had another week to get things settled and to pack. Her heart was racing, and her head was beginning to pound from the increased blood supply.

"Let me help, Leah, please? It'll be a lot easier for you if you don't have to worry about your little girl. You can't take her to the hospital with you, you know." Cap grinned his dimpled smile, the one with the power to persuade a nun to go to bed with him.

Leah did not like the slightly patronizing tone dripping off his tongue like honey. She hated being talked down to; she loathed being treated like a child, as if she didn't always consider all the contingencies in advance. But she didn't feel like arguing with him, and she *did* trust him to take good care of Glory.

She'd be a lot happier here with him and Keeper than caged up in Aimee and Anthony's tiny house. "Alright, fine. If you're sure. I can run home and get her kennel and some food if you want."

"Don't be ridiculous," he chided her. "Just go to your friend and don't worry about us. We'll be just fine, won't we?" He reached down to run his fingers up Glory's neck to her chin. She shook her little hind end and wagged her tail in agreement with him.

"Okay. I'll call and check on her tonight," Leah promised. She retrieved her purse from the coffee table and made her way toward the door at the back of the room, making a mental list of everyone from work she could call to cover her shift.

"What, I don't even get a kiss goodbye?"

She met him where the kitchen transitioned into the

living room. He slid his arm around her waist and pulled her tight to his body.

"Thanks for last night," he whispered into her ear just before planting his lips on top of hers and lingering there for a moment, their mouths touching just enough to create a wave of electricity between them.

● ● ●

She sat in her Jeep for two whole minutes before deciding what to do. She was paralyzed by the thoughts that had stormed in, but she needed to turn the key in the ignition. It was cold, and her breath was steaming up the windshield. Her fingers were numb and her knees locked into position.

What the hell did I just do?

She couldn't help but envision the proverbial angel and devil sitting on opposite shoulders, poised to debate the issue with each other. She hated all things cliché, but the dichotomy of her Good Girl and Bad Girl selves going head to head couldn't be ignored.

Leah's inner thighs were burning where Cap had been the night before. A soreness permeated her groin, but it was a delicious soreness that painted her memory with visions of his silhouetted frame against the Christmas tree lights as he sank into her, filling her with his throbbing cock.

You know what? I'm not going to feel bad about this. It felt amazing. He felt amazing...and I don't think I did anything wrong.

The little she-devil perched on her shoulder grinned victoriously.

● ● ●

The hospital room's curtains were drawn, blocking out the bright Christmas sun that shone over Philadelphia. Music played in the background, but not the soothing melodies she expected to hear in a labor and delivery suite. Aimee was headbanging to heavy metal as Leah rushed into the room.

Father-to-be Anthony was propped up in the corner, relaxing in a cushy-looking recliner, his feet resting on a peach and sage-colored ottoman. He wore headphones and had an iPad open on his lap, but his eyes were closed, and he appeared to be sleeping.

"Some support he is, huh?" Aimee rolled her eyes.

"Why are you listening to such loud, clanging music?" Leah asked, covering her ears and searching for the source of the cacophony.

"What, you don't like Slayer?" she gasped with fake disbelief.

Leah smirked. "So, you must have had drugs, right? You seem really calm and relaxed."

Aimee grinned and pointed to the monitor next to her. "See those mountains? Those are contractions, and I haven't felt nary a one since I've been here. Not bad, huh?"

"Epidural?" Leah inquired, and her friend nodded. "Well, good. I don't know what I was expecting... I guess that Hollywood portrayal with the mom all sweaty, her hair in a ponytail and matted to her face, huffing and puffing as she tries to push the baby out."

"Yeah, we're not quite there yet," Aimee assured her. "I'm only dilated to six."

"Oh, okay, so I guess we just wait, then? You have to get to ten, right?" Leah confirmed.

"Huh, you know more about this than I thought!"

Aimee teased her. "Is that 'cause you grew up on a farm?" She laughed so hard that a nurse came in to readjust the monitors on her stomach; the pressure from the laughing made the readings go haywire.

"I didn't grow up on a farm, and you know it," Leah retorted. "Although I did have to take Ag class in eighth grade. Wow, that was a trip! I can tell you a bunch of different breeds of hogs and dairy cattle, but I assure you that's not where I learned about human gestation."

Anthony's eyelids slowly fluttered open. His dark eyes looked glassy and not quite capable of focusing. "Is it time yet?" he mumbled.

"No, not yet. Hold your horses," Aimee complained. "Gee whiz, I guess we're not getting this done fast enough for your Daddy," she said to the baby, patting her belly.

"Hi, Leah," he offered, ignoring his wife as he finally recognized they had a visitor in the room. "Can I get you anything? Soda? Water? Earplugs for when our families get here?"

Leah giggled. "Oh, I think I'm just fine. I was going to ask if I can get either of you anything."

"Oh, hey," Aimee interrupted them. "Leah, spill the beans about last night. What were you doing out on Christmas Eve, you little vixen?"

"I was working," Leah lied. "It's no big deal."

"You were only working till midnight. Why weren't you home when I called you this morning at four?" Aimee pressed.

Leah looked down at the floor, trying to decide if the truth was really in Aimee's best medical interests. *Might as well tell her. She's not going to believe anything else anyway.*

"Well...Cap made me Christmas dinner...and...I..." She

looked up just in time to see Aimee's eyes bulge out with surprise.

"And you spent the night?" she asked expectantly. "Oh, please tell me you spent the night!"

Aimee is more excited about this than I am.

"Thank God, it really is Christmas! Leah got laid! Glory, glory, hallelujah, it's a Christmas miracle!" she sang.

Leah tilted her head in Anthony's direction, silently begging her friend to give it a rest. "Yeah, it was nice," she offered by way of description, and that was all she intended to say on the matter.

Moments later, the heavy metal music gave way to its human speech equivalent. The door burst open, and over the top of the nurse's pleas for compliance rose the sound of Aimee's mother, Francine Minnelli. She was a small, round, but extraordinarily animated woman whose voice was about seven levels louder than it needed to be at all times. Whether she was happy or angry mattered not, she was just loud.

Right behind Mrs. Minnelli were Aimee's two sisters, Carmen and Michelle, and her sister-in-law Gina. The volume these four women could generate en masse was formidable. Leah suddenly wondered if they'd all get kicked out of the hospital.

Anthony recognized trouble when he saw it and began slowly backing toward the door. "I'm going to run out and grab something to eat real quick if that's okay," he announced, but he was halfway out the door before anyone could protest.

"He looks tired," Mrs. Minnelli observed before he'd made it down the hall.

"Yeah, we've been up all night. The drugs are making me sleepy, so I've gotten a little rest, but he hasn't gotten any at all," Aimee replied. "He's been very supportive, though, even when I yell at the nurses."

"Yell at the nurses?" Leah raised an eyebrow, but it wasn't difficult for her to imagine her feisty friend spitting out some choice words while in pain.

"When they stuck that huge fucking needle in my back, I just about went ballistic!" Aimee explained, getting worked up enough to appear just a touch animated, despite the drugs that had subdued her a great deal.

"Why are you listening to this trash?!" Aimee's oldest sister Carmen said with disgust as she searched for the off button on the radio. "I listened to classical music when I had Tommy and Zoe. Nothing but the best for my two babies!"

"So, Leah was just telling me about her new boyfriend," Aimee announced to divert the attention away from herself.

"Is that so?" Mrs. Minnelli gushed. "I always wondered why a cute girl like you didn't have a man! What's he like?"

Leah blushed. "He's not really my boyfriend; he's just someone I'm getting to know." She hoped her dismissive tone would convey her desire for privacy on the matter.

Fortunately, that was the last word anyone spoke about Cap that day. Soon after, Anthony's mother arrived, and she and the Minnellis took over labor duty. Leah was cast aside. She and Anthony sat in the corner like caged puppies making idle conversation until it was time for Aimee to push.

Then everyone got kicked out of the room, except for Anthony, who was clearly out of his element and appeared as though he would have gladly traded places with any of the women.

Leah was ushered into the waiting room along with the rest of the clan. Mrs. Minnelli made an attempt at conversation, but otherwise Leah was left to listen to the thoughts bouncing off the corridors of her brain.

Anthony finally emerged from the delivery room, his face glowing and eyes wet with tears. It was just like a scene in one of a hundred movies where the proud papa comes out to announce the birth to the rest of the family.

"It's a girl!" he proclaimed.

Leah expected her heart to leap with excitement, but she just drew it in, trying to reconcile the image of her best friend holding a newborn to her breast with the one of her downing tequila shots during some sort of harebrained drinking game in college.

She knew Aimee was well-prepared, having read tons of books, and she had no fewer than five women close by who could show her the ropes, but still, the consequences of a mistake...a tiny oversight...a misjudgment...could be fatal. Leah was bludgeoned by the realization of all the things that could go wrong while raising a child, everything from choking to accidental poisoning to drowning.

She scolded herself for having morbid thoughts during such a happy occasion. *Why does my overactive brain have to ruin everything?*

When it was finally her turn to hold that precious bundle in her arms, she looked into the tiny red, scrunched-up face with her eyebrows and eyelashes delicately painted on, and remembered how many billions of people had been born and lived and gone on to pass their genes down the lines of history.

Somehow we make it through. I don't know what's the bigger miracle, conception and birth or just life itself, the way we figure out how to survive despite everything stacked against us.

Leah turned the key and pushed open the back door to the small house that Aimee and Anthony rented so she could feed their cats and stay the night. She'd go back to the hospital in the morning to visit with the newly minted family of three. Her phone buzzed in her purse as she was dumping the cat food into the dishes while three hungry felines crossed between her legs, rubbing against her calves and shins appreciatively.

"Hey, Cap, how's it going?" Her involuntary smile shone through her voice.

"All's well here. Just took Glory and Keeper for a run down the boardwalk, and they are plum tuckered out." He laughed. "What's the scoop? Baby come yet?"

"Yes, I was just getting ready to call you. Seven pounds, seven ounces. She's absolutely gorgeous with a head full of black hair. They named her Natalie, which means Christmas. I even got to hold her. She's so tiny and sweet!" Leah gushed.

"Uh oh," Cap grunted. "Guess your biological clock was activated, huh?"

"Oh," she said, surprised Cap would assume something like that. She spent a moment trying to decide whether or not she should be offended. "No, nothing like that. I don't think I have one of those."

"Really?" Cap asked. "I pegged you for the domestic type. You know, someday, when you're bored with the world of hotel management...figured you'd wanna pop out a couple of babies."

"Nope, you couldn't be further off. I've never wanted children," Leah corrected him. She decided she was definitely offended now, if she hadn't been previously.

"You just haven't met the right man," he asserted, further delving into the disfavor zone. "Trust me, when you meet the right man, you're gonna want to have his baby."

Well, that's it, he's hit rock bottom now. She seethed as the blood rose to the surface of her skin. "Of all the stupid misogynistic things I've ever heard! Seriously, Cap?"

He chuckled in response to her ire. "Calm down there, sugarplum, I'm only teasing. Thou doth protest too much!" He delivered the line in his best Shakespearean accent. After he was met with silence, his native Eastern Shore tongue was restored. "I'm sorry, I didn't mean to offend you, Leah. I was only kidding."

"Alright," she managed. "I'm going to go now. Give Glory a kiss for me, okay?"

"Will do, although I'd rather be giving you a kiss," he admitted. "Or something more..."

Leah washed and put away all the baby clothes, piled diapers in the diaper stacker, and sterilized every item that could possibly come into contact with the newborn. She made sure that the new mom was comfortable and had everything her heart could desire at her fingertips.

They don't call me the Guest Experience Strategist for nothing.

She had no doubts when she left Philadelphia a few days after Christmas, Aimee would be getting her adventure into motherhood started on the right foot. Even Anthony admitted he wasn't sure how they would have managed without Leah's help. "You know," he remarked, "if you ever decide to leave the hotel business, you could probably make a killing providing this service to new moms!"

"I promise I will return the favor when it's your turn," Aimee vowed in their last few moments together before Leah made the three-hour trek back to Maryland. Aimee's smile fell when her friend's brow furrowed. "You know, if you ever change your mind about having kids."

Cap's statement from their last conversation burned in Leah's ears. *Trust me, when you meet the right man, you're gonna want to have his baby,* he'd said. *That's the most sexist thing I've heard in a long time,* Leah thought.

She considered venting to Aimee about it, but she had decided not to say anything else about Cap. Every time Aimee tried to pry out more information, Leah changed the subject.

Fortunately, little Natalie was the baby version of "saved by the bell." Her tiny lips would curl into a pout, signaling that a huge wail of discontent was about to be unleashed on all within earshot. And then all discussion regarding Cap was abandoned, much to Leah's relief, while everyone scrambled to soothe the little one.

Leah patted Aimee's hand and shook her head, "Can't see that happening now, but you never know, right?" She smiled to show it wasn't a sore subject. Then she stroked the newborn's silky black hair as she finished her breakfast, her blissful face revealing a trip to dreamland was imminent now that her belly was full of milk. "Although this little angel...she's so sweet, she's liable to make anyone want a little doll baby of their own."

Aimee broke the suction between Natalie's mouth and her nipple with her index finger. "She's asleep again mid-feeding. I never know if I should wake her up, burp her, or just let her sleep."

"I vote let her sleep," Anthony said, eavesdropping from the doorway. "I'll take her so you two can say a proper good-bye." He stepped toward the bed where Aimee was propped up with a half dozen pillows and a yellow gingham Boppy decorated with tiny bees and butterflies. The new dad scooped up the tightly wrapped pink bundle from her mother's arms.

"It would be so much fun for our kids to grow up together, wouldn't it? Can't you just see them running along the beach together? Laughing and playing in the waves?" Aimee asked with a dreamy look in her dark eyes.

Leah sighed, wishing she could stare into her future via the proverbial crystal ball. Was Cap's sexist statement a one-way street, or did he feel the same was true for men? *When they meet the right woman, they want her to have their babies.* Was Cap still able to have kids, or did he get a vasectomy after his daughters were born?

All the way home, she beat herself up for wondering, especially that last item.

● ● ●

She drove south through Ocean City all the way to the inlet. Despite not knowing what she should say to Cap, she wanted to be reunited with her puppy as soon as possible. She hoped she would be able to slip in, retrieve Glory, and be back on her way in a flash, but she had a distinct feeling a certain pair of ocean-blue eyes and irresistible dimples would work in tandem to detain her as long as possible.

She was disappointed and irritated to see that Cap's truck was not in its usual parking place in front of his shop. "Oh, that's just great," she muttered under her breath as she dug her phone out of her purse.

"Oh, so you're alive after all?" was Cap's way of answering the phone.

"Where is my dog?" Leah cut right to the chase.

"Relax, Sugar, we're on our way back from Salisbury. We had to pick up some stuff. I called earlier to tell you, but you didn't answer."

"How long?" Leah snipped.

"Ten minutes. Go on upstairs; the door's unlocked."

Leah tapped her screen to end the call without saying goodbye. *He leaves his door unlocked? Who does that?* she wondered, but when the fishy smell in the entryway smacked her in the face, she realized it was probably deterrent enough.

She held her breath as she made her way up the stairs and pushed the door open. Marlina the cat greeted her by brushing against her legs affectionately but skulked away as soon as she realized she wasn't getting any food out of the deal.

Leah glanced around Cap's small but tidy apartment. It resembled a ship the way each precious square foot was maximized to its greatest potential. Built-in cabinets flanked each side of the living room, lined a wall in the bedroom, the kitchen and bathroom. She assumed he had all his personal items stashed away because very few things were visible except a couple of fishing magazines and a cup and bowl from his last meal.

Spread on top of the cabinets in the living room was a collection of small framed prints, each of them featuring a grinning person holding up a rather large fish. He had a small laptop stowed in a bin beside the sofa alongside a remote to the TV and a few dog toys. The Christmas tree they'd made love under a few nights before had already been whisked away, not even a single pine needle remaining.

The window from his kitchen looked down on the street below. The lone streetlight guarding his block cast its orange glow onto the sidewalk and pavement, revealing fresh snow falling. She shivered thinking about having to clean off her Jeep before driving sixty-some blocks to her painfully cold, lonely apartment.

How many more days till summer?

Before she could snoop around the apartment further, Cap's navy truck whipped into its usual space along the curb. Out popped Cap with two leashes wound around his hand. The pair of canines bounded toward the door, pulling Cap behind them like sled dogs getting the heave ho on the arctic tundra.

The door handle turned, and the two dogs leaped over the threshold before Cap could fully swing the door open. Glory jumped into Leah's waiting arms, and soon her face was covered with wet puppy kisses.

"She looks pretty happy to see her mom," Cap observed as Keeper sniffed Leah for a moment and then indulged in a series of loud gulps of water from his bowl.

"Awww, I missed my baby girl too!" Leah cried, not even bothering to wipe the puppy slobber off her cheeks. She gave her wiggly beagle a kiss and plopped her back down onto the wood-planked floor so she could scurry off toward the water bowl to join Keeper.

"Those two have been pretty much inseparable. It's sorta made me feel guilty for not having a little sister for my boy all these years," Cap confessed. "I sent you a few pictures of their shenanigans. Did you get them?"

Leah nodded. "Sorry I wasn't really in touch. I was trying to focus on Aimee and the baby. I just wanted to..." She let her voice trail off as the tension in the four feet of space between them rose up like a tornado, making her almost dizzy with its sudden onslaught of unexpected emotions: frustration, resentment and regret—spiked with a surprising dose of arousal.

He took one giant step toward her, and in a tick of the

clock, his arms were wrapping around her and drawing her to his chest. Her nostrils filled with his scent, and she instantly remembered what it felt like when he slid inside her, when his heavy, lust-laden breaths fell on her cheek. There was something miraculous about his touch; it dissolved every emotion in the tornado that had been spinning around her. Every emotion except for arousal.

One thing about Cap was that he didn't need words. Not that he didn't have an impressive vocabulary—even if his words were colored by his twangy accent—but his most effective communication required no words at all. His mere presence, his skin against hers, spoke volumes more than his lips could ever utter. She felt all the words he might have spoken seeping into her as she melted into his embrace.

After several minutes of silence, he offered a sincere apology for his statement about her biological clock, but it was unnecessary at that point. She'd already felt it through his touch.

He guided her to the loveseat in his living room, and all she could think of was how she'd straddled him on the cushion and he'd gripped her hips while he'd relentlessly drilled his cock into her. Those dizzying impulses of arousal traveled up and down her spine again as she took a seat on that exact cushion, reeling with disappointment that she wasn't sitting on his lap instead.

What is wrong with me? One time and I can't even control myself in his presence.

"So I'm just curious, and if it's something you don't want to talk about, just tell me to mind my own business," Cap started, "but I really am kinda surprised you don't want kids. Have you always felt that way?"

Leah allowed herself a deep breath. There was no reason to feel defensive. It was a legitimate question.

"I know it seems weird, coming from the Bible Belt and a pretty big family. All that was expected of me growing up was that I'd find a man, settle down and make babies. I guess I'm sort of defying my roots, but I've never felt like I have maternal instincts. I don't think motherhood is for me."

Cap laid his hand on her knee and leaned toward her. "Fair enough. Not everyone is cut out to have kids, and a lot of people who do shouldn't have them, you know?"

She nodded. "What about you? Did you always know you wanted kids?"

"Hell no." He laughed. "God no." He crossed his leg so his ankle rested on his thigh. He was wearing his heavy work boots, which were wet from the snow that had begun to stick to the ground. "My ex...her name is Sharon, by the way... I always thought she trapped me. You know, got pregnant so I'd stick around? I thought she was on the Pill, but come to find out a few months later...we had a baby on the way. But it was right then that I made up my mind. I wanted to be the best daddy ever."

"I've always wondered about women who do that. Seems like a pretty big risk... The guy could just run away, right?" Leah conjectured.

"I suppose. But you should know me well enough by now to know I'd never do that. And besides, my father was a great man. I was his shadow my entire life. He taught me everything I know, and I spent at least eight hours a day out on the water with him until he had a heart attack at age forty-two...and..." He stopped abruptly, the memory still choking him up, decades later, leaving a tear glistening in the corner of his eye.

It dawned on her that forty-two was Cap's current age. She tried to imagine being the same age as one of her parents when they'd passed. How that would weigh on someone, always feeling like you were living out time that wasn't afforded to your parent. She expected Cap to swallow hard, push that memory back down deep inside him and go on talking about raising his daughters, but instead, he continued to speak of his father.

"I was out on the boat with him, just the two of us. He'd been out on a charter earlier in the day and had spotted some large stripers down by the jetty. He wanted to go back and see if we could get one of the bigger ones. He seemed a little off to me that evening. Just so damn determined, like he couldn't rest until he got this catch. He had always been stubborn and strong-willed, not the type to tell you how he was feeling.

"There was a fiery sunset on the bay that night; I'll never forget it, the image of him silhouetted against that crimson canvas..." Cap took a sip of the beer he'd grabbed from the fridge when he'd first gotten home and swallowed it down with the tears threatening to break free.

"He had one on the line, and boy, it was a fighter. He was really struggling to get him reeled in. I was just about to grab the rod and take over when he clutched his chest and fell onto the deck. He was moaning and writhing in pain. I'd seen this guy take blows and get thrashed by shark fins and hardly flinch. I knew he had to be hurting real bad to carry on like that."

Leah now had her hand on his thigh, wishing there was a way to take away the pain that still seemed so real and fresh. Maybe she could dull it, flatten it out, roll it into a tiny manageable ball and hand it back. He could stick it in his pocket, and his heart would feel lighter. She was pretty sure she knew how his story would end, but it seemed like he needed to tell it, to get it out.

"I panicked, Leah. I should have given him CPR, but I

didn't know what to do. I was eighteen years old, getting ready to start college in the fall, and I should have known better. But all I kept thinking was I had to get him back to shore. No cell phones back then, so I couldn't call, and even if we'd had 'em, I doubt we would've gotten reception way out there on the water.

"I whipped the boat around and fired up the motor, trying to haul ass back to the dock. My plan was to get him into my truck and rush him over to Salisbury to the hospital. I figured it would be faster than waiting for an ambulance by the time I was able to find a phone." He tried to choke back the tears that had formed but lost one down his cheek.

His body heaved beside her as three more tears chased the first one down. "I couldn't make it in time."

He took a deep breath and straightened his shoulders. "I didn't think I could ever forgive myself. My mom...God bless that woman, she kept trying to tell me it was okay; God had just called him home. It was his time to go; his number was up. But I never believed her. I kept telling myself it was my fault. It was my responsibility to save him, and I couldn't.

"And then my daughter was born a year later. I looked into her sweet little face, and there was something there, something that reminded me of him, like his spirit was looking out at me through her big blue eyes. I knew I had a chance for redemption. I vowed right then and there to be the best damn father in the whole world. I wasn't ever going to let anything happen to that precious baby girl."

Leah was speechless. She had never expected to see such a vulnerable side of Cap; she never imagined he'd feel close enough to her that he could share such a deep and personal story. She wanted to throw her arms around him but settled for resting her head against his shoulder and whispering, "You have some lucky daughters, Cap. They're really blessed to have you for a father."

Cap's story affected Leah so much that it made her heart ping with sadness. Her parents had never seemed like protectors, only fortresses keeping her from discovering who she was and what she wanted out of life. They did it out of moral obligation, not out of love or for redemption like Cap had for his daughters.

It was what the Bible said to do, not what their hearts told them to do. *And maybe that is why I've never wanted kids.*

The epiphany creeped up on her, enveloping her in its shadow. *Maybe I've just been waiting for my heart to tell me it's what I must do.*

SEVENTEEN

Leah lurched awake, alarmed to find herself ensconced in unfamiliar plaid flannel sheets. Then she remembered how it had gotten late and snowy, and Cap had pretty much demanded she spend the night. They didn't make love, but they curled together under the covers until they both drifted off, their dogs slumbering away at the foot of the bed. She grabbed her phone off the nightstand to check the time and was relieved to learn it was only 5 AM. She wasn't going to be late for work.

I should probably get back home and prepare myself for returning to a stack of invoices, a litany of complaints, and a slew of emails. She cringed when she considered how many voicemails had likely been left on her office phone in the past three days.

"Voicemails are the worst," she groaned under her breath.

Cap sat straight up in the bed before she could fully contemplate her exit strategy. "Where are you going?" he asked, his voice a little hoarse.

"Just thinking I should take Glory home and get ready for work," she explained. "I didn't mean to wake you up."

He grunted and grabbed her arm, pulling her back down onto the mattress. "Don't go." It did not sound like a suggestion.

He turned onto his side and slid his body so it was adjacent to hers. One of his arms wrapped around her waist, and one of his legs hooked her thighs, effectively locking her in his embrace. "I'm holding you hostage."

"If you're expecting a ransom, don't hold your breath. My parents don't make much on a minister and teacher's salary," she laughed, "and although my boss loves me, he'd probably rather replace me than put up his own money."

"Bummer," he teased her. "No matter, you're worth more than they could pay anyway." He flung himself onto his back and effortlessly pulled her on top of him in one swift motion, surprising Leah with his agility and brute strength. He pushed her head down so her lips pressed against his.

"I haven't brushed my teeth yet," she protested, trying to pull away.

"Does it look like I give a fuck?" He ran his tongue over her dry lips. "Oh, hey, leave Glory here today, why don'cha?"

"What? Why would do I do that?" Her eyebrows rose.

"Because she's gonna like being here a hell of a lot more than being cooped up in a crate all day," he explained with a heavy dose of "duh."

"But then I—"

"Have to come back here tonight to get her? Gee, hadn't thought of that!" Even in the darkness, she could see he'd said it with a devious grin and wink.

"Are you sure she's no problem?" Leah asked. "I don't

want her to get confused about where her home is and all that...you know?"

"I wouldn't worry about it too much. Besides, you'd be making Keeper pretty sad if you took his playmate away," he tried a new angle.

"Okay, yeah, I guess that will work. I won't have to work quite as late since I won't have to let her out on my lunch break. I can skip lunch altogether. I'll still be kinda late though; is that alright?"

"I've got nothing but time," Cap assured her. She couldn't quite tell in the dark, but she was pretty sure his dimples were winking at her.

● ● ●

Roughly half of the messages on Leah's voicemail were from Casey Fontaine. Before checking in with Barry, Leah grabbed her office phone and dutifully punched in Casey's number.

Even at eight in the morning, Casey's voice sparkled like diamonds. "Well, Leah Miller, I was just talking about you last night at dinner. Were your ears burning?"

Leah couldn't help but smile when she talked to the woman. "Is that so? All good things, I hope!"

"Naturally, my dear! I have a niece who is planning to get married in Ocean City in the fall, and she's looking at reception venues and accommodations for out-of-town guests, which is practically everyone but me. You better believe I gave her your number. So if an Olivia Darcy calls you, that's my niece. Just take twenty percent of whatever you quote her and my sister and send that bill to me, understood?"

"Oh, of course, Casey, no problem at all." Leah furiously scribbled down a note: *Olivia Darcy – Casey Fontaine's niece – 20% to Casey.*

"Don't tell them about the twenty percent, though. They'll think it's the cheapest rate in town, and they won't be able to refuse. Just remember when the fam is all here for the wedding, mum's the word about the lifestyle stuff. They know I run a charity group, but they think it's a bunch of old biddies playing cards one night a week, and getting dolled up and dragging their old, decrepit husbands out for a stodgy cocktail party once a month!" She laughed at her red herring description of the group.

"You have absolutely nothing to worry about," Leah reassured her. "I would never disclose details of our clients' personal lives to anyone. Hotels are in the business of discretion, you know."

"You're such a doll," Casey cooed. "Okay, now let's get down to the real reason for my call. I want to set up the Valentine's Party."

"No party for January, then?" Leah asked, failing to disguise her disappointment. The group's monthly events were certainly helping to keep The Pearl in the black even during the off-season. Barry had been blown away by their numbers for December, a notoriously slow time for the hospitality industry in Ocean City. January was usually their worst month, though, and Leah was hoping to keep Barry's mood elevated with the promise of a lucrative event.

"No, I decided to take January off. I'm having some minor surgery next week, so this gives me plenty of time to recover before February's party. Last year in January we had a football-themed party, which was a lot of fun, but it's just not in the cards this year, unfortunately," Casey explained.

"I'm so sorry to hear you have to undergo surgery," Leah offered. "I hope everything goes smoothly."

"It's elective surgery, so don't worry; I'm in perfect health! Alright, so if you can pull out your calendar, we can look at Saturday nights in February?"

By the end of the phone call, Leah had Casey's group confirmed for the second Saturday in February. The Pearl was going to be decked out in red from floor to ceiling, with the charity proceeds going to the American Heart Association. Casey also disclosed she had bought the perfect red velvet evening gown to wear, accompanied by an exquisite set of pearls that belonged to her grandmother. If nothing else, Leah was impressed by how attentive Casey was to details.

She would be pretty damn good at my job, actually, Leah had to admit. *She is as dedicated to making her group members as happy as I am.*

Before she had too much time to reflect on her conversation with the one and only Casey Fontaine, Barry waltzed into her office with the advertising budget. "They're screwing us, Leah. We need to re-shoot that one commercial we aired last summer, and it's going to cost a freaking fortune. And get a load of what they're charging now to do our social media. It's a fucking racket, I tell you." He only cursed in front of Leah when he got really worked up.

Leah finished entering the details into her spreadsheet for the Casey's Group Valentine's Party and looked up over her computer monitor at her severely agitated boss. "Well, why don't we save some money and do our own social media?" she calmly suggested.

"We were doing that when you first came on board; don't you remember? It was a disaster! No one ever had any time for it." She could see faint impressions of veins popping out of Barry's temples.

"I know it didn't work before, but our staff is much more

technologically inclined now; everyone is in this day and age. I say we buy a few iPads, form a Social Media Task Force, and let them have at it. That new hire for the front desk is really sharp. I bet she could help. And I know a few other people who would be great at it too."

"Leah, you are, hands down, the smartest person I know. So I can dump all this on you? You can get it all set up?" He was clearly ready to wash his hands of the whole thing.

She nodded with her most confident smile. "Of course! I really think having a team like this will help build rapport among the staff too. It's a win-win, really."

"God, Leah, I missed you when you were gone. I know it was only three days, but, damn, we need you around here. You're never allowed to quit, got that?" Barry shook his finger at her in mock teacher fashion.

Leah just laughed. She loved that Barry always made her feel appreciated. No wonder she didn't mind putting in long hours.

Of course, she'd never had anyone special enough to trump her desire to work. She remembered the way Cap played at holding her hostage that morning, pressing her body tightly to his as if he never wanted to let her go. Would he be the one who kept her from being a workaholic? Only time would tell...

◆ ◆ ◆

Just moments after she sent Aimee a text at lunchtime, her phone rang with Aimee's picture glowing from the display.

"How's it going?" Leah instinctively whispered into the phone.

"You don't have to whisper, silly." Aimee laughed at her. "Anthony is changing Natalie's diaper across the room, and she's wide awake. She just had lunch. She'll be alert for a little while now, then she'll want to nurse and snooze again when she gets tired."

"Is she sleeping at night?" Leah questioned.

"Not more than three hours or so at a time, but it's been okay. She'd just stay attached to me all day if I'd let her!" Aimee's complaint didn't sound too serious. "She's so damn cute, though. I'm already in love with her, what can I say?"

"Awww, of course you are," Leah replied. "So...Cap asked me to spend New Year's Eve with him."

"Oh yeah? You'd hardly said anything about him when you were here. I was afraid you didn't actually like him after all," Aimee observed.

"I didn't want to distract you from your first few days of motherhood," Leah explained. "But now that you're getting the hang of things, oh my gosh, I'm going to need a lot of help. I don't even know what to do!"

"What do you mean? You go out, you have fun, you drink, you eat, you get laid. How fucking hard is that?" Aimee teased her. "Sounds pretty easy to me! Not to mention enviable as I probably won't get a night out for the next six months."

"The New Year's Eve thing he wants to take me to is a house party." There, she'd said it. She'd hardly been able to wrap her brain around it since he asked her. Now she'd actually gotten the words out of her mouth.

"House party? So what?" Aimee asked. "I don't get what the big deal is about that."

"A *swinger* house party," Leah returned her voice to a whisper. "I just don't know if I can go. I don't belong at a swinger party. It's all so crazy!"

"What are you going to do for New Year's Eve if you don't go with him?" Aimee was always one to play devil's advocate.

She's definitely in cahoots with that little imp on my shoulder, Leah mused. "Probably stay home with Glory and paint my toenails or something. Or work."

"Oh god, Leah; that sounds lame. Take it from me, there is nothing more depressing than spending New Year's Eve alone. I did that once. I am still in therapy."

Leah was not surprised to hear such a colorful exaggeration from her melodramatic best friend. Motherhood had not mellowed her out. Yet.

"But I don't know if I'm ready."

"Well, just because you go doesn't mean you have to get busy with anyone, right?" Aimee asked. "I mean, I don't really know how these things work. Are keys involved? They don't use keys anymore, do they?" She bubbled up with giggles.

"Come on, be serious, Aimee; this is really hard for me! I like him, but I don't know if I'm comfortable with all this swinging stuff. It's so nice when it's just the two of us. I don't want to think about there being anyone else in the middle of us. I barely even know him one-on-one at this point!"

Aimee sighed. "I know, I'm sorry, sweetie. Sometimes my imagination runs wild, you know. You really are in a situation, aren't you?" She had clearly taken charge of Natalie again because Leah could hear her bending down to coo in her daughter's face. Then she heard lip-smacking sounds like she was kissing the baby's soft, round cheeks. "Oh my god, Leah, I could just eat her up!"

"I guess I'll talk to Cap tonight when I go pick up Glory. I'll ask him what to expect, and then I'll decide. I don't want to be alone for New Year's...I don't...but I don't want to do anything I'll regret either." She hated having decisions hanging over her. She preferred to gather the information, analyze it, and make a swift decision without a lot of hem-hawing around.

"That sounds like a perfectly reasonable plan," Aimee agreed, her attention coming back to Leah now. "But don't be afraid to make mistakes, Leah. We'd all lead really boring lives if we never took any risks. Sometimes the best things in life are the result of a risk."

"Okay, I'll keep that in mind," Leah promised, though making mistakes was one of the things she loathed most—even more than being indecisive.

EIGHTEEN

Leah still felt a twinge of guilt for not agreeing to work on New Year's Eve. She was sitting in church on a frosty Sunday morning waiting for the service to begin and trying to forget that the shroud of guilt she wore wasn't just for taking off work. She had skipped church the prior week, then she lied to her mother about it.

At least I'll be able to tell her with a clear conscience that I went today.

Leah sighed as the worship team took their places on stage. When she glanced at the program, she noticed the sermon was covering the passage about the woman at the well in the book of John.

Oh, great. Just want I need to hear is a lecture about how this slutty woman repents and follows Jesus. My dad always said that God puts the right message in your ears just when you need to hear it.

She spent a great deal of time the night before discussing the impending New Year's Eve house party with Cap. He'd smiled at her questions and tried to answer frankly.

"Look, a house party is just like any party you went to in college. You know, people drinking and flirting, and getting it on. It's just that these people are a little older, probably won't get as tanked, and aren't likely to regret anything in the morning," was the way he'd characterized swinger parties.

"Does everyone participate? How many people will be there?" She felt like she was interviewing him for a position at The Pearl: trying to be objective, looking for all the pros and cons.

"No, not everyone plays. It's fine if you don't. Sometimes people are just there to socialize, and that's cool. No one is going to pressure you, especially since I'll be there to step in if there's any hint of trouble or pushiness. Not sure how many people John and Monica are expecting for this party, but there were probably about thirty at their last one."

"Are there rules? Etiquette? Things I need to know so I don't embarrass myself?" She was still envisioning walking through a room of writhing bodies piled up on the floor. "Do people just get it on out in the open? Is it like an orgy?"

Cap put his arm around her and tried to keep his poker face. "No, no, only the best parties turn into orgies!" Then he erupted in laughter at how wide her eyes grew. "Darlin', it's not like that, seriously."

He cleared his throat, and the playful, dimpled smile vanished. "Most vanilla people who walked into a swinger party wouldn't even know that's what was going on. You won't usually see a lot of stuff other than kissing or making out happening in the public areas of the house. Most of the time people go to the bedrooms to play—not unlike the hotel parties you've already witnessed."

"You keep saying 'play.' And you said 'vanilla people.' I don't know what all that means. 'Playing' makes it sound like it's a sport or something." She was still trying to wrap her head around all of the new vocabulary.

Cap seemed happy to impart his years of swinger knowledge. "We call sex with others in the lifestyle 'playing.' If two couples get together, and sex is on the agenda, they might call it a 'playdate.' And 'vanilla' is someone who isn't part of the lifestyle. Like you, right now."

"Ah, okay. So what about the rules?" It was starting to slowly crystallize.

"Basic party rules are just to use common sense, courtesy and respect. If a door is closed, don't enter. If a door is open, you can watch but ask before trying to participate. I don't exactly see you jumping into a pile or offending anyone, anyway. We try to clean up after ourselves, you know, respect the hosts. Pick up condoms and put down plastic or towels if you're a squirter."

"I'm sorry, what?!" Leah's eyes exploded to maximum shock size. *Just when I thought this stuff was starting to make sense!*

"Um, *squirter?*" Cap repeated. "Female ejaculation?" He watched Leah's head vigorously shake back and forth, revealing they were venturing into quite unfamiliar territory.

"I thought that was a myth?" Her head was spinning. *Maybe I'm not ready for this after all...*

He raked through her strawberry blonde waves with his fingertips, smiling when the silky strands slid through his callused hands. "I've seen it. Trust me, it's no myth."

"Alright, so what else do I need to know?" She wanted him to just give it to her: the good, the bad, the ugly.

"Every couple has their own rules. Soft swap, full swap, same room, separate rooms, kissing or no kissing, bi stuff or no bi stuff...you know, whatever floats their boats," he rattled off.

"Um, I pretty much didn't understand one word of that. Slow down and try it again, please?" Leah asked, resisting the temptation to become frustrated.

"Soft swap means fooling around but intercourse only with your partner; full swap means intercourse – 'swapping partners' – is on the table. Same room means the couple plays only in the same room with each other; separate rooms means they are able to play in different rooms. Some couples will kiss other people; some reserve that just for each other. And bi stuff? Well, most of the women are bisexual to some degree. Bisexual males are kinda frowned upon. Yes, it's a double standard, but that's just the way it is," he explained with a shrug.

Bi stuff? She hadn't even considered that would be part of the equation. The scene she'd viewed at Casey's Christmas party didn't include much interaction between the two women. She had honestly never thought of a woman sexually. *I don't think I'm ready for that.*

I can't believe I'm thinking about all this in church. She jolted herself back into the present and looked around, wondering if anyone seated around her had even a vague inkling of what was running through her mind.

She thought about how crazy this worship service might seem to a non-believer if they were to walk into the sanctuary and witness it. *Not unlike a vanilla person stepping into a swinger party for the first time, I suppose. It's all in what you know, what you're used to, right?*

●◌●

Leah had not admitted to Aimee that she was going through with attending the party. For two days, she'd kept her conversations with her best friend focused on the baby and how crazy Aimee's mom and sisters were driving her. So she didn't feel like she could call Aimee at 7 PM on New Year's Eve to beg for advice about what to wear to her first swinger party.

She tossed a pile of clothes onto her bed and started sorting through them, throwing rejects back into her closet.

Cap had given her a great deal of advice, not only about swinger party fashion, but also about how to interact with men in the lifestyle:

Be flirtatious.

Be yourself.

Be honest.

Be adventurous.

Don't judge a book by its cover.

Keep an open mind.

Don't be afraid to say no if you're not feeling it.

He said that men would like me, that they'd think I was really hot. He kept reassuring me that I was desirable. Who would've ever thought I'd be listening to advice about how to get a man to fuck me from a man I'm already fucking?

Leah finally settled on a silver sequined tank top and a slinky black velour skirt when she remembered she had tall black leather boots that she'd worn exactly once the prior winter because she didn't feel they were really "her." They had shiny silver buckles up the side and came to just above her knees with a thick three-inch heel.

Maybe they weren't "me" last winter, but this winter they are? It's completely crazy.

She stepped in front of the mirror and put her hands on

her hips, jutting one out so she could exaggerate the femi-nine curve of her torso as it gently sloped into her thighs. *So, this is what swinger chicks do, huh? Dress to impress. Bait their hooks to lure the men in? And women too, I suppose, for the bi girls. But I'm sure that brings the guys in too.*

Cap was due to pick her up in fifteen minutes. *Better take Glory out one more time before I leave.*

Cap had encouraged her to leave Glory at his house with Keeper indefinitely since she had been working so much, but she was leery of making such a leap. *It's one thing to stash a toothbrush at the apartment of the man you're dating, quite another to keep your dog there.*

Is that what we're calling it? Dating? She shrugged, still looking at her reflection in the mirror. *I guess so.*

She watched the reverse-image Leah shrug back at her. *Except I can't think of any other dating relationship where you go trolling for other partners on a...what is this...fifth date?*

She heard his truck rumbling into the parking lot before she saw it. She threw a kiss to Glory, who was occupied with a new bone in her crate, locked the door and headed down to Cap.

"I trust you look stunning under that long coat," he said as she hoisted her leg into the cab of his truck and then pulled her body into the seat.

"I look something." Leah sighed, straightening her skirt under her wool coat. Even when she pulled it down, it remained several inches above her knees.

Cap stopped the truck with a jolt in the middle of the parking lot, fifteen yards or so from the exit. "Tell me now if you don't want to go. We'll go back to my place, open a bottle of wine and ring in the new year, just the two of us," he suggested, with no trace of bitterness.

"I know how much you're looking forward to this." Leah looked down at her boots. The silver buckles gleamed in the ambient lighting from the street lamps.

"I am looking forward to it," Cap agreed. "I have a sexy date I can show off to my friends. What man wouldn't look forward to that?"

He paused to see the corner of her lip curl up in response to his compliment. "And I know you will really have fun if you just keep an open mind and get to know some of these people. I think you'll enjoy yourself."

"But?" Leah pressed.

"But I don't want you to feel uncomfortable. I don't want you to do anything you'll regret. And I don't want you to go just to make me happy." He tossed the ball back into her court.

"As long as you promise you won't leave me alone, and I won't be pressured into anything, then I want to go," she said decisively.

"Oh, of course, Sugar. That's a given." He winked at her.

"I have to admit I'm dying of curiosity...to see how people react to me being there. Oh, one thing... This isn't going to cause me any problems at work, right? It won't get back to my boss? I mean, he's cool and all, but it's just none of his business, you know?" She'd been meaning to broach that subject with him, but she kept her work and private lives so compartmentalized, when she was in Cap Mode, her mind wasn't anywhere near Work Mode.

"It's the Swinger Code," Cap promised. "We all want discretion; it's expected. If you were from around here and knew as many people as I do, you'd probably be surprised at some of the folks you run into at lifestyle meet and greets, parties and clubs. There are actually some pretty powerful people...well, Casey Fontaine, for instance."

"I know she's a realtor, but...there's something else about her?" Leah's curiosity was even further piqued.

"Her dad was a U.S. Congressman. Oh, he's retired from politics now but still serves on all sorts of boards and is in DC hobnobbing with famous types all the time. Everyone in the state knows who Casey Fontaine's dad is. But only a select few knowshe swings or she's bisexual. By the way, you didn't hear that from me, if you know what I mean." He winked again.

"Wow, I had no idea!" Leah considered that if Casey could work in a field like real estate, where her reputation was literally her lifeblood, she had much more at stake than Leah. "Okay, okay. You know I trust you, right?"

"It makes me happy to hear you say that." Cap reached for her hand and squeezed his thick fingers around hers before shifting his truck back into drive.

● ● ●

Fifteen minutes later, the heels of Leah's black boots clicked against the brick path leading up to a bayside townhouse in North Ocean City, just south of the line sepa-rating Maryland from Delaware. Cap's fingertips pressed against the small of her back as he guided her from the rear. *Like he's steering a boat*, she mused, trying to distract herself from the butterflies dancing in her stomach.

Yeah, forget flitting about causing mild anxiety—they're having the freaking Olympic Opening Ceremonies in there.

"Before we go in, I want to remind you that if you feel uncomfortable at any time, just let me know, and I'll take care of it." Cap lifted her chin toward him with his index finger, capturing her eyes with his. "I'm not going to let anyone hurt you or disrespect you, okay?"

Leah bit her lip and nodded, smiling at him in understanding. Then she took a deep breath and faced the door. But before she could knock or ring the bell, a woman pushed the glass storm door open and ushered them inside.

"Well, Captain Chris Sheldon, it's been damn near forever since I saw you!" she gushed as soon as they were through the door.

"You didn't see me at the Christmas party?" he asked, and she shook her head, still beaming at him. He gestured toward Leah. "Oh, Monica, this is my date, Leah. She's new to all this, so be gentle."

The hostess was in her mid-fifties with short, dark hair with highlights woven in. She wore a purple halter-top A-line dress with fishnet stockings and black boots that didn't look too different from Leah's. "Welcome, Leah! Glad to have you here." She leaned down and pressed a kiss to Leah's cheek.

"Thanks for having us." Leah smiled graciously as the moisture from the kiss evaporated in the cool winter breeze that had followed them into the house.

Cap led Leah into the kitchen, where he wasted no time in mixing them both a drink. "Guess this is a turn of events, huh?" Leah smirked. "When we first met, I was the one mixing the drinks."

"Good point. I think I make a better bartender, though!"

When his laugh echoed throughout the kitchen, she fake-punched him on the triceps right about the same time Rhonda slunk up to the kitchen counter beside him. Leah watched her put her arm around Cap and squeeze his posterior while whispering something in his ear. He grinned, dimples exposed, but said nothing.

"Not working tonight?" Rhonda asked Leah through her fake smile. She appeared as though she had been spending a lot of time in the tanning booth recently. Her skin was darker, and her hair was lighter.

"Nope, every once in a while, I'm allowed out to play." Leah tried her best to appear relaxed and confident, even though there was something about Rhonda that made her claws want to come out.

But she was quickly distracted from Rhonda when she noticed a youngish man, maybe in his early or mid-thirties, staring at her from across the kitchen. He wore his thick, reddish-brown hair in a conservative cut, and his deep brown eyes were covered by trendy black-rimmed glasses.

He looks like a teacher. Or accountant. Definitely not like someone you'd expect to run into at a swinger party.

A thought washed over her that was so ironic that she nearly spit out the delicious, not to mention strong, cocktail Cap had concocted for her. *What if I actually meet the man of my dreams at a swinger party?*

The Teacher/Accountant slowly made his way through the crowd toward her. Cap noticed the advancing figure and stepped into his path before he reached Leah. "Hey, Jeremy, what's new, brother? Haven't seen you in ages!"

"I've been so god-damned busy this year, I haven't gotten out much. I was coaching girls' volleyball this spring, and I swear I didn't know if I was coming or going most days. This is a well-deserved reward for all my hard work."

Oh, definitely a teacher, Leah surmised, patting herself on the back for her superior observation skills.

"I'll drink to that!" Cap raised his glass. "Oh, Jeremy, I noticed you had your eyes on my date. This is Leah, and she's new to all this, so be gentle, got it?"

"Oh, I don't bite," Jeremy promised. "Not too hard,

anyway!" The two men laughed again, and on that note, they both took another swig of their drinks.

"It's nice to meet you, Jeremy." Leah extended her hand politely. But he ignored her offering and moved in close enough to plant a soft wet kiss directly on her lips.

She grabbed the kitchen counter to steady herself in her high-heeled boots as a shock of electricity bolted through her. She doubted she had ever shared a first kiss while so many people watched.

So this is how we're supposed to greet new people. Cap definitely neglected to share that little tidbit with me.

She looked out from the kitchen toward the living room, her eyes landing on a woman sitting on the sofa with her breasts exposed, pulled out the top of her shirt and resting on her bra, squeezed together into two huge mounds. Two women flanked her, bending over her to each take a nipple into their mouths. Leah watched their tongues encircling the areolae, flicking the hardening nipples and then closing their lips around them.

The woman in the middle rested her head back against the sofa cushions, her eyes closed and mouth gaping open as she sighed with pleasure, her fists beginning to clench and cheeks and chest flushing with arousal.

Several drinks later, Leah was feeling giddy, free, and unencumbered by inhibitions. Cap had introduced her to so many people throughout the course of the night, she had started playing a "drinking game" in which she took a shot when she met someone new and then recited the names of everyone she had met thus far. The party guests were wildly amused.

"Your girlfriend is a lot of fun," one of the women, Tricia, told Cap. "Not to mention really cute. You've done well, Cap!"

Cap nodded in agreement. "You know how much I love bringing them into the fold."

"And, of course, you have impeccable taste," the woman's brunette friend chimed in.

"Monica, Jeremy, Beth, John, Tricia, Alan, Bruce, Lila, Paul, another John, Mike, Audrey, Mary... How'm I doin', guys?" Leah spouted, the last several names slurring together.

"I think you left out Bart and Allison, but otherwise pretty damn good." Cap patted her on the head.

"I have to be good at this shit for my job," Leah announced. "My whole job is pleasing people!"

"Well, you've come to the right place then," Jeremy boisterously proclaimed with a wide grin spread across his handsome face.

"Oh! You're that lady from The Pearl!" Tricia bellowed with pride for her powers of recognition. "The bartender!"

"I'm actually the Guest Experience Strategist," Leah slurred. Cap immediately grabbed her and pulled her into his arms in an attempt to get her to stop talking.

"Mixing business with pleasure, eh?" asked one of the two Johns, who was standing behind Tricia and intermittently grinding his pelvis against her plump, curvy backside.

"Alright, that's enough," Cap warned. "Let's keep Leah's job out of this, okay?"

"Oh, don't worry, Cap, you know we'd never get anyone in trouble," Tricia promised. "Relax! Have another shot!"

"I'm pretty sure I'm the D.D.," Cap politely refused.

He steered Leah into the hallway. "You doing okay, Sugar?" he asked in a low voice once they were alone.

Leah heard moans and playful squeals coming from the doorway next to her. She peered into the room and saw a woman with wispy blonde hair, someone she didn't remember meeting earlier, her face buried between Mary's spread legs while the other John pumped his cock into her from behind.

Leah looked just in time to see John's palm smack the blonde's fleshy ass cheek, eliciting another high-pitched wail *that is partially muffled by Mary's...muff*, Leah joked as she narrated the scene play-by-play in her intoxicated head.

She felt herself lured into the room by a siren of curiosity. The threesome was occupying one half of the king-sized bed, and Leah took a seat on the floral comforter on the opposite corner for a better view.

All of that debauchery in college and I never once witnessed other people having sex. Guess I was missing out!

She watched Mary's face as she locked eyes with Other John. The way he was slamming his cock into The Blonde was forcing her face further down into Mary's pussy. Leah imagined that all of The Blonde's squeals and moans were humming deliciously against Mary's clit.

She wondered what it would be like to be Mary, to be staring intensely into a man's eyes as he fucked another woman, and having that woman bring you to orgasm with her tongue as she's being fucked. She wondered what it would be like to be The Blonde, to know she was giving pleasure to two people while simultaneously receiving it.

Desire washed over her like a tidal wave. She glanced back to see that Cap had followed her into the room and was standing beside the bed, also observing the scene playing out before them. She looked up at him with eyes gleaming green with lust and insistently tugged the dense fabric of his jeans.

He crouched down next to her and whispered in her ear, "Like what you see?"

In lieu of a spoken answer, she forcefully yanked him

down on top of her, aching for his weight against her body, for his lips to press down on her mouth. He was more than happy to oblige, shifting to station himself between her legs. His erection pressed through the thick denim of his jeans into the exposed flesh of her thighs.

"I want you now," she demanded, trembling with her sudden and all-encompassing need.

Other John's eyes bored into her as Cap eagerly ripped her black velour skirt down past her ankles and pulled her sequined tank top over her head. "It's almost midnight," John warned Cap. "Looks like we're all going to ring in the New Year the right way!"

"Fuck yes!" Cap agreed and began to strip away his own clothes.

Mary screamed as an orgasm ripped through her, which coincided with the exact moment Cap's engorged cock came springing out of his boxer briefs. "Hey, look at that, didn't even have to touch her!" he joked.

John cracked up laughing but didn't miss a stroke, and The Blonde briefly came up for air long enough to nod in appreciation of Cap's humor.

"Quit fooling around and slide your cock inside me!" Leah begged, her back arching as she impatiently waited for him to resume his position between her legs. She was at that precise point of inebriation where she was fully cognizant of her inhibitions having been thrown out the window, but too far gone to give a damn about it.

"For fuck's sake, Cap, give the girl what she wants!" Mary shouted, having regained the capacity for normal speech after her orgasm subsided.

Leah felt every last bit of Cap's eight-inch cock push past her lips till he was buried to the hilt inside her. He stalled there, balls-deep but denying her any movement.

Other John, still rhythmically drilling into The Blonde, watched as Leah's brows furrowed and her teeth clenched. Her breath hitched as she ground her hips against Cap, desperate for him to move inside her.

"Let's tease her a bit more, shall we, Tess?" Mary suggested.

Tess, The Blonde, looked up from her "dessert" with a slick, red face, across which an evil grin was rapidly spreading. Other John slid his cock out, and the three inched closer to the young nymph writhing under the boat captain's thick, sturdy body. Cap, fully in support of the diabolical plan, shifted onto his knees, taking the weight off Leah's torso and exposing her breasts, which were all but popping out of her black lace bra.

Mary slipped her hand under Leah's already arched back to release the bra hooks, and Tess whisked the lacy contraption away in just a breath of time, sending it flying across the room. The two women set about inspecting the lush, creamy, now fully exposed mounds decorated with small strawberry-hued nipples like tiny bows on a wrapped gift.

Other John stroked his fingers down Leah's torso toward her pussy, where the base of Cap's cock, still on "standby," could be seen parting her lips. "I see the carpet matches the drapes." He trailed his finger first over her mound of springy reddish-blonde curls, then brushed against her clit, keeping a good one-inch margin from Cap's throbbing organ.

Leah's body jolted from the sensation, but her attention was soon captured by the pair of mouths poised to taste her strawberry nipples. She felt their tongues first, warm and wet, teasing her pink areolae like they were made of cotton candy.

Leah wondered if the alcohol had relaxed her enough to

enjoy this amount of attention, or if she had been missing out on the pleasure of being a human playground her entire adult life. As she was contemplating how long she could bear having two mouths, a set of fingers and a rather hard, massive cock teasing her, she noticed Jeremy had wandered into the scene. He crawled across the bed and perched on his knees perpendicular to her waist.

Fuck, how many people can fit on this freakishly large bed?

She had a woman on either side of her upper half, Jeremy at her right side in the middle, Other John on her left side at her thighs, and of course, Cap on his knees between her legs, holding them steady against him so she couldn't cheat and move herself up and down on his cock.

Jeremy glanced up and down her body, pinned to the bed by all her admirers, and decided to change his position so he was above her head. The two women slid down to give him a little more room. Now when she peered up, it was into his deep brown eyes as he towered over her. He had unbuckled his belt and unzipped his pants before bending into place. The very tip of his erection peeked out the top of his black underwear.

She thought he was going to reach in and pull it out, but instead he leaned down and pressed his lips against hers. His tongue invaded her mouth, and at the same time, Cap finally began to stroke ever-so-slowly in and out of her pussy. The two women were gently grazing on her breasts, sucking her nipples in and out of their teeth, sending tingly shocks traveling in tandem lines down her torso and directly into her clit, which was being attended to by Other John.

I can't believe I'm lying here and letting all of them do this to me, she thought with one breath and with the next: *Oh. My. God. Every nerve in my body is being stimulated all at the same time. It's overwhelming. Consuming. But absolutely, indescribably euphoric all at the same time!*

Jeremy pulled away from her lips and rose back to his previous height above her. She was staring into his thighs and pelvis now, her eyes locked onto that tempting-looking tip of cock straining to get out of his pants. It looked wet and glossy now; a bit of pre-cum had oozed out while he was kissing her. The sight made her want to lick it. She found herself yearning for him to bring it to her mouth.

She peered up at his eyes again, narrowed and wanton behind his black-rimmed glasses. "I want to taste it," she said, feeling bold and still intoxicated.

She uttered the words along with a moan and then immediately looked toward Cap, who nodded in approval. The ladies sat up on their knees to watch her take Jeremy's thick, swollen cock into her mouth. She licked around the head with her tongue, tasting those pearly drops that had seeped out, savoring their saltiness as he moaned with delight.

"Good girl," Cap complimented her and began to pick up his pace, thrusting into her pussy now more intently. Other John moved off the bed and stood so Tess could turn and wrap her lips around his cock as well.

Mary looked from face to face as if contemplating where she should place herself in the scene. Cap was beginning to thrust into Leah so hard that she could barely maintain her oral attention on Jeremy's cock. She sighed, realizing where she was needed, and then knelt down on her hands and knees to help Leah take care of their hot teacher friend. She paused for a moment to unbutton Jeremy's shirt. She revealed his wiry but muscular build, with very little chest hair in between his well-defined pectoral muscles.

"That's more like it," she announced before getting back down to the business of helping Leah lick up and down his broad shaft.

Leah loved the contrast of Jeremy's hard cock and Mary's soft lips as they intermittently met up with hers. At times it felt like she was kissing Mary as much as fellating Jeremy.

And he was clearly relishing the pair's enjoyment of each other over his rigid cock. Leah let Mary take over for a moment while she looked down her body to Cap, who had repositioned her legs to rest on his shoulders. He was penetrating her so deeply, she could scarcely catch her breath, let alone concentrate on assisting Mary.

He looks as though he has tuned out everyone else in the room, and all he sees is me.

She remembered how his breath had sounded when he was close to climax on Christmas night, and she heard that pattern again, the exhalations quickening, and every third breath punctuated with one syllable grunts of "Yes," "Oh," and "Fuck."

Knowing he was about to explode inside of her sent her over the edge on which she had been teetering for what seemed like an eternity. The waves of her orgasm engulfed her so completely, she cried out in ear-splitting ecstasy. While she was still riding the waves back to reality, an explosion of cheering rocketed through the house. At first Leah thought the entire assembly of party guests were celebrating her crowning achievement, but then she realized the ball had just dropped. The clock had struck midnight. It was the new year.

What a way to ring in the new year!

Just in time to hear Cap's grunted announcement: "First orgasm of the new year!" He grabbed the sides of Leah's thighs as he continued to impale her like a piston. "Oh, God...oh fuck!" His face flushed and grimaced as the surge of pleasure seared through him like an uncontrollable blaze of fire.

Her buzz had completely vanished, and the soreness from the ravage of her delicate female anatomy—untouched for the past three years—was quickly setting in. After Cap finished and pulled out, the two men moved out of his way. He slid his body next to Leah's and cradled her in his arms.

Mary and Tess assumed positions on the other side of the bed, allowing Jeremy and Other John to stand at the edge and fuck the ladies in tandem. The thrusts reverberating through the mattress gently lulled Leah to sleep in Cap's arms.

The last thing she remembered him saying before she drifted off was, "I hope you had fun, Sugar...and don't regret anything in the morning."

NINETEEN

Regret was not the right word. Leah had tried to explain how she felt about the party the next morning, but she failed to find the words.

She couldn't articulate her feelings or sort through all the twisting, turning layers of them—and she didn't know how to tell Cap she didn't think swinging was for her. All she knew was that something had shifted between them.

She drove down to Cap's nearly every night after work, along with Glory, and fell asleep in his arms, returning home before dawn to ready herself for work. Every morning she told herself she was going to sleep in her own bed that night, but after ten hours at The Pearl, all she wanted to do was collapse in his embrace, anything to avoid sleeping in her cold, empty bed.

Not one of those nights did they have sex. The first week after the party, she was sore, her delicate tissues swollen and bruised.

Cap offered the appropriate measure of concern and apology but also remarked, "I hope it brings back good memories at least?"

She really liked Cap but had a distinct feeling that he and swinging were a package deal, despite what he'd said on their first date. And she wasn't sure she could ever be okay with that. She didn't want to force him to choose between his lifestyle and her.

Sure, he shared her willingly, enthusiastically even, but could she share him? Could she watch him with another woman now that she'd had him for herself? And was she even morally okay with this sharing business in the first place?

She was on a constant pendulum, swinging between the extremes of "He's a great guy, and I enjoy our time together" to "He's a bad influence on me, and I should have known better than to get involved with him."

The next week, right after he came back from his long weekend fishing trip to Florida, she started her period. That explained her volatile emotional roller coaster during the previous week and gave her a reason to hold him off when he returned from his trip hungry for her.

Do I feel like he has to prove he's into me for more than sex? Am I just coming here every night so I can be certain he's not with another woman? Like Rhonda, for instance?

She wished she had someone to talk to about the battle raging within herself, but there was only Aimee, and it didn't seem right to harass a stressed, sleep-deprived new mother with her problems. And eventually, she had to face the conflict head-on. That meant talking to him.

Saturday night came again with a frigid rain that wouldn't quite push itself over to snow. There was a coziness, a security, at Cap's that she never felt in her tiny, sterile apartment with its gleaming white tile floors and flat ecru walls. In the summer, it seemed airy and breezy with her wicker furniture and tropical flower decor. But in

January, it felt as chilling and uninviting as the bitter winter wind.

He wanted to know what specific aspects of the party she regretted. He peered at her through serious, almost-gray eyes, his usual ocean-blue color hiding out with his dimples in an undisclosed location.

I'm making him so miserable he's not even himself. And that thought made her stomach turn sour.

"Regret is still not the right word," she repeated, just as she had two weeks prior.

"If regret isn't the right word, then what is?"

Her cheeks began to burn and head began to throb only moments into the conversation as all the thoughts she'd had walking the boardwalk earlier in the week swirled inside her. She was fighting to drill down to her thoughts about swinging, about this lifestyle that had been sprung on her. It all started when she had to bartend that party.

If the bartender hadn't called out that night...I never would have met Cap. Or Casey. Or any of these people.

Despite seeing that the participants were normal, everyday people, she remained skeptical that she, Leah Elizabeth Miller, was cut from the same cloth. Although there were people with political ties like Casey Fontaine, teachers like Jeremy, and fishermen and nurses and cops and firefighters and computer geeks and people from all other backgrounds and walks of life, she just didn't know if she, the daughter of a minister, hailing from tiny, rural, corn-fed Wahoo, could be one of them.

And that was essentially the question, right? Because with Cap came either her involvement or at the very least her consent for his involvement. She had learned enough from previous relationships to know she could never expect someone to change himself for her. And that was what she would be asking if she demanded he give up the lifestyle for her.

That morning she was walking Glory along the deserted boardwalk, she'd had a vision of walking their two dogs there—in the prime of summer. The picture painted in her mind was so romantic, so appealing. It filled her with hope that she might be in love and happy.

But where was Cap in that fantasy? Why could I see Keeper and not him?

"So, regret is not the word. Maybe *disappointment* would be more accurate?" Leah finally answered when it seemed like Cap's solemn gray eyes had turned to glass while he waited for her to speak.

He slowly nodded while he took that word "disappointment" and rolled it back and forth in his mind, trying to squeeze out the meaning. "Disappointed in me or disappointed in yourself?"

"I don't know," she admitted. "Both? More me than you."

"What could I have done differently?"

"Oh, I don't know, Cap, I feel so stupid for even being upset with you. You patiently and thoroughly answered all my questions, and you gave me multiple chances to change my mind. Maybe I shouldn't have had anything to drink that night. That was my mistake," she said, resigned.

She felt like running away. She'd made a fool out of herself and probably made a fool out of Cap too. *What are his friends going to say when I'm cold and businesslike at Casey's Valentine's party? They're going to think I'm a stupid, immature drama queen.*

She shifted her feet squarely to the floor and began to rise from the loveseat, but he grabbed her wrist and pulled her back down and into his arms. "Don't go," he said, then added in a near-whisper: "Please?"

The tears had already fought their way to the corners of her eyes, the tears she'd kept at bay for two weeks. She'd held them off so she could get through all the looming tasks at work, all of her obligations to Barry and to keeping her staff happy and operating smoothly. She'd poured so much energy into The Pearl that she hadn't had enough left over to deal with the emotional storm brewing inside her. And that was by her own design.

Now, with his arms around her, and after the vision on the boardwalk, her previously submerged feelings had come to a head, and there was no other way than out. She felt the barriers break and release themselves in the form of violent sobs into Cap's strong shoulder.

He held her for some time, letting her body shake against his sturdy frame while all the demons haunting her were exorcised. Finally, when her body had relaxed and melded to his like it was made of clay, he asked, "What do you want, Leah?"

Her green eyes were glowing, her cheeks flushed and tear-stained as she pulled back from his arms. She searched his face for clues that he could give her the answers she wanted, although she wasn't even sure what the questions were.

"I just want to know what we're doing here," she said, her voice fragile like eggshells.

"What do you mean?" He was still patient, still comforting. "Like with our relationship?"

He said the R word.

She sat up straight and found her bold voice. She wasn't accustomed to struggling to find the right words. Her entire livelihood depended on her being assertive, being able to ask for what she wanted in an articulate, diplomatic manner, and on being able to find common ground and compromise anywhere and everywhere.

So why is this so hard for me?

"I want to know what you want from me. From this." She gestured to the space between them.

He took her hand into his and caressed his thumb across her smooth ivory skin. "I really like you, Leah. I'm enjoying getting to know you. I don't have a specific agenda, but there is something about you, within you...an inner light or something... I don't know exactly, but it's something that makes me want to peel away your layers and get to your core. I think there's something there you haven't tapped into yet. Something I may be able to bring out of you."

"And you think it has to do with my sexuality?" Leah asked.

The waves of his voice vibrating across her eardrums were making the hair on her arms stand on end. It was like he was speaking to a different level of her consciousness, a level buried deep below the surface.

"Maybe."

"I like you too, Cap, and I've been trying really hard to be open-minded," she said. "But I'm having a lot of trouble reconciling all this with my beliefs. And I'm not only scared of burning in Hell...but I'm also scared of getting burnt here on Earth too." She let something from her deepest depths seep up to the surface.

"You said you trusted me." His brows drew together in what looked like frustration...or disappointment.

"I did say that," she agreed. "Maybe the problem is that I don't trust myself."

"Why wouldn't you trust yourself, Sugar? You are such a bright, grounded young woman, so mature for your age.

You've got a great head on your shoulders, and from what I've seen of your work, you're gonna just keep climbing. Your boss loves you; your staff respects you. Everyone who met you at the party thought you were... Well...you wanna know the word Other John used, and Mary and Tricia agreed?"

One corner of her mouth turned up. "What's that?"

"They said you were a 'keeper.'" He laughed. "They don't know my dog is named that. But, come on, that's funny, right?" The blueness seemed to be returning to his eyes as he worked to elicit a full smile from her.

"That's sweet." Her temporary smile faded, and she scrubbed her hands down her face when she realized she needed to take responsibility for this chasm that had grown between them. "I think one of the problems is that I don't trust myself to keep my heart from getting broken again."

"Again?"

She didn't like using the past as an excuse. But there were very good reasons she had built walls around her heart and guarded it from invasion. Not only did she need to focus on her career as she climbed the management ladder at The Pearl, but she never again wanted to experience the heartbreak she'd felt after Will and the confusion and despair she'd felt after Todd.

"What do you mean by 'again'?"

She buried her face in her palms and searched for a way to make the story of her failed love life short and sweet. Determined to cut to the chase, like pulling off a Band-Aid, she answered, "I had two boyfriends in college. One cheated on me with someone who was supposed to be my friend. And the other turned out to be gay. So there you have it."

He could only manage to spit out the word, "Ah."

He leaned back against the cushion of the loveseat and ran his fingers through his silver-streaked blond hair. She noticed how much it had grown since she first met him and how it was beginning to curl up at the ends.

"Well, Leah," he finally said, "if you close off your heart, you won't ever find that part of you I see buried deep in there. And I don't know what else to say except that swinging isn't cheating, and I'm sure as hell not gay. Not that there's anything wrong with it."

In approximately one millisecond, she went from feeling paralyzed on the loveseat to springing to her feet and heading toward the door, as if a huge reserve of energy caught fire under her feet.

I'm not being fair to him. He's a man who knows what he wants, and it's not a twenty-something-year-old prude.

"Where are you going?" Cap rose to his feet.

"I'm going home, Cap," she answered sharply when he stepped into her path. "I'm clearly not what you want or need, and I'm not ready for a relationship, anyway. I'm just wasting your time. And you don't deserve to have your time wasted."

He stepped out of her way as she went to the bedroom to wake Glory from her curled-up puppy nap. She snapped her leash onto her collar, grabbed her purse off the kitchen counter and rushed to the door.

"So that's it?" Cap stood in the kitchen watching her, his volume staying steady. "You're just going home, and then what? It's over? Goodbye?"

"I'm sorry, Cap," was all Leah could offer him. "I wish I could be who you want me to be."

In another millisecond, she was gone.

TWENTY

Sunday morning's sunrise chased Saturday's thick layers of clouds away like unwanted guests. Glory was sniffing and pawing at the front door of Leah's apartment by the time the light broke through the curtains.

Leah stumbled out from her bed and into the tiled foyer, feeling the cold seep into the soles of her feet. She was dizzy, her head throbbing again, and just as she was starting to question why she felt so disoriented and fuzzy, she caught a glimpse of an empty bottle of wine turned on its side on the kitchen counter.

"Oh yeah," she muttered under her breath.

Glory looked up at her owner with shiny almost-black eyes, cocking her head to one side as if to ask, "Are you talking to me?"

Leah clipped on her leash and opened the front door. The beagle bolted out toward the steps, dragging her owner behind. When the fresh air hit her, Leah swallowed hard, willing herself to keep the contents of her stomach safely locked inside.

Glory was completely oblivious to her owner's plight.

Leah headed toward the bay, only a half block from her apartment complex. The sky was a shade of periwinkle where it touched down on the deep teal water. She liked the contrast of the dark glossy currents rocking against the feathery sky.

Oh, it's Sunday, she remembered. *Church.*

Even though she knew it was a completely irrational thought, there was a small part of her afraid to darken the door of church out of fear that God would strike her down with a lightning bolt for her actions at the party.

Does God really care that two women sucked on my tits and another guy played with my clit while the guy I'm dating fucked me? Does it make Him angry that I also put another guy's cock in my mouth during all that? Does it make me a bad person? Does it mean I'm going to Hell?

The gauzy periwinkle curtain seemed to be lifting off the bay, fading a little more with each moment she stood in the chilly breeze. If she stayed there long enough, the sky would turn to a sun-kissed blue before her very eyes. Looking back east toward the ocean, she witnessed the pink tendrils of dawn caressing the sparse golden clouds that hung over the water.

Doesn't God have enough to worry about just making the sunrise happen every single day, day in and day out? I may have fooled around at a party, but He's still making the sun rise and set. The earth is still spinning. Gravity still seems to be in working order. Maybe no one else gives a damn about what I did except me.

I bet my parents would give a damn.

A sudden flush prickled her wind-bitten skin. *And Aimee, what would she say? What would Barry say?*

That's it; I've gotta get out of here.

The past two weeks she oscillated between sluggish

inertia and swift, decisive action, like when she abruptly left Cap's the night before. She half expected to hear from him, a text or call to check on her, but her phone was silent, and she was left only with the image of his bewildered face embossed on her memory. It was what she deserved after leaving him like that.

She didn't want to stay in Ocean City. She needed a break, and the off-season was the perfect time to use vacation days she'd never touched. She would call Barry and tell him she needed a little time away from the office. She could do a lot of the more pressing parts of her work via email and phone.

By 9 AM she was steering her Jeep toward Philly.

* * *

By noon, she was knocking on Aimee's door. Her face was tear-streaked and blotchy, and her nose was swollen. Her best friend took one look at her, and her maternal instincts kicked in. She wrapped her arms around Leah as best she could, being about eight inches shorter, and ushered her inside. Anthony was dozing on the sofa, his feet propped on the ottoman with a pink bundle wrapped up in his arms.

"I'm sorry I didn't call first, I...I just had to get away," Leah apologized as Aimee led her back to the bedroom where they'd have more privacy to talk.

"Don't be ridiculous," Aimee assured her. "You know our door is always open." She patted Leah on the back and smoothed her strawberry blonde waves so they fell against one shoulder. "Tell me what's going on." Her voice was soothing and gentle.

"I went to the swinger party," Leah blurted out. Just admitting it caused another outburst of tears.

"Okay...and something went wrong? Did Cap not take care of you?"

She shook her head as she struggled to work her voice past the block of phlegm that had settled in her throat during her marathon crying bout. "It's not that. He was fine. It's just that I feel so guilty and so confused about what I did."

Aimee's eyebrow shot up with curiosity. "What exactly did you do?"

I knew she was going to ask. "I don't want to tell you." She looked up to see Anthony in the doorway with the baby, who was starting to sob and flail her tiny arms. *And I definitely don't want to tell him.*

"I think she's ready for lunch," he said, and Aimee lifted the wrapped bundle from his arms and brought her to her chest. Leah could barely see her soft rosy cheeks peeking out over the blanket. She wore a little white cap with delicate pink roses and a fuzzy pink pom-pom on top.

He stood there for a moment until his wife shot him a look that said, "Scram! It's girl time!" When he got the hint, he finally vanished. "He'll be entertained as soon as the football game gets underway," she promised.

Hailing from Philadelphia, Anthony and Aimee were naturally Eagles fans. Leah had completely forgotten it was a Sunday during football season. She was keeping Aimee from the game too. "Oh, no, I don't want you to miss the game."

"I won't," Aimee assured her. "We're going to discuss your problem, get it solved, and go drink some wine while we watch the game. Don't worry, the Eagles didn't make the playoffs this year, so it's not like I'm missing my team if our talk runs over." She winked and ran her fingertip along her breast, stroking it from the outside toward her nipple, which was large and dark brown in color.

"Why are you doing that?" All Leah could think of was Mary and Tess playing with and sucking on her nipples at the house party. Watching Baby Natalie use her mother's breast as God intended made all the guilty feelings rush back.

"I'm stimulating my mammary glands," she explained. "Trying to get my let-down going."

"What?" Leah asked with wide eyes. She looked at her best friend reclined on her pile of pillows like royalty, comfortably cradling her newborn daughter against her bosom. *She looks like the freaking Madonna, and I'm feeling like a dirty whore.*

"Let-down is when the milk starts to flow, that's all."

Leah stood watching for a moment, mesmerized by the fact that mammals sustain their young by making their food. *It is truly amazing when you think about it.*

Aimee propped Natalie on her shoulder and patted the baby's back until she let out a very unladylike belch. "So are you going to tell me what you did at the party or what?"

"Well...at the beginning of the party, everything was great. I was drinking and buzzing and being all charming and funny. Everyone was telling me how sexy and beautiful I am, which is not a bad thing for the old ego, you know?"

"Hmmm, maybe I need to go to one of these parties." Aimee laughed. "I could use a little ego boost myself now that I have this saggy tummy and big ole leaky boobs."

"Oh, please." Leah waved off her friend with an eye roll. "You're a beautiful new mom, Aimee."

"Tell me more about this party," was Aimee's response.

Leah sighed. "So then we went into a room where some

people were fooling around, and next thing I knew I was sort of in the middle of them."

"What do you mean by 'in the middle'?" Aimee asked incredulously.

Leah sucked in a sharp breath before launching into the explanation. "Cap was fucking me... No one else did that, by the way. But I had a guy playing with my...ahem...clit. And two ladies playing with my tits. And then I gave a BJ to another guy while all that was going on," she stated matter-of-factly.

"Oh. My. God. You did WHAT?!" Aimee was completely shocked by her friend's scandalous confession.

"Well, I'm not repeating it!" Leah exclaimed with a smirk.

She didn't expect Aimee to be so surprised. She sat there for a moment scanning her face, trying to tell if her reaction was solely shock, or if it was colored by a big heap of judgment too.

"You remember some of the stuff we did in college, right?" She stared at Aimee again, waiting for those memories to register in her friend's mind. There'd been more crazy nights than she cared to count.

Aimee made a little gasping sound before making the argument, "Yeah, but that was in college. And we were drunk. We're grownups now."

Leah wanted to say "speak for yourself" so badly, but she couldn't. Despite being successful in her career, a lot of the time she still saw herself as that awkward teenager who never felt like she fit in, always questioning and over-analyzing everything she did and said.

Is that what this is about for me? Sowing my wild oats before I'm too old to use my age as an excuse?

But Cap is a grown-up. He is over forty years old. And

what about Casey Fontaine? She has to be at least fifty. She's definitely a mature, responsible adult. This is who they are. They don't make excuses or blame their choices on youthful ignorance. They own it.

This was the argument forming in Leah's mind. She realized age had nothing to do with this. It was just a different mindset than what most people had.

Leah's arms suddenly felt prickly and cold as if she'd stepped out into a brisk wind. She only told Aimee because she thought she was the one person who could be objective and keep an open mind.

Leah purposely built it up to be so terrible that she expected her friend to laugh it off and accuse her of overreacting. She thought Aimee would tease her a little but ultimately say something like, "Way to go; that's awesome you put yourself out there and tried something new." She'd never known Aimee to shy away from adventure.

But watching her friend lean down and press her lips ever so gently against her newborn daughter's cheek, Leah realized her old friend was a new mother. She'd now look at any adventurous, experimental behavior and think, *would I want my daughter to do this?* She'd never be the same again.

● ●

That night Leah crashed on Aimee and Anthony's sofa. Her phone had remained silent for hours. Even her mother had failed to make her weekly phone call to ask how church was, which at least relieved Leah of the temptation to lie about attending. Now she was cold, lonely, and her stomach twisted with thoughts and feelings she could no longer suppress. She yearned for Cap's warm body next to hers and the gentle snoring of two contented dogs at their feet.

There was something so domestic, so natural about their arrangement, even though they had waded through two weeks of thick tension about the party. She wished she was only ten minutes away instead of three hours so she could drive down to the inlet and endure the fish stench to ascend his stairs.

There was no denying it: she missed him.

She thought confessing her sins to Aimee would make her feel better, that she would come away absolved, validated. But what if Aimee wasn't the only person who understood her anymore? What if that person was now Cap?

TWENTY-ONE

Makeup sex is fun.

That was Leah's take-away from her reconciliation with Cap when she returned from Philadelphia. She tried to launch into a big speech about how sorry she was for leaving so abruptly, and that she was still having trouble sorting things out, but she had missed him so much, and—

He claimed her lips, snuffing out any further words she had planned to say. After spending the entire day and night in bed, only leaving for the bare necessities, the next morning, she attempted her apology speech again. After all, she'd spent the entire drive home from Philly composing it in her head. But Cap pressed a finger to her lips and told her to pack a bag for New York City.

She stared at him blankly. "Why?"

"Because I'm taking to you New York? Why else would I ask?" He chuckled at her wide-eyed stare.

"I can't just up and go to New York!" Leah gasped, astonished he would suggest such a ridiculous thing. "I was just off last week. And what about the dogs?"

"Oh, geez, Leah, you're so uptight! Just relax, will ya? First, you told me yourself that your boss gave you the whole week off. Secondly, my buddy Jim over in Berlin will watch the dogs. He's got a huge farm, so there's plenty of space. We'll drop them off before we leave." He left the room and returned with a small suitcase. "Do you have enough of your stuff here, or do we need to stop by your apartment too?"

"So you're serious then?" She searched his face for a clue. His eyes sparkled like the sea when sunlight dances on the waves.

"Of course I'm serious!" he said with a mild degree of exasperation, then mumbled under his breath as he made his way back into the kitchen, "Try to do something romantic, and she doesn't even appreciate it."

She ran into the kitchen and tackled him from behind. "I heard that!" In just an instant, he grabbed her wrists that were latched around his neck and spun her around his body to face him. Her breath was momentarily taken away at his show of speed and strength. "Oh!"

He grinned when she squealed. "You like that, Sugar?"

She was continually amazed by her infatuation with Cap's body and the power it could wield over her. His large, bulky frame and heavy labor-molded muscles aroused her more than she ever thought possible. Sometimes when he was on top of her, she'd run her fingertips across his broad shoulders and down the firm outline of his triceps and immediately orgasm, she'd be so turned on.

"I do like that," she agreed. "And I like that you surprised me, even though I don't normally like surprises. It's not so easy to surprise me, you know."

"Tell me about it, Miss Plan Every Damn Thing Out!" He squeezed her affectionately. "I think we'll have fun."

"I know we will!" she corrected him.

Since Leah returned, he had treated her like a princess. There had been very little talk of swinging. She told him she was still trying to come to terms with what happened at the party. She asked if they could focus on getting to know each other for a little while and leave everyone else out of the equation for now.

To her surprise, he said yes.

Despite her relief, sometimes when they made love, she felt a tension deep inside him that never seemed to dissipate, no matter how many climaxes he reached. Other times she'd be curled in his arms, and he'd stroke her hair and down her back, and hope he could be satisfied by what they had filled her heart. Those times left her waiting for the other shoe to drop.

As they were driving to New York, she flashed back to the night she drove home from Philly. She'd only stayed with Aimee and Anthony for one night. Aimee encouraged her to go back and face Cap, although part of Leah wondered if her friend lacked the required energy to deal with her problems.

Nevertheless, Leah knew she was right. Avoiding Cap wasn't going to make her feel any better. Besides, she missed him. It thrilled and scared her all at once that she missed him so much.

When she knocked on his door, she was worried he'd had enough of her anguish and indecisiveness and would send her away. But he threw open the door, and there were the dimples, so happy to see her.

"When I'm away from you, I don't want to be," she'd confessed. "And I don't know what I want or where this is going, but for right now, I just want to be here with you."

He had taken her into his arms and pressed his lips

against the top of her head. He whispered against her hair, "That's good enough for me, Sugar."

When she turned to Cap and put her hand on his knee, he looked at her with a grin, as if he knew she was thinking happy thoughts of him. "Thank you," she offered up, glad he recognized he was the source of her happiness.

"Thanks for what?" he asked, still grinning.

"For this trip, for being so patient with me, for being you," she answered.

He removed one hand from the steering wheel and used it to squeeze her hand that rested on his knee. "It's my pleasure, Sugar. My pleasure."

● ● ●

Leah had never been to a Broadway show before. She slipped on a little black dress and pulled up her black boots with the silver buckles. Cap emerged from the bathroom in a fitted button-down dress shirt that was every bit as blue as his eyes and perfectly accentuated his muscular frame.

"Well, aren't we the best looking couple in New York!" He grinned, dimples flashing.

"I want a picture of us," Leah said. They didn't have any of them together.

"You want me to take one of you?"

"No, silly, I want one of us together!" she cried. "Come here!"

She stepped in front of him and handed him her phone, directing him to take a picture of the two of them. She leaned back into him with her cheek against his ear and his chin on her shoulder. He snapped the photo, and she quickly assessed that it was a keeper. She wished she could upload it to her social media, but then how would she explain it to her family back home?

That night after the show and drinks in Times Square, they returned to their hotel room on the seventeenth floor. Cap turned on one light at the far side of the room and led Leah to the eight-foot-tall windows overlooking the busy street below. He swiped the window seat covered with upholstered cushions with his outstretched hand, flinging three small pillows to the floor. Then he pulled the little black dress she wore over her head, hurling it toward the pillows.

His command was simple: "Sit."

Her bare shoulders pressed against the cold glass as he pushed her back and pulled her legs up onto the bench, spreading her thighs wide while her ankles rested on the cushion where she sat.

"And just what do you think you're doing?" she asked as he lowered himself to the floor and began stroking his fingers down her inner thighs.

He followed up his fingers with soft kisses, lingering between her legs to drink in her scent. "I've been staring at you in that dress for the last five hours, and all I could think about doing the entire time is tasting you."

He filled his lungs with her natural perfume and hooked his index finger under the fabric of her red silk panties, tugging insistently till she lifted her hips. After he succeeded in removing them, she was completely nude except for the matching red bra that lifted her stunning cleavage to glorious heights.

I wonder if people down there can see me?

She envisioned what it would be like to drive down a street in Manhattan and look up to find a naked woman silhouetted against the window. *Oh, it's Manhattan. It probably happens all the time.*

Nevertheless, there was a little charge of electricity surging through her at the thought of anyone noticing and becoming aroused by the sight of her.

Meanwhile, Cap was parting her labia with the tip of his tongue, very gently licking up her slit just shy of her slowly swelling bud. "Oh my god..." He breathed against her delicate flesh, savoring her wetness on his tongue. "You taste even better than I dreamed."

As more and more blood rushed between her legs, Cap recognized each new signal her body gave him: the soft sighs, the widened legs, the quickening pulse, the growing moisture, the arching back, and expertly took his cue. He increased the pressure of his tongue against her clit as well as the speed at which it moved. More cues: deep moaning, her fingers ravaging his thick, wavy hair, the tension in her body growing with her need for release.

She wanted to tell him how good it felt, but she had been rendered speechless. *I'm going to explode any minute, and we didn't even kiss yet! He just sat me down and went to work, as if I get no say in the matter.*

Not that I'm complaining.

Then, just as she was about to surrender to the impending hurricane of pleasure, he stopped. His tongue ground to a halt, and he pulled his face away from her thighs.

It took a moment for the blood flow to stop and reverse itself back into her head so she could speak. "What the hell? Why did you stop?"

"I want you to come on my cock," he explained matter-of-factly. "Just wanted to tease you a little first." He winked at her and then pulled her to her feet before she had a chance to protest. Her legs were shaking with frustration, her body punishing her for denying its climax.

Before she could think too much about her aching pussy and legs of jelly, he spun her around facing the window. She was still standing as he pushed her forward hard. She caught herself with her hands against the glass, leaning over the bench seat. He slid his fingers up the inside of her thigh and used both hands to force her legs further apart.

"Don't move," he warned her.

Part of her wanted to move just to see what he would do, but she remembered how badly she wanted him—even though he'd just driven her nearly to the point of no return and then abandoned her there.

Cruel. So damn cruel! I'll have to get him back for that someday.

But when he began to rub the head of his cock against her ass and zeroed in on the entrance to her pussy, she instantly forgot about retribution and instead fought the urge to beg him to take her.

She saw the line of headlights moving slowly down the street below. Even well past midnight, the city was buzzing with traffic. As his cock burrowed into her waiting hole and the walls of her pussy stretched to adjust to his girth, she hoped someone driving down there was looking up at her breasts pressed against the cold glass, a bulge growing in his pants.

Now she was thinking about someone watching her, being turned on, maybe to the point that he'd need to go home and take care of the insistent erection she caused. He'd stroke his cock to the memory of her mouth gaping open as her partner slammed into her. He'd imagine her rapturous screams, even though he couldn't hear them. Maybe he'd imagine how she smelled, how she tasted.

Those thoughts were the last ones she had as she finally exploded around Cap's cock, milking it with wild spasms of ecstasy until even he, the master of stamina and self-control, could no longer hold back his own release.

That night they collapsed in each other's arms after two more rounds, completely drained and satiated, peacefully slumbering in the city that never sleeps.

●●●

By the time they awoke the next morning, sunlight was streaming through the window that had been their backdrop the night before. A wide beam of yellow splashed across Leah's face, urging her to wake up. "Wow, it's almost ten o'clock already!" she gasped. "I never sleep that long!"

"It's amazing what being well fucked will do for you," Cap mumbled, turning his body back over to face her.

She playfully slapped his arm. "No, silly, it's what not having your dog around will do for you!"

"Ow!" he groaned, drawing back as if she'd actually hurt him. "I'm not even awake yet, and you're already beating me up."

She kissed him on the cheek. "I'm sorry, honey. So what are we doing today? Central Park? I've always wanted to go there." She regretted not spending more time in Manhattan when she was in school at Cornell, only four hours away.

He looked at her, blinked twice, but said nothing.

Her eyebrows creased as she tried to figure out what she'd said wrong. "Oh, I didn't tell you, did I? Last night was amazing. The show, the dinner...the...um, after show part... Thank you so much. I had a wonderful time!"

His expression brightened for a moment and then faded again, the dimples slipping into oblivion. "We can't stay that long today, actually. Since it's already ten…I think we better be heading out by noon, don't you think?"

Now it was Leah's turn to wear the blank expression. "I thought we were staying all weekend," she said, unable to hide her disappointment.

"Don't you have to be at work tonight?"

Her mind scrambled to figure out the date. As soon as it came to her, she felt as if a ton of bricks had collapsed on top of her, leaving her buried in the rubble. *Casey's Party.* She had completely forgotten that it was the weekend of the Valentine's party.

Since taking a few days off, spending time in Philly and coming back to Cap, she had lost track of time. And she'd disassociated him with Casey's Group out of necessity, lest her mind drive her absolutely crazy.

Now her buried feelings of inadequacy and paranoia and the nagging leaches of insecurity were threatening to suck the wind out of her sails. All she could think about was having to work that party while Cap circulated amongst the guests, staking out potential partners, plotting how to get one up to a room. Just the thought made her stomach churn.

"Are you going?" she asked, her voice quiet and neutral. She needed him to state his intentions and not take a cue from her reaction, so she was trying to stay calm, even though her insides felt like they were melting in sour bile.

His face scrunched up, making his brow wrinkle as if he might be able to squeeze an answer out if he only concentrated hard enough. He rubbed his hand across his jaw, raking his fingers through his silver-streaked beard. "What would you prefer I do?"

Smart man—deferring to me. And now if I say, "Don't go," then I look like the bad guy, not him.

She wasn't going to let him off that easily. "I would

prefer you do whatever you'd like." She tried to remove the sharpness from her tone but didn't quite succeed.

He took her reply as an open door for diplomacy. "Alright, how about this?" he proposed. "You know, couples who swing have rules. And rules are good, as long as everyone is in agreement, because they can mitigate jealousy and uncertainty and all that negative shit, right?"

Leah slowly nodded, anxious to hear his potential solution.

"Many couples have the rule that they only play together in the same room," he said.

She nodded again, remembering all of the advice he shared with her shortly before the New Year's Eve Party.

"So what if I went to the party, confined myself to the ballroom, and then when you finished your shift and the ballroom is closed up, if we wanted to, you know, mingle upstairs, we could do it. Together."

Her question about whether or not he was willing to just give it up, to stop cold turkey, had been definitively answered. He clearly didn't want to stop. She fought to keep herself from getting angry, but she couldn't deny the stinging spines of her temper starting to pierce through her skin.

Even after all that fucking last night, I'm still not enough for him.

But then her rationality jumped in on the action too. *Well, he's a swinger and has been for a long time. What did you expect him to say? At least he's willing to compromise. And he didn't say that he expected you to play. At least he said he wouldn't do it alone.*

"What if I don't want to play?" she played devil's advocate.

She was trying to imagine a circumstance in which she

would, but couldn't. But then she remembered the thrill of last night in front of the window when she hoped she was being watched. That was also the part of the New Year's Eve debacle that she couldn't deny enjoying, the part where others were turned on by watching her.

She had a sudden moment of clarity. *I'm an exhibitionist. How could I be twenty-seven years old and never realize that about myself?*

"I don't want you to play unless you want to," he assured her.

She wasn't going to end this conversation until she was sure she had the answers she needed. "What if you want to play and I don't?" she pressed.

He smiled and took her hand into his. "Sweetheart, I would never want you to take one for the team. I promise."

"Take one for the team, huh? What is this, baseball?" She laughed at what seemed like a very silly analogy to her. She immediately conjured up a crazy vision of skimpy uniforms where everyone wore the number 69 and a highly animated manager walking out to the pitcher's mound to give him a piece of his mind. Even the word "mound" made her chuckle, despite trying to remain serious.

Cap's face was painted with confusion at first, but then she witnessed the triumphant return of the dimples. "Oh, no, that is actually a phrase you hear all the time in the lifestyle. Just means one partner wants to play, and the other doesn't but goes ahead with it anyway to make their partner happy. It's generally a frowned-upon thing."

"You swingers sure have colorful lingo," Leah observed. She was still mulling his suggestion over. They'd had such a wonderful night, and the sun was so glorious as it streamed through the huge window overlooking the busy street. It now enraptured the entire bed in its golden embrace. It didn't seem like the right time for boat rocking.

She couldn't think of a better solution to their dilemma other than him staying home with the dogs while she worked. But it was pretty unfair to ask him to miss out on seeing his friends. Not to mention there was some allure to the idea of being seen with him...as his date.

"So, what about tonight? Are we on the same page?"

"Okay," she agreed. "Same room, if we play, soft swap, and no taking one for the team." Her lips curled into a devious smile as she tossed out her newly-acquired swinger vocabulary.

"Got it." He quickly glanced at the digital clock on the nightstand on his side of the bed, then turned back to Leah with an even more devious grin. "Looks like we only have about an hour and a half till we need to leave. We better make the most of it!" And with that, he pulled the sheet up like a cape around him and descended upon her like a superhero.

TWENTY-TWO

Casey looked radiant in her red velvet gown and pearls, her hair done up in an elegant French twist and just the right makeup and contouring to make her look like a starlet from days gone by. Her vivacious personality was flowing in abundance as she stood giving directions to her team at the check-in table when Leah and Cap approached.

They had arrived early as Leah needed to make sure everything was set up on time and ran smoothly. Casey was instructing her team about the charity event for the evening, which was a silent auction to benefit the American Heart Association. Two huge tables with gift baskets and gift cards from local businesses flanked the hallway leading to the ballroom.

The woman did a double-take when she saw Leah was accompanied by Cap. "Well, my my my!" her melodic voice burst forth. "I didn't know you two had become so well acquainted."

Leah was surprised. She assumed Rhonda would have told Casey all about the incident at the New Year's Eve party. *But maybe Rhonda didn't notice?* She had slipped off with two other men early in the evening, and Leah didn't see her after that. *I guess I just assumed people talked about it, though. Maybe they really are that discreet?*

"Yes, ma'am." Cap nodded at her. "I've corrupted this sweet little thing, and now there's no turning back." He laughed deviously, but his youthful dimples made him look almost innocent.

"Well, that's just wonderful, Chris! Now you listen here, darling," she said, drawing him closer to her by pulling his tie, "Leah is one of the most lovely people I have ever had the pleasure of meeting. You better be good to her, or I'm going to make you regret it!" Casey had the magical power to make her voice sound like a choir of angels even when she was delivering a threat.

"But of course!" Cap grinned. He wandered off to chat with a man Leah recognized from the New Year's Eve party, and Leah went over last-minute details with Casey.

Hours later, the party was wrapping up, and more and more guests were vanishing from the ballroom and slipping into the elevators to make their way upstairs. Sometimes the elevator carried a man with two women—he was always wearing a smug smile on his face. Sometimes it was two couples, the women chatting and the men trying to avoid looking nervous. Sometimes it was just one couple, and both parties were silent and frowning. Maybe they'd struck out for the evening and were returning to their room alone.

"My feet are killing me," Leah sighed as she pulled her strappy silver heels from her feet. "I don't know why I think I can walk around all night on shoes like that."

"Because they're sexy," Cap answered. "You know men really do appreciate the great lengths you women go to to lure us in, right?"

She had been watching him all night. He flitted back and forth between different groups, shaking the hands of men, kissing women on the cheek, certainly not the life-style-typical greetings she'd seen him give at Casey's parties in the past. He had practically abstained from drinking, toting around the requisite glass of booze for a couple of hours and only sipping from it periodically.

Now they were alone in the ballroom; the last of the kitchen crew had cleared away every bottle, glass, tablecloth and centerpiece. The D.J. had unassembled his equipment and packed it away. Even Casey had left the building. They were the only two who remained.

He was studying her face. "Everything okay?"

She sighed, glanced down at the floor and then back up into his eyes. "Besides my feet, you mean?" He nodded and looked at her expectantly. "I guess I'm just a little nervous about going upstairs."

"We don't have to," he offered. "We could just go back to my place if you'd rather."

She weighed her choices against each other. "I guess we can go upstairs," she decided before she could change her mind. It was what she'd agreed to before the party started. She hooked the straps of her heels under her index finger and followed him to the elevator.

The entire third floor was full of Casey's Group guests. Someone was having an after-party in the suite at the end of the hall. The door was open, and Leah heard music and noise wafting down the hallway to the elevators. The professional side of her cringed. This was exactly the sort of thing that guests called the front desk to complain about.

Suddenly, over the thumping bass and commotion, she heard a woman's voice shouting. She unclasped her hand from Cap's and sprinted down the hall, her stocking-clad feet pressing into the plush navy carpet with each step.

Her heart was pounding, more from anxiousness than from the impromptu jog. She reached the open door and peered past the door frame to assess the situation before going inside. She stood there for a moment getting her bearings, almost enough time for Cap to catch up with her.

There was a group of eight or ten people on the "living room" side of the suite, huddled on the couches and the two chairs, a couple of people standing. The shouting had come from a short, heavyset woman with layered, shoulder-length brown hair and feathered bangs that poufed up, underscored by a layer of fringe resting against her forehead, a hairstyle Leah hadn't seen since she was a little girl. The woman's face was flushed, and she was visibly trembling. In the corner, a man was being restrained by two other men, who were speaking to him in calm, low voices.

Leah reached deep within her throat to bring out the most authoritative voice she could muster. "What's going on here?"

"Just stay out of it, sweetheart," said a man from the living room side.

"I'm the assistant general manager of this property, and I need to know what's going on." She looked around the room at the faces that suddenly looked pale and sober. Cap remained in the doorway, his eyes glued to her, still watching out for her but refusing to interfere unless necessary.

A crowd of people gathered near the entrance to the bedroom of the suite cleared to make a path for Leah to follow. A mass of voices, all giving accounts of the story, began to rise up all around her as she made her way into the bedroom. There was another man seated on the edge of the bed, his head in his hands, which were covered with blood. A woman emerged from the bathroom carrying a wet towel, which she handed to him.

"What happened here?" Leah demanded, her voice becoming more insistent, yet still calm.

"That guy out there punched my husband," the woman with the towel whined. She began dabbing the towel against the man's cheekbone and Leah watched it turn dark with blood.

"Why did he punch him?" Leah asked.

"Because I didn't want to play with him, and my husband told him no, we weren't going to play. He's pretty drunk," she answered matter-of-factly.

"Do I need to call an ambulance?" she asked the man, who was lucid and still seething with anger. He looked up at her and shook his head but didn't seem to want to speak.

"Alright, I'll be back in a moment," she stated and then went back to the living area to talk to the alleged perpetrator. The men who had contained him had wrestled him into a chair, and he sat rocking back and forth, his eyes bloodshot and his skin mottled with rage.

"What's your name?" Leah asked, trying to get a quick read on his level of inebriation.

"It's Jason. Jason Barnes." His speech seemed only slightly slurred.

Leah shouted to Cap across the room, "Call security for me, would you?" He nodded and walked over to the phone that rested on a table near the door.

Leah spent the next fifteen minutes interviewing the witnesses and piecing together what had happened, and by the time she had finished, two security guards arrived to take over.

On the way to the truck, she relayed the entire story to

Cap, "Earlier in the night, Jason and his girlfriend Amanda had approached Dan and Trina to ask if they'd like to hang out after the party, apparently sweetening the deal with the promise of Jell-O shots.

"Trina was quick to say no, but later in the evening, Dan was chatting with and dancing with Jason's girlfriend like he was interested in getting to know her better. Jason had gotten the false impression that they'd be hooking up, which was apparently corroborated an hour or so later when Dan went with Amanda to her room to partake in the Jello shots.

"Then Jason found Trina hanging out with some other people and told her Dan had apparently changed his mind and asked if she was ready to go upstairs. Trina was mad and sent her friend Heather to retrieve Dan from their room. Well, I guess Jason was pissed, and Dan was pissed, but he left their room and then they all reunited at the after party. By that time, Jason had finished the rest of the Jell-O shots, and that's when it all went down. Heather was the one shouting for them to knock it off, and I heard her when I stepped off the elevator."

"Wow," was all Cap could say at first.

"Yeah, talk about drama!" Leah shook her head. "That stuff doesn't happen very often, does it?"

"No, not physical fights." He started up his truck and blasted the heater for their short ride down to the inlet.

"Not physical fights...but drama?" Leah questioned.

"Any time there's sex, there's bound to be hurt feelings, jealousy, or misunderstandings on occasion, you know? Human nature and all."

There was potential for all of the negative things he mentioned in just plain vanilla one-on-one sex, too, so obviously, with so many more potential configurations, the chance of drama in the lifestyle was magnified. "Well, I'm just glad I was there."

"You did an amazing job handling it," Cap assured her. "Seriously, very calm and very in charge. I rather liked seeing that side of you."

She grinned and looked over to see his dimples in the faint light that filtered into the cab of the truck. "Is that so? That turned you on?" She laughed at him.

"I think all the sides of you turn me on," he confessed, putting his arm around her and squeezing her shoulder. "Especially if any of those sides are naked."

●◎●

L ater that night she woke up with a relentless thirst, so she stumbled out of bed and into the kitchen to get a drink of water. She tiptoed back to bed so as not to wake the dogs and slid back under the blankets, pressing her body against Cap's back. She wrapped her arm around him and snuggled her face into his shoulder.

As she listened to his deep, steady breathing, she had a vision of him holding a baby. A tiny baby wrapped in a bundle of blankets, just as Natalie had been when she'd seen her last. That "sexist" prediction Cap had made... *When you find the right man, you're going to want to have his baby...* came rushing back to her.

In the quiet of the cold February night, she conceded that he may have had a point.

TWENTY-THREE

She was sandwiched. One body beneath her, their flesh pressing together as if it would meld into one. Behind her was a steady and rhythmic force against her posterior. Inside, she felt completely stuffed, and there was so little room that the movements were restricted to very slight ones. A strong fist firmly gripped her hair like reins, and she felt a drop of...sweat?...fall onto her back and roll down her side, tickling her...till it seeped between her torso and the body underneath, lubricating the joint where they met.

She arched her back as the fist clenching her hair pulled her away from the other body. Her breasts were released, and she felt the cool air rush in against her skin and in the space where her soft, creamy globes had been smooshed against the solid, well-defined chest beneath her. The coolness evaporated off the hot sweat that had accumulated between them, and her nipples hardened in the sudden chill.

The body underneath her pulled her back down by her shoulders, just far enough so the tip of his tongue could taste the points of her nipples, but not quite enough to suck them into his mouth like he wanted to. She was caught between both bodies, each pulling her in opposite directions but uniting at her core.

Suddenly the passage seemed wider, more forgiving. She heard a groan from behind her, and the force increased, each thrust pushing her against the body underneath her, who was now gripping her hips with strong fingers, his breath punctuated with grunts as he began to move his pelvis up toward her following the same rhythm as the body behind her.

The face below her came into focus, and the voice was now recognizable. Cap was behind her and Jeremy underneath. They were sharing her, both deriving pleasure from a single source in her body. The intensity she felt was because it was both of them together, stretching her walls as far as they could go.

How did they talk me into this? Am I drunk?

Before she could tend to another thought, pleasure spiked around her like a lightning bolt, sending her crashing through a narrow tunnel of pulses and spasms. The electricity it created sparkled like a shower of stardust raining down upon her. She felt suspended in space, tethered only to what was within but not a part of her.

"Leah?" She felt a hand gripping her shoulder, shaking her, then warm breath on her neck, in her face. "Leah? Are you okay?"

She sat up, still trembling, her throat parched and scratchy, with beads of sweat clinging to her forehead. "Cap?" Her voice barely squeaked out.

"Are you alright? Were you having a bad dream?"

Her mind flooded with flashbacks, moon-drenched arms and chest muscles, deep moans and the slap of skin against skin. "Oh no," she revealed, as surprised to say it as he would be to hear it, "quite the contrary, actually."

He settled down on his pillow and turned toward her, propping his head up with his hand. "Oh, do tell," he implored.

"I think I just had my first double penetration," she confessed, remembering the impossibly full feeling in her pussy, the delicious sensation of being stretched to her absolute limit.

Cap nearly gasped with surprise but covered it up with a, "Mmmmmm, regular or vaginal?" slipping through his lips as an erotic growl.

"Vaginal," she replied, the word feeling a little foreign on her tongue. *Did I really just say that?*

"I really have corrupted you, haven't I, Sugar?" He pulled her body to his so her head rested on his shoulder and biceps.

"That's a good thing, right?" she asked, her last vestiges of innocence on full display.

"A very good thing," he assured her. "Now, quit dreaming of cocks and get some sleep, okay?"

"Aye, aye, Captain." She laughed and in a flash had drifted off again.

•◦◦

Leah stared at Barry, too stunned to speak. The best she could manage was to suck in the edge of her lip and bite down hard enough to prevent her from crying.

"Leah? What's wrong?" Concern spread across his face. "I just want to know why you were up on the third floor at 1:30 AM. You look like I'm about to fire you or something!" He laughed uneasily.

The perplexed expression painted on his face told her he wanted to believe there was a perfectly reasonable explanation. He'd gone over the security guards' report of the incident in the third-floor suite following Casey's event several times, and it clearly stated that Guest Experience Strategist Leah Miller was on the scene. He'd squinted and reread.

"I just couldn't figure out why you'd stay at work so late unless you had a feeling something bad was going to happen after the party. And honestly, as lucrative as having her group book with us is, it's just not worth the risk if bad shit goes down. Not if it's going to be all over town that a bunch of swingers take over The Pearl once a month, and the management condones it, you know? I mean, grown men fighting, Leah? I don't even want to know what would have happened if you hadn't been there to intervene...but I just don't get why you were."

During his speech, she'd run a list of competing strategies through her mind with computer-like speed and precision. *When in doubt, honesty is the best policy,* her mother's voice echoed in her head. It was followed closely by Aimee's voice instructing her to *Deny, deny, deny.* She prayed for the right words to come out of her mouth.

"Leah, is there something you want to share with me?" Barry asked, the edge of his voice tinged with condemnation after her pale, anxious face shattered his faith in the reasonable explanation theory. He seemed half angry and half incredulous that his star manager would ever cause him the slightest moment of worry.

"I'm dating someone in Casey's Group," Leah declared as if she were taking a stand on some groundbreaking political issue. She knew Cap would be proud of her for admitting it. She just hoped she wouldn't regret it.

Barry's reaction was not at all what she expected. Instead of disapproval, he burst into a wild explosion of laughter. "You?" He chuckled, struggling to recapture his breath. "You're dating a swinger?"

She glared at him through indignant emerald eyes. "I'm dating Chris Sheldon, and, yes, he's a member of Casey's Group."

"I'm sorry, I'm sorry," he apologized, but he was still laughing. "I'm having a hard time picturing it, that's all. God, it's just too much!"

She stood tall, fighting the urge to put her hands on her hips and assume a defensive position. "I happened to be at the right place at the right time. I'd just finished supervising clean-up in the ballroom, and Cap and I went upstairs to see how the after party was going. I heard shouting as soon as I got off the elevator and got in there as quickly as I could."

Barry had finally regained his composure, and the ramifications of all he'd just discovered began to coalesce. Leah could practically see his mind processing it, neuron by neuron and synapse by synapse.

Casey's event resulted in a physical altercation. Leah stopped the altercation but was only there because she's now part of the group. Having his assistant general manager be part of a swinger group, especially one known for assaults, is not the best idea.

After drawing those conclusions, he was still at a loss for solutions. "I don't know what to do," he admitted like he was asking for her advice.

"I don't understand what the problem is. Fights happen when people drink. They happen at bars, hotels, anyplace that serves alcohol. It goes with the territory."

"You told me Casey's Group was a charity organization,

and it was all on the up and up," he argued, his tone leaning toward accusatory.

"And they are!" Leah fought back. "Casey is a very well-known local realtor. Cap is a respected local businessman. There are doctors, nurses, lawyers, teachers and cops in the group too. Now I don't know about the guy who threw the punch, but the guy who received it didn't even retaliate. Basically the entire situation was caused by one drunk, unreasonable guy. A newcomer to the group, if I understand it correctly. And Casey said she'd deal with him on her end. That's it. I've definitely seen worse from vanilla groups."

"Vanilla?" His eyebrows rose. "Okay, okay," he sighed. "I trust your judgment. I do, Leah. I just feel a little uncomfortable with you participating, that's all. What if it impacts the reputation of The Pearl?"

I can't believe this is happening.

Leah's eyes threatened to well up with tears again; no amount of lip biting was going to stop it from happening. "I didn't participate in anything here," Leah testified. "I wouldn't do that. It's not professional."

"But the group members know you work here," he stated. "What if one of them tells one of their friends, and then that person tells someone else, and then next thing you know, it's all over town? Ocean City is a pretty small place, you know."

"It's a small place to the locals," she agreed. "But let's face it, most of our clientele are from out-of-town. Not only that, and you may be surprised to hear this, but OC is a veritable mecca for lifestyle folks!"

"So, what are you suggesting, that we should cater to them?" he asked.

"I'm not suggesting that they be treated any differently than other guests," Leah clarified. "We have gay and lesbian guests pretty frequently. Would we treat them differently? What if I were a lesbian and that got spread around town? Would that impact The Pearl's reputation? This is the same thing. And even if we did have a reputation for being life-style-friendly, it could translate into really big business, especially during the off-season. I believe it already has. Our bookings are way up since Casey's Group started coming here."

Barry crossed his arms over his chest and studied Leah's face as if trying to discern what had happened to the prim and proper ingénue he'd hired several years ago. But he couldn't form an argument to counter hers. Looking at the bottom line already indicated that the risk was paying off.

"Okay," he conceded. "Like I said, I trust you. Just don't participate while you're working, and try to keep things hush-hush. Remember you represent The Pearl, alright?"

She nodded and silently turned to exit his office. As soon as the door closed behind her, the inevitable flood of tears blurred her vision until they came cascading down her inflamed cheeks. She'd never been reprimanded at work before.

What the hell am I doing?

TWENTY-FOUR

She didn't feel like going to Cap's that night after work, but Glory was there, so she didn't have much of a choice. She dragged out the end of her work day, filing away some paperwork and cleaning out some other older files. She decided to give Aimee a call too, half afraid to hear a hint of disappointment or judgment in her best friend's voice after she explained what happened earlier in Barry's office.

Maybe I'll get a pep talk instead. A "you're not doing anything wrong, so fuck Barry" would be awesome right now.

Aimee sounded weary when she answered the phone, but her voice pepped up once Leah explained that she had a work issue to discuss. She listened attentively, eager to hear of something happening in the real adult world she'd abandoned for motherhood.

"That's a sticky wicket," Aimee concluded once Leah's story was relayed from top to bottom.

"I know," Leah agreed. "But I don't want to stop playing. I'm not ready to stop yet." Her mind spun with images from her earlier dream about Cap and Jeremy. Just thinking about it sent sparks racing up and down her spine, causing every nerve in her body to dance an electrifying tango.

"Are you going to tell Cap?" Aimee asked.

"I'm not sure yet." She tried to imagine what he'd say. "Part of me is afraid he'd want to break up with me...because he wouldn't want to be responsible for me losing my job. And I know he wouldn't want to stop swinging either."

Aimee was not much for beating around the bush, which was, naturally, one of the attributes Leah valued most about her friend. So she was not surprised when the elephant in the room was finally addressed: "Do you love him, Leah?"

That was the question that had not yet been discussed but that everyone would want an answer to. Herself more than anyone...

"I really don't know." She tried to breathe and settle her heart back down into a normal rhythm. "I haven't thought about it very much."

Aimee laughed. "You say you don't know, and you haven't thought about it much as if it's something your mind can decide. It doesn't work like that, girly. It's something you 'feel,' not 'know.' It's in your heart, not your brain."

"Well, geez, Aimee, when did you become The Love Guru?" Leah giggled. Sometimes it was easier to laugh than to delve deep into the scar tissue that Will and Todd had left across her heart. "And anyway, what does that have to do with Barry?"

"I just think, if you really love Cap, and he loves you, maybe you should quit the swinging stuff. At least for now. And just focus on each other. I mean, didn't you ask him to be exclusive for a while?"

"I did, but that was a while ago, and our last agreement

was to do same-room-only stuff. And I guess I'm okay with that," Leah explained. "Of course, we haven't even done that yet; we haven't done anything since New Year's Eve other than going to Casey's event. But we didn't play. The altercation I took care of kinda ended the evening for us."

"So how do you know he's being faithful to that agreement?" Aimee questioned.

"What do you mean?" Leah laughed nervously, "I've been sleeping with him every night!"

"Sure, but people don't just knock the boots at night, you know. You're at work, what, eight to twelve hours a day? And what does he do? I'm guessing he's not running a lot of charter fishing trips in the dead of winter, right?"

A wave of nausea washed over her, chilling her so much that the hairs on her arms began to stand on end. *What **does** Cap do all day?* she wondered in a sudden panic, her mind reeling from Aimee's questions.

He had been meeting frequently with a web developer to redesign his shop's website. He had been over to Baltimore picking up new fishing and boat equipment a few times. He had done some inventory in his storeroom. But other than that, the winter was his downtime. *It leaves him ample opportunity to meet up with someone.*

It was rare that she didn't dream up every possible anxiety-provoking scenario, whether in the realm of work or her personal life. But here was a scenario she had refused to acknowledge until she was forced to.

How do I know he's not playing without me? How can I be sure?

"Gee, thanks for making me paranoid now on top of confused and angry at myself for having my boss call me out." Leah shook her head in disgust at herself. Tears threatened to form in the corners of her eyes again.

I need to be stronger. I need to take charge.

"Oh, honey, I didn't mean to make you feel bad," Aimee consoled her. "I guess I just don't understand your relationship, that's all." She heard her best friend sigh in response. "It sounds like I'm not the only one."

"I guess I have to decide what to do." Leah was trying to convince herself as much as Aimee. "I wish this wasn't so hard. I wasn't expecting to get involved with someone who made me question everything I believe in."

"You must be really drawn to him," Aimee observed. "Because the Leah Miller I've known since our days at Cornell would need someone pretty compelling to make her compromise on any of her beliefs."

"That's the problem exactly." She loved how Aimee had a way of distilling things down to their pure, simple essence. "I knew as soon as I met him that he was the type of man who sucks a woman in like a magnet. I knew I was risking that, but I let it happen anyway. And now I feel so very stupid."

There was no way she could blame Cap for all of this. *He was just being himself. And he charmed the pants right off me. Literally. Just like I knew he would. A self-fulfilling prophecy.*

"If you love him, he's worth compromising for," Aimee reminded her. "But you need to make sure he's willing to compromise for you too."

"You mean, if he loves me, he will compromise for me, right?" Leah knew the writing was on the wall.

"I know Anthony and I haven't been married forever," Aimee said, "so I'm no expert, but I am pretty sure I have figured out at least that much about relationships and love. If you love someone, you will compromise for them. And if they love you, they won't want you to compromise too much, certainly not who you really are."

"Now that you're a mom, you're like Dear Abby or something." Leah laughed. "Thanks for listening and helping me out. I really do appreciate it. I know you're busy with the baby and all."

Leah could hear the glow of gratitude in her friend's voice: "Hey, it's nice to know I'm useful for something other than lactation!"

* * *

Cap was not home when Leah finally arrived. He hadn't left a note or texted his whereabouts either. Leah wondered if he was out visiting a friend, *and by visiting, I mean fucking*, she thought with a twinge of nausea churning her stomach. Her heart was weary from trying to examine her feelings for him. It was much easier to shut those feelings down and let her business side take over.

This is where we cut our losses, she thought, borrowing a phrase from one of her favorite college professors.

She grabbed the leashes off the table and called the dogs, who had briefly greeted her at the door but then wandered off to resume their snoozing on the living room rug. They came running to her, tails wagging, clearly refreshed from their naps.

"You guys are going to miss each other, that's for sure," she sighed as she clipped each leash to its respective collar.

She headed down the stairs and out the door. She thought she saw Cap's blue truck coming from down the street, two stop signs away from his shop, but she ignored him and proceeded toward the boardwalk. The sun had exploded behind her in a fiery death, and the moon was rising over the Atlantic like a silver angel. The lavender blue dusk spilling down onto the white-crested waves beckoned her as she made her way up the slight incline where the horizon was at last revealed. It was brisk but warm for February.

Maybe we'll have an early spring. She let that temporary brightness illuminate the dark caverns where she'd hidden the thoughts she was avoiding. She wanted to clear her mind once and for all of all worry, indecision, and tribulation.

Remember last summer when I first got Glory? Everything was so simple. I had work and Glory and phone calls with Aimee. That's it. That's all I had to worry about.

Glory and Keeper bounded toward the waves, not at all deterred by the chill of the water. They enjoyed tormenting the sea gulls that dared to land within a twenty-foot radius.

See? They have a simple life. Eat, sleep, play. That's all they have to worry about.

She shook her head, and her hair caught the wind, blowing it back into her face. She sputtered and used her free hand to tuck the strawberry blonde waves behind her ear. *I can't believe I'm jealous of dogs.*

Why am I making this so complicated? I'm putting myself in a bad position at my job. I'm turning my back on my faith and everything I've been taught about love, sex, and the sanctity of marriage. This is a no-brainer, right? I need to move on. Clearly.

She looked down the boardwalk to the south, past the jagged rocks jutting away from the point of the inlet, toward Assateague Island, where wild ponies roamed the marshes and beaches. It was amazing that just a few miles south, the same beach existed but there was no boardwalk lined with shops and restaurants, no smells of boardwalk fries or tattoo shops buzzing with fresh ink. There were no Ferris wheels or cotton candy. No giant sharks coming out the side of a Ripley's Believe It or Not museum. There weren't arcades lit up in neon or throngs of people carrying bags of cheap souvenirs or moms pushing strollers with screaming toddlers. No formerly pale girls with thick coatings of aloe plastered to scarlet, sunburned skin, pulling up their bikini tops just in time to avoid flashing their freshly minted tan lines for the entire boardwalk to see.

No, Assateague Island was the same exact beach but an entirely different environment. The beaches were wide and often vacant, windswept and desolate. There was a purity that permeated every molecule: the water, the sand, the air, the sun. Loblolly pines proudly towered over the bay side of the island. Tall reeds with fluffy plumes lined the trails. Low scrappy-looking bushes dotted the sides of the roads. White broken shells and dried seaweed were strewn across the sand, and piles of dung marked where the wild ponies had ventured.

Every single thing was born of nature, and when its life was spent, returned to nature. But there was a loneliness that echoed across the island, from the bay to the beach. Even with regular visits from humans, there was an understanding that this world belonged to nature, to the seagulls and the ponies and the deer. To the crabs and the dolphins. To the pines and the seashells. To everything that existed in that realm that was not human. To everything that would someday return to the earth or the sea.

Leah recognized the contrast between the two beaches was a metaphor for the way her life had diverged since she met Cap. She had gone from the pureness but steadfast loneliness of Assateague to the frenzied hedonism of the boardwalk, where her body and mind enjoyed constant stimulation. It left her wondering if there was any middle ground, any way to have the best of both worlds. But looking south from the tip of the Ocean City inlet to the beginning of the long, narrow stretch of Assateague, the only things in between were rocks and water.

TWENTY-FIVE

She didn't mean to slam the door when she went to return Keeper to Cap's apartment. She intended to slip in, leave the dog, grab her things and head back to her apartment. After all, it had been several days since she'd been there, since before the trip to New York.

I can't believe how much has happened in less than a week.

She tiptoed across the kitchen to retrieve her purse. When she glanced into the living room, she noticed Cap was asleep on the couch with the television blaring. *No wonder he didn't hear the door slam.*

She unhooked Keeper's leash but kept Glory on hers. Naturally, the Labrador bolted straight for his owner, covering his whiskery face with "I desperately missed you!" kisses.

So much for slipping out unnoticed, Leah lamented as Cap sputtered and flailed in reaction to the big dog's gratuitous affections.

"Where have you been?" His question was barely

coherent as he pushed it through an open mouth stretched wide by his yawn.

"Um...taking the dogs on a walk?" she snapped back, pointing to the leash on Glory. "Where were you when I got home?"

His face contorted for a moment as if he were trying to decide how to answer, but his features slipped into what looked an awful lot like a lie in the meantime. The result was something like a smarmy, sheepish grin.

You've got to be kidding me.

Her cheeks flushed with anger as her hand flew to her hip, gripping Glory's leash so tightly, she thought she might melt the material. She was giving him one minute to offer her a plausible explanation before taking her dog and leaving.

"I have a surprise for you," he finally said, his smile so wide that the dimples were out in full force.

It seemed like a stall tactic to her, a distraction from the real question. Her patience was wearing thin, and her temper was about to take over. In a moment, every bit of red in her strawberry blonde hair was about to reflect in the fiery words her tongue would spew.

"You didn't answer my question." She paused for about three seconds as his dimples disappeared into oblivion. His face registered the realization that she was truly upset. "I asked you where you were. I have a feeling you were doing something I wouldn't like."

He took a step back, and Glory lurched toward him on her leash with a growl. *Amazing! She's mad at him too!*

Glory's reaction sent Keeper dashing into the kitchen to see what the fuss was about. Suddenly the four of them were facing off, Cap looking defensive, and Leah looking about to cry. Her nerves were completely shot from all the stress that had been heaped upon her throughout the day, and this was the situation she had most wanted to avoid.

"What in the world is going on, Leah?" Cap stepped toward her again, and Glory moved out of his way. His eyes searched her face for answers, and when he saw the tears, his arms stretched out, reaching for her.

She fell into them despite her determination not to. When she felt them wrap around her, she collapsed in heaving sobs against his shoulder. He pressed his lips to the top of her head and said nothing, just absorbed her tremors into his tall, strong body.

Minutes later, her eyes drying and her throat finally opening back up to allow sound through, she pulled back and looked up at him. She could see he was still confused about why they were in his kitchen with Glory still on her leash and her bawling into his chest.

"Are you fucking anyone else?" she asked in almost a whisper.

"Oh my god, what?!" He laughed. "Are you serious?"

She straightened her back and looked him in the eyes. "Yes, I'm serious. You're a swinger, Cap. You like to fuck multiple women. As far as I know, it's been months since you've been with anyone but me, and I need to know if that's true, if you're really following our agreement."

"What is our agreement exactly?" he asked with feigned innocence.

"Really?" Any evidence that she'd just been crying in his embrace had vanished into thin air. "I can't believe you're pretending you don't know what I'm talking about."

He put a heavy hand on her shoulder and leaned in close to her face. "I am not sleeping with anyone but you. And I believe our agreement was that we would only play together in the same room, am I right?"

She bristled at the weight of his hand on her. *It feels patronizing, but maybe that is just the paranoia I've been feeling since Aimee asked me if he's been faithful.*

She studied his face: the clear teal-blue eyes with their long blond lashes, the thick eyebrows that were just shy of being shaggy, and the square jaw carpeted with a thick mat of silver-streaked beard. She had looked at his face so many times now that she knew each expression it was capable of forming by heart. She had never questioned his honesty before now, and it made her wonder if he had a "lying" face. Would she be able to tell if he did? Was he showing it to her now?

"I don't know what to say," she admitted quietly, wishing she could crawl through his ear and worm her way through his mind to examine what was really happening in there.

"Do you really think I would cheat on you?" he asked, his voice filled with disappointment that she didn't trust him.

Why was she doing this? Sabotaging them? Because of what happened with Barry in his office today? Because of what Aimee said? Was she really this hell-bent on making things as difficult as they could possibly be?

"I don't know. I don't know what I think anymore."

"Come here," Cap beckoned her. "I really do have a surprise for you. Will you go with me to see it?"

"I don't know, Cap, I've had a really awful day. I think I'm going to just go home and go to bed," she sighed. Her skull was throbbing with the beginnings of a tension headache.

"What happened, Sugar? Why don't you tell me about it on the way there? Then, when we get home, I'll draw you a hot bath and give you a nice massage. What do you say to that?" He smiled, dimples and teeth in full view. He reached out to grab her hand and pull her into his arms again. "I'll make it all better, baby, I promise."

She rested her cheek against his firm chest muscles and sighed again. *He always knows exactly what to say. He reels me right back in. Damn good fisherman.*

Next thing she knew, she was hoisting herself into the cab of his truck, and he was whisking her across the inlet bridge toward West Ocean City and Berlin. They turned down Route 611 toward Assateague Island, and her heart began to pump faster when she remembered the metaphor she'd thought about earlier when she was walking the dogs. They headed south for a few miles; then he turned down a gravel road heading east, back toward the ocean.

The gravel road wound around a bend of pine trees and then straightened into an empty field where a large, abandoned building rose up from the earth. It was industrial-looking, perhaps a warehouse, and the metal siding was faded around the place where a sign had announced the name of the business in days gone by.

Leah looked over at Cap, who was still beaming, and shook her head. "Why are we here?"

"I bought this place," he announced, his dimples at maximum depth. He sat in the truck staring at the building, his eyes afire with visions and ideas.

Leah opened her door and stepped out onto the sandy, weed-dotted soil. The first thing that came to her mind was a television series she'd watched on Netflix where the characters built a meth lab in a similar-looking structure.

"I know it's not much to look at now, but picture this." He spread his hands out as if making a frame around the building. "Looks like a warehouse from the outside, right?

But we clean it up on the inside and build a bar and some rooms, and voila, it's a swing club."

"Really?" She looked back at him and then toward the building again. The excitement Cap was radiating was beginning to seep into her pores as if it was contagious. But her body wanted to fight it off like a virus.

"Yes, really. Look, it's so out of the way back here on this gravel road, it will be discreet yet still close to OC, so people vacationing at the beach can find it. There's plenty of parking. And wait till you hear the plans I have for the inside. It's going to be amazing!" He looked like a kid on Christmas morning, unwrapping the gift he'd anticipated all year long.

He took her hand and pulled her toward the concrete slab and double glass doors at the entrance of the two-story metal-sided building. The doors were chained together, and he wrestled with a huge ring full of keys to find the correct one to unlock them. He pulled off the chain and opened the right side door.

"After you," he offered as he ushered her into the lobby.

There was an office area on the left with large windows on each side. He flipped a light switch, and three bare bulbs on the ceiling faintly illuminated the space. "This will be the reception area, where staff will take IDs and money."

He led her down the hall, where a square opening revealed the building's cavernous interior. "The sky's the limit in here."

He pulled a flashlight from his belt and waved it around. "I think the middle area will be a huge dance floor with a bar at that end. It'll be bring-your-own-booze, but you'll have to check them in with the bartender. That's pretty much standard procedure with the clubs I've been to. And then flanking both sides, there will be a series of private playrooms. Oh!" he exclaimed, as if the ideas were flooding his mind so quickly, he couldn't get them out fast enough. "The name! The name is fucking brilliant!"

"What's that?" Leah's eyes struggled to adjust to the dim light coming from the bulbs they'd illuminated in the foyer. She looked toward the ceiling as Cap shone the flashlight on exposed steel beams and massive pipes. "What did they do in here, anyway?"

"I was told they processed crabs back in the early part of the 1900s. Then, after the crabbing industry started declining here, it was mainly used for boat and fishing equipment storage. That's how I found out about it. This old fisherman from here in Berlin who comes down to my shop every now and again told me the owner had died, and his son was trying to sell this place off. He'd had it on the market for about a year and was about to tear it down. He was gonna try to sell the land to be developed for real estate. You know the real estate this close to the water is big fucking business.

"I've been negotiating for a couple months now—had to move around some assets to make it all work. And I have a partner too. I didn't say anything to you or anyone else at her request. We both wanted to make sure it was going to work out. Well, today we met at the bank, signed the papers, and got the keys!"

"Partner?" Leah asked, her eyes wide.

"Casey Fontaine," Cap revealed. "She's probably twice as excited as I am. It's about time Ocean City had its own club, that way we don't have to keep hosting stuff at local hotels, where we have all these rules, and we're tiptoeing around all the vanilla people, trying not to offend them all the time."

Leah was still trying to process everything. Slowly the intricate details were being filtered through her mind, and she began reconciling them with what had happened during her meeting with Barry earlier in the day. A web of ideas and emotions started to take shape.

If Casey's Group stopped using The Pearl for their events and used Cap's club instead, then there'd be much less risk to me professionally. We'd still be out the revenue from the parties, but I'll just have to figure out a way to make it up...

"So, the name," Cap brought her back to the present. "The Factory. What do you think? We're going to keep the industrial look, all the exposed beams and pipes, just paint all of that dark, like a midnight blue, we're thinking, and the accent colors will be lime green and fuchsia. That's all Casey's idea, of course. She's hired a contractor, and we're going to meet out here on Monday to go over everything."

She'd never seen him so impassioned about anything, except when he spoke of his father or his daughters. Even in the dim lighting, he looked decades younger with his eyes lit up and the color rising to the surface of his cheeks.

She was in awe of this side of him she had never before seen. He was usually so laidback and even-tempered, always going with the flow, projecting an easy, southern gentleman type of charm. Now he was borderline hyper, he was so animated. The energy radiated off him and bombarded Leah's exterior, only to bounce back to him with twice the force.

"You're not saying anything, Leah." His enthusiasm levels waned as his eyes swept her face looking for answers to why she wasn't equally enthralled by the new venture.

"I don't even know what to say. I'm happy for you, Cap; I really am," she said stiffly. There was a chill in the unheated building, and she felt it permeating her wool coat. She shivered, then wrapped her arms under her chest and curled her fingers around the opposing elbows.

"Be happy for US," he corrected, emphasizing the pronoun. He turned to her and pried her hands away from her folded arms. He gripped them in his own and yanked her so close to him that there was only an inch of space separating their bodies.

"What do you mean?" she questioned.

He squeezed her hands tightly into his. "This is for us, Leah. Casey and I want you to run this place. We want you to be the manager."

She stepped back, an instant wave of vertigo twisting around her like a tornado. She watched his hands drop to his sides. "You want me to leave The Pearl and work for you?"

He nodded. "Wouldn't it be great? You'd be perfect, absolutely perfect."

"Cap..." Her mind was spinning so rapidly, she thought smoke would start puffing out her ears at any moment. "I...I don't know if I can do that."

So many questions and scenarios were jumbling up inside, her brain felt like a clogged drain. She couldn't choke anything out, and the furiously flowing thoughts were backing up throughout her entire body, threatening to spring a leak.

"Why not? Casey adores you. I adore you. We are going to make a fucking killing, there's such a great opportunity here. The closest clubs are in Baltimore and DC, you know. People from Delmarva drive two or three hours to go. There are so many tourists in the summer, and they end up meeting at someplace like Seacrets since there's no club here. That's why Casey's Group has taken off like it has; there's a real need for a local place for lifestyle people to congregate."

Leah nodded. "I get that, and it does sound like a

wonderful opportunity, but what do I tell my parents? What do I tell my friends? I can't exactly say I'm leaving this great job at The Pearl to run a swing club. I mean, really, Cap? Did you even consider that?"

She watched his excitement fade and frustration take its place. "We'll think of something else to tell them," he suggested. "Where there's a will, there's a way. And we're willing to make you an equal partner, so you'll be sharing in all the profits, even though you're not investing anything. And that's fine! We both want you to succeed, of course."

"What about your fishing business and Casey's real estate job? How will you have time to do this too?"

"That's why we need you to handle all the details. You'll need to hire an assistant and some security and a bartender. But we can get started with a pretty small staff, and it will only be on the weekends, at least at first. Of course, we need to get all the renovations done before we can do anything. But I want to open the doors to the public by the winter. When everything is dead in OC, we'll be having this ridiculous grand opening party here at The Factory!"

"Where is the capital coming from?" She felt like she was shooting down every golden star of joy and hope he'd hung in the sky. *But someone has to be realistic, right? Someone has to play devil's advocate.*

He scratched his head with disappointment, and it seemed as though he was deflating before her very eyes. But he took in a deep breath of patience and explained, "Casey comes from money. And I sold my grandparents' farm in Pennsylvania. We have half a million in cash to get this thing off the ground. Plus I have some other assets I can liquidate if need be."

Leah struggled to keep her mouth from gaping open at the idea of half a million dollars. *I didn't even know his grandparents had a farm in Pennsylvania.* She was suddenly sad that he gave up a property that may have been in his family for generations.

He watched her wrap her head around the staggering sum as she started to make mental calculations. But she was still frowning. "This is a lot to take in, Cap, especially after the day I've had. I just don't know how it will all work out. I have a lot of questions, you know? I don't like to jump into things without knowing where I'm going to land."

He intertwined his hands with hers again. "I understand that, Sugar, I do. I am not asking you to decide tonight. Let's talk to Casey, and you can come with us to meet the contractor, and we'll get all your questions answered, I promise."

She turned and began to walk toward the front of the building, suddenly needing to fill her lungs with something other than the stale air that had been trapped inside those walls for years. She made her way through the lobby, her steps illuminated by the faint lights overhead. She nearly stumbled over a thick gray mat that was curled up against the threshold as she pushed her way out into the open air.

The night winds swirled around her, but the cool crispness was welcome as she inflated her lungs, breathing in and out, in and out. She heard Cap locking the doors as she stepped farther into the stubbly yard. The sky was pierced with tiny white stars, glittering through the clear and cloudless heavens. She recognized the constellation Orion, his belt gleaming with its trio of brilliant orbs.

Cap moved in behind her, pressing his body against her back and bottom, wrapping his arms around her waist and pulling her flush so they were sealed together. He rested his chin on her shoulder. "Leah, we can make this happen. I know we can."

She whipped around to face him. "I don't know what we're doing here," she admitted, realizing that all her trepidation stemmed from that overarching dilemma.

"What do you mean? I just told you about the club I want to build."

"I mean us, Cap. I don't know what you and I are doing. Together."

I've only known him for three months, yet we sleep together every night, and in some ways it feels like we're together, a couple. She considered those elusive, magical words that had not yet been uttered. *Three magical words all in a line, like those three stars in Orion's belt.*

Instead, the constellation hanging in the sky over us is a giant question mark. And the answer seems as far away as the stars.

"Leah, I want this for us. For our future. I want us to be together...to be partners in every sense of the word." His voice was deep and husky as the words spilled out of his mouth with no hesitation.

"I don't know if you're ready for that, so I've been trying to take it slow. You're so much younger than me, and you have your whole life stretched out in front of you. I don't know if you can see yourself with an old man like me, one with skeletons in the closet and so much goddamn experience, I could write a fucking book.

"You know, after I got divorced, I was positive I wanted to be alone, you know, the single stud, notching my bedpost with all the lovely women who came to the beach to play. I didn't know women like you were out there. You're so smart and independent, and you have no clue how fucking sexy you are.

"The first time I saw you that night at The Pearl, I wanted you. Yeah, I wanted to put the notch in my bedpost, but then after that, there was so much I saw in you, so much substance, so much potential... I wanted more. I needed more. But I didn't want to scare you with that. I didn't want to chase you away."

Her lips trembled as she answered him, "Well, I'm still here, aren't I?"

His speech made her eyes well up with tears, stinging and soothing all at once. These were words she didn't know he was capable of saying. She felt it from him, that their lives were growing into each other, but she didn't expect him to say it, to admit it. And still that elusive word hung in the air unsaid.

"I always feel like you're one step from running away. Like I've pushed you too far, too fast, and all I want to do is hold you and promise you that no matter what happens, I'll make it right," he vowed. "But I'm afraid you won't let me."

"I'm just scared, Cap, scared of trusting you, scared of trusting myself. I'm scared of all these thoughts and feelings that contradict everything I've always believed. I get so scared, sometimes I think I have to escape. Even tonight when I was walking the dogs, I was planning my exit strategy, but you always pull me back in. You make me want to stay."

"Do you love me?"

She didn't answer at first, still as confused as when Aimee asked her the question earlier. She'd searched her heart all afternoon and evening, and she kept coming back to the fact that she *did*—but she *shouldn't*. Like Aimee said, it was a matter of the heart, not the mind.

My heart says yes, and my mind says no. It's not an answer. It's more of a contradiction.

"I do, Leah," he confessed.

He took a deep breath as if he'd been holding it inside

for an eternity, then he drew her body close to his. "I've fallen in love with you, Leah. I didn't want to; I didn't think I needed to... But I did...and..."

"And what?" she asked when his voice trailed off into the dark winter night.

Her heart was pounding at the utterance of that word, the word she kept trying on and taking off again like an outfit in a dressing room she liked but was too afraid to buy. She was sure he could hear her heart thundering against her ribcage.

"And I hope you feel it too," he answered, more vulnerable than she'd ever heard him sound.

The stars swirled above her head in crazy elliptical orbits, but maybe it was just the dizziness she'd felt inside the building returning for an encore. Her thoughts were falling like bombs around her, but she felt a clear, ringing voice rise up from somewhere deep inside her, someplace she had locked up years ago. It passed over her vocal cords and through her lips like strands of silk being woven together, tumbling out into the cold night air in a misty vapor that wrapped around Cap's ears and then his heart.

"I do feel it. I want to trust you, and I want to let my heart feel what it wants to feel, Cap. But I need your help. I need you to promise you'll always be honest with me, no matter what. That's the only thing I'll ever ask of you. Complete and total honesty. I've been lied to before, and I just can't...I can't have it happen again."

She wrapped her arms around his waist, locking eyes with him and searching for a promise. "If I can trust you, I can love you. It's as simple as that."

"You have my word," he promised, pressing his lips against her forehead. "As well as my heart."

She looked up at the sky, and her gaze followed a line of

stars pointing to the southeast, where moonlit-crested waves were crashing upon the shores of Assateague's simple, natural beach. She thought about the relation of The Factory to Ocean City and the island—it was almost directly in between the two. The metaphor from earlier had come alive.

She glanced at Cap, then down to her feet as they pressed into the sandy soil.

Maybe there is a middle ground after all. Maybe I'm standing on it.

TWENTY-SIX

The plans were coming together for The Factory. Casey's mantra was "If we build it, they will come." Only she didn't mean "come" in the literal sense.

Leah had been involved in every decision from what color of tile to put in the bathrooms to writing the code of conduct each member would sign upon joining.

The earth spun quickly through the next two months. Spring touched down onto Delmarva tentatively, like a butterfly wandering among the flowers, one day flying close and bringing warm golden sun and the next flitting away and sending cold gray skies.

Cap was beginning to prepare for "The Season," as he and most of the locals called it. The shop was inventoried and cleaned, seasonal help was hired, and his equipment and boat had been scrubbed down and readied for action.

"You know you won't be seeing me as much once business picks up, right?" he warned Leah one night in April when an early heat wave caused them to throw the blankets off and the windows open.

She lay with her back against his bare chest, her legs curled toward him and his arm wrapped around her waist. They slept like that most nights; she loved feeling the steady rhythm of his breathing falling against her hairline, lightly tickling her ear.

"I know, honey, and don't forget my work will be picking up too," she reminded him.

"Okay, but I don't think you realize how busy it will be. I'm gone from sun-up till eight or nine at night some days. Especially days I do three charters. I barely drop off one crew and pick up the next."

"I get it, Cap. I'm prepared," she promised.

"When are you going to resign from your job?" he proceeded to question, clearly not receiving the hint that she was ready to nod off.

She pushed the air out of her lungs and filled them again before answering. "Not until the end of the summer. Things are back to normal now, and Barry was pleased with the way Casey's last event went. He really needs me this summer. Besides, you said the club's doors won't open till January, anyway. I figure I have at least till September or October to break the news to him."

"I'd really like to have you out of there by August," Cap said. "Because that's when we're going to need to start hiring and training, and I'm still going to be full up on charters until a few weeks after Labor Day."

"I don't know, okay? We'll just have to see how things go. I don't want to leave Barry in a tight spot. He's done a lot of stuff for me, and I don't want to burn any bridges. And besides, I haven't exactly figured out what I'm going to tell my family yet."

"Speaking of which..." Cap slid his torso out from under her head, sat up in the bed and leaned his back against the headboard. He pulled the sheet down, exposing Leah's shoulders, which prompted her to roll over and sit up next to him.

"What?"

"When are you going to tell your parents about me?"

Oh my gosh, where is all this coming from? And why isn't this man tired?

She realized it was because he hadn't worked all day. He'd hung out with his fishing buddies and drank beer at M.R. Ducks, a bar not far from his shop.

"The plan is to tell them next weekend when I'm home for the bridal shower," she explained as nicely as she could muster. Ever since she met Cap's daughters, Emma and Ashton, when they'd celebrated Emma's birthday last month, he had been asking more about her family.

"Don't you think you should tell them before I just show up at your brother's wedding with you?" He laughed.

She bristled. She hadn't quite made up her mind that she would take Cap to her brother's wedding in June. She'd assumed he would be too busy with charters and wouldn't want to lose out on any business. But he was so confident the club would do well the following winter that he insisted he could take some time off this summer, when the bulk of his income was normally earned.

In many ways, it was easier to pretend she wasn't quitting her job at The Pearl than to deal with the fact she was about to become the manager of a swing club. It was easier to pretend on the phone to her mother that she was still happily single than to deal with the inevitable outrage that would ensue when her family learned she was dating a forty-two-year-old divorced father of two grown daughters, who just happened to be building a club that was essentially a "den of sin."

And it was easier to make love to Cap and pretend her faith wasn't condemning her to hell for it. *Not going to church is making that a heck of a lot easier too.*

At least we've been monogamous for months now. Since New Year's Eve.

He had accepted her promise to revisit the idea of them participating in the lifestyle at some point. But she couldn't imagine he would be okay with permanently taking themselves out of the proverbial "lineup," especially being owners of a swing club.

"Don't worry; I'll take care of it. Honey, I'm really tired, aren't you?" She turned to him and laid her head on his chest. He stroked his fingers down her silken back.

"I want to be tired, but I think we need to take care of this first." He smirked, pulling back the sheet to reveal his cock standing at nearly full attention. He nudged her toward it. "Please, baby? Don't you want to taste it?"

Leah had cultivated a fondness for giving blowjobs since meeting Cap. As he gently guided her training, she began to see it as an art form, and with very little coaxing, she had developed mind-blowing skills. She was close to being able to take his entire eight-inch organ deep into her throat, spurred on by the discovery that she loved watching the way his eyes rolled back in his head in complete and utter bliss when she attempted it.

She adored teasing the tip with her tongue and then plunging her mouth down on it, taking it so deep she'd gag, then coating it with saliva as she slid her mouth back up the shaft. Cap claimed most women couldn't bring him to climax with their mouths alone, but with practice, Leah mastered the feat. And she was proud of her accomplishment.

"I only want to get it wet," Leah remarked, running her

tongue around the ridge under the glans. "And then I'm going to climb on top and ride it."

She slurped his cock into her mouth, swallowed it nearly to the base and then held it there, feeling it stiffen and throb as she brought her lips back up to the head. She let it spring out of her mouth and wave in the air, glistening with saliva and aching for more.

She slid herself up Cap's body, stopping along the way in a zigzag pattern to enjoy a nibble here and there, across his nipples and then all the way to his neck. Once her hips were aligned with his, she lowered her pelvis on top of his cock and felt each inch pass through her lips to penetrate her tight, wet hole.

"Good girl," Cap groaned as she began to grind her hips into him.

She pushed herself up off his chest, her hands balancing herself on the firm mounds of his pecs. Riding him upright, her breasts bounced each time she brought her hips down on top of him.

"That's it, baby, ride that cock," he moaned, looking up at her through hooded, lust-filled eyes. "You love that cock, don't you, baby?"

She began to pick up the pace as the pressure built within her core. "I guess I need to fuck you harder to get you to shut up," she teased him, her lips curling into a smirk. "How else is a girl gonna get some sleep around here?"

"If you keep moving like that, we're going to be done and asleep in no time, Sugar," he winced as she slammed down hard, her ass cheeks slapping onto his thighs.

"The quicker the better," she announced, "cause I'm about to come all over your cock, baby!" Just as the words were slipping out her lips, her pussy began to spasm with pleasure. The waves rocked through her, and in seconds she heard Cap's telltale groan. He grabbed her hips and pumped his cock like a piston up into her body until he convulsed and shook beneath her.

She let him come back down to earth as she patiently perched on his cock, the aftershocks making him twitch inside her. Once he regained his breath, he pulled her down onto his chest till her head rested on his shoulder and wrapped his arms around her. "That felt amazing, Sugar; sorry it was so quick."

"That was by design." Leah smiled against his lips. "Now, let's get some sleep."

She rolled off and curled up next to him, once again the inside spoon. Just as he began to drift off, he whispered, "I love you."

TWENTY-SEVEN

She stepped off the plane and headed toward a terminal on the opposite side of the airport to meet her connecting flight. The trip from Salisbury to Philadelphia on the little puddle jumper was always loud and often choppy, but she took consolation in the fact that it was only twenty-five minutes in duration.

She walked as fast as she could down the long corridor, dragging her carry-on bag behind her. Even though she had plenty of time before the next flight, she was anxious to see Aimee and Natalie waiting for her. She hadn't seen either since she'd sought refuge in Philly shortly after the infamous New Year's party.

Aimee was sitting by the windows looking out across the tarmac, bouncing her four-month-old daughter on her lap. The baby was decked out in a leopard-print coat with matching shoes and a red rose affixed to a velvet band crowning her head. She was giggling at the older woman sitting across from them, who was smiling and gesturing to her.

Leah approached slowly, watching how proud Aimee

looked of her little girl. *The last time I saw her, she was this tiny sleeping bundle, and now she actually looks like a miniature human with expressions and a personality. All that in four months. Truly remarkable.*

The only experience she had with babies was working in the church nursery. It only took one time of being spit up on and a few nasty diaper changes to turn her off them. But watching the little girl's arms and legs waving as she gurgled and cooed and blinked her huge brown eyes, Leah could see the appeal.

And, yes, there was also a tiny part of her that dared to wonder what a baby with Cap might look like.

"Leah!" Aimee's shrill voice burst out of her mouth as she jumped to her feet. "Oh my god, it's so good to see you!" She threw the arm that wasn't full of baby around her best friend.

Leah bent and gave Aimee a kiss on the cheek and then scooped Natalie out of her arms. "She's gotten so big! Oh my gosh, look at those cheeks! She is so adorable, Aimee."

"I know! Look at her little leopard-print Mary Janes. Do you have any idea how much it's going to cost me to clothe this child over eighteen years? There are too many freaking cute clothes!"

Leah was grateful Aimee had agreed to travel to Nebraska with her to attend her future sister-in-law's bridal shower. Leah felt like she needed a buffer between her parents and herself, a distraction to help her avoid unwanted discussions. She knew having Natalie there would send her mother into baby crazy mode, which would hopefully prevent her from digging too deeply into her daughter's personal life.

The airline staff called for passengers with small children to board, so Leah and Aimee headed toward the podium with their boarding passes, luggage, and Natalie in her stroller. Minutes later, they were settling into their seats for their flight into Omaha.

"So what are we telling your parents?" Aimee asked as the flight attendants readied the cabins for departure.

"As little as possible," Leah answered. "I mean, I might mention I'm dating someone, but I don't want to give any details. And nothing about the new job. We're not crossing that bridge till we come to it. I'm hoping everyone will fawn over you and the baby so much, they'll just forget about little old me."

● ● ●

She had time to send Cap a quick text to say she'd landed safely, and then as soon as she, Aimee and Natalie passed out of the terminal, they were bombarded by the Millers. Pastor Miller got to Leah first, then her mother, then her brothers and her sister-in-law-to-be. Her Aunt Jane and Uncle Bob were there, as well as her cousins Lilly and Ruth. And, of course, her Grandma and Grandpa Yoder had joined them as well. Aimee and Natalie received just as many hugs and squeezes as Leah, and by the time all their affection was exchanged, Leah was certain they were the hugging-est family in Nebraska.

On the drive to Wahoo, she had a sudden pang of homesickness as she counted down the stop signs and turns till her father pulled into the driveway of their modest two-story house with its half-brick and half-siding exterior and neat stone-lined lane that led up to the brick porch. The dogwood trees on either side of the lawn were just about to bloom. This was one of her favorite times of the year.

By the time she came back in June for the wedding, all

the spring flowers would be replaced by the summer ones. She didn't usually get to come home in the summer since The Pearl was so busy with tourists, but this year was an exception. She couldn't miss her brother's wedding.

Her parents' house was exactly the same as she remembered it: tidy and quaint with country decor. The kitchen windows wore green-checked valances with small red apples stenciled along the bottom edge. The living room was done in peach and country blue. Antique baskets and kitchen implements decorated the kitchen walls.

Leah showed Aimee to her bedroom, which looked virtually the same as it had ten years ago when she was graduating from high school with its white eyelet comforter on the brass daybed and matching curtains framing the windows. The wallpaper was a lilac and pink floral print on a pearly white background, and the carpet was mauve. A trundle bed pulled out from underneath the daybed to accommodate a sleepover friend. Leah helped set up Natalie's pack and play in the corner near the closet doors.

"So far, so good, right?" Aimee laid Natalie down on the bed to change her diaper.

"The real grilling will start after dinner," Leah predicted.

As usual, she was right.

Pastor Miller said the prayer as the family gathered around the heavy oak dining table, hands clasped together and their noses filled with the aroma of pot roast, green beans, mashed potatoes and homemade yeast rolls. Little Natalie cooed and babbled through most of it from her mother's lap.

"Oh, Aimee, that baby of yours is just so adorable. Is she eating solid food yet?" Mrs. Miller gushed as she began passing dishes and bowls around the table.

"We just started her on cereal last week, actually," Aimee replied. "It's such a mess. I'm not sure if any of it actually makes it into her tummy!"

"Oh, your parents must be in heaven," Mrs. Miller sighed. "I can't wait to have grandbabies. I hope Andrew and Mikayla have babies right away!" She smiled hopefully across the table at her son and his new bride, who blushed.

She seems like a sweet girl, bright and eager to please, but also young and naïve. I hope she doesn't let my mom walk all over her.

Mikayla tossed her honey-blonde curls over her shoulder and giggled at her future mother-in-law's comment. Leah's brother Andrew put his arm around his fiancée.

Look how happy they are!

She was stricken by a sharp twinge of jealousy that Andrew was sitting at the table with his betrothed, but her family didn't even know about Cap.

"I thought Leah would have given me a grandbaby by now," Mrs. Miller said with no attempt to disguise her disappointment. "I know she's doing great work out there on the East Coast, but I sure hope she decides to start a family before it's too late."

I love it when she talks about me like I'm not even here. Leah bit her tongue to prevent her from saying what she really wanted to say. "I'm twenty-seven, Mom," she finally responded as calmly as possible. "I don't think my biological clock is in danger of expiring any time soon."

"That's true." Aimee swooped in to back up her friend. "She still has a long career ahead of her. And plenty of time for babies!"

"Are you at least dating? Are there any nice young men

at your church?" Mrs. Miller asked, begging like a dog for a bone.

"I have been seeing someone for a little while," Leah said boldly. She glanced toward Aimee, who was desperately trying to conceal her shock at Leah's admission.

Mrs. Miller's eyes lit up like a Fourth of July fireworks display. "Someone from work? Someone from church?"

"I met him while I was at work, yes," Leah offered. "He owns a business. He's a really nice man."

"Well, that sounds promising!" Mrs. Miller exclaimed, looking down the table at Pastor Miller, who nodded in agreement.

"We'll see," Leah replied, and that was all she intended to say on that matter.

●○◦

Weekend trips, no matter how relaxing, always speed by. Leah couldn't believe her time in the homeland had already drawn to a close as she stared out the window at the whizzing scenery on their way to the airport. She had felt restless, defensive, and out of sorts all weekend, especially at church that morning.

Her father's sermon was on purity. He preached about purity of the mind, the heart, and the spirit. He condemned impure thoughts and actions and reminded his congregation of the passage from Philippians 4:8, "...whatever is true, whatever is noble, whatever is right, whatever is pure, whatever is lovely, whatever is admirable—if anything is excellent or praiseworthy—think about such things."

She was thinking about each of those adjectives: true, noble, right, pure, lovely, admirable, excellent and praiseworthy. *Don't those words describe Cap and our relationship?*

Pure is a funny word, she had thought as she sat on the hard, unforgiving wooden pew and doodled a little design on the back of a prayer request card. The drawing kept expanding as she thought, spirals and arrows and little roses on vines climbing up cross-hatched trellises, until all the white space was filled in.

Pure, pure, pure. P-yer. The more she repeated the word in her mind, the less meaning it had.

It really just means something is 100% one thing and 0% anything else, right? As if anything is really 100% one thing, she thought back to high school chemistry, *unless it's an element. Even water is two-thirds hydrogen and one-third oxygen. But we talk about water being pure.*

Now, sitting on the plane, she started to miss Cap with a vengeance. There was a small shadow growing around her, a shadow of insecurity that caused her to wonder if he strayed while she was gone. She couldn't be back to Maryland and in his arms fast enough, but of course, there was nothing she could do to speed up the flight.

Her mother had surprisingly disbanded the inquisition about her personal life that first night after dinner. She tried to interrogate Leah after she admitted she was dating someone, but all Leah would volunteer was that her beau was named "Chris," that he came from a long line of fishermen, and that he'd grown up in the Ocean City area.

She closely guarded the secrets that he was forty-two and had two adult daughters. But she did as Cap had asked: she'd told her family about him, even if she shared minimal information. Mrs. Miller seemed to finally understand that Leah would not divulge anything further, and then, as if a miracle had just occurred at 614 Primrose Lane in Wahoo, Nebraska, she just stopped prying.

What did I think she was going to ask? If I'm sleeping with him?

Her mind wandered to the house party she and Cap had been invited to the following weekend. No matter how many times she had played the memories of the New Year's Eve party across the movie screen in her mind, she still found it exhilarating and arousing. Even though she didn't want to.

There were parts of her that continued to fantasize about starting where her New Year's Eve experience had ended and taking it to a whole new level. A room full of spectators. A blindfold. Not knowing whose hands, mouths and cocks were on her and in her. Being taken and used for pleasure by a roomful of men. And maybe by women too.

What would Cap say if I told him these naughty daydreams of mine?

She had a feeling he would be elated. She wondered what kept her from sharing her fantasies with him when she knew they'd make him so happy—not to mention turned on.

Because I've been taught it's wrong. Because I've been told my whole life that sex is only for marriage, only for two people, two people who are a man and a woman.

Anything else is not pure.

TWENTY-EIGHT

"So you're sure you want to go?" Cap asked again.

"I kept thinking on the plane," Leah explained, "the whole flight, while Aimee and Natalie were asleep, I kept thinking about the New Year's Eve party. How erotic it was, how turned on I was. How much I loved being watched by all those men who gawked at me through the doorway. How much I loved losing myself in pleasure and not worrying or caring where it was coming from or what anyone thought."

"Wow, just hearing those words come out of your mouth made me so hard," Cap confessed, pulling her hand toward his crotch. She felt his erection begging for her touch. "You know, there's someone you should talk to about the religious stuff, how you feel conflicted and all that."

"Oh yeah?" Leah raised her eyebrows. "Who's that?"

"Mary," Cap answered. "You remember her from the party? She's an ordained minister. She performs weddings and preaches and all that."

"Really?" Leah asked, searching her memory for an image of Mary. The last time she saw her up close, she wasn't wearing anything. It was hard to reconcile that image with one of a minister. "I can't believe you're just now telling me this."

"Sorry, I don't know why, but I just thought of it," he apologized. "I'll give you her number."

Later that week, Mary agreed to meet Leah for lunch a few blocks away from The Pearl. They grabbed a booth at the back of the restaurant for privacy. Leah knew how sensitive listening ears could be in a small town, and she certainly didn't want to get called into Barry's office again to be reamed out about lifestyle issues.

"So, I guess I just feel conflicted about all these fantasies I have and about my relationship with Cap," Leah initiated the conversation as soon as their drinks were served. "I feel like God is probably going to strike me down with a lightning bolt or turn me into a pillar of salt or something." She let a nervous giggle float into the space over the table.

Mary joined her in laughing at first, then sipped a long drink of her iced tea. She had a calm demeanor, and everything she did was measured and careful. "Well, that hasn't happened yet, right? You don't look like a pillar of salt to me!"

"No, of course not. You know, when I'm in the moment with Cap, or when I was at that party, I don't think about all that. I just do it. And it feels so good. It's later that the guilt creeps up on me, and my mind is flooded with Bible verses. And I hear my dad's pulpit voice thundering down on me. God's voice always sounds like my dad's in my head," she confessed. She had never admitted that to anyone before.

"Having a minister for a father probably does some crazy things to your conscience," Mary guessed. "But you need to turn that voice off and learn to listen to your own voice. I find that God speaks to me in whispers, not in a hell-fire and brimstone baritone."

She sat for a moment and absorbed that thought. *How lovely is that? To think of God whispering lovingly instead of yelling in anger.*

"So you're ordained? You've studied the Bible a lot, then?" Leah asked.

"I have," Mary answered. "And let me just give you some food for thought. There are dozens of commandments in the Bible that we have long since abandoned since they don't fit our cultural values. For example, what is that dress you're wearing made of?"

Leah wrinkled her nose in confusion. "What does that have to do with anything?" She laughed.

"In the Old Testament, the Israelites were forbidden to wear clothing that has more than one type of fiber. So that means anything that's a blend – like cotton and polyester together – would be a sin."

"That's so weird!" Leah gasped. "I never knew that." She couldn't believe that in all of her years of studying the Bible, she'd never read that. "What book is that in?"

"Leviticus," Mary responded. "There are other things too. Like when a woman had her period, she was unclean for seven days and could not be touched."

"That's ridiculous! I don't even have my period for seven days." Leah tried to imagine Cap refraining from touching her for seven whole days.

"My point is there are a lot of laws and commandments in the Bible that we don't follow anymore. Not only that, but most of the scriptures regarding marriage and sex are completely outdated today because marriage was a much different institution than it is now. Back then, wives were property, bought from their fathers for a dowry. Adultery laws were more about stolen property than about infidelity. And what about the multiple wives thing? Men could have as many wives and concubines as they could afford. Polygamy is illegal in our society."

"I guess I never thought of it that way," Leah remarked. "But what about having multiple partners and premarital sex and all that?"

"This is the thesis I wrote when I was in seminary, and I want to share it with you. It's about the mistranslation of the word 'fornication' from the original Greek. There are also some references to other mistranslations."

She handed Leah a thick nondescript-looking binder. "Look, I can't tell you what to believe," she explained, "but I can share what I've learned in my own study of scriptures. I think about how back in Bible times, women were married off at twelve or thirteen. They didn't get any choice about who they married or had sex with. We live in an entirely different culture where women have equal rights; we decide for ourselves what happens to our bodies.

"I personally believe that if we're honest and loving in our interactions with people, that is much more important to God than who we sleep with. I also believe that God made sex as a beautiful expression of love and closeness. And I believe that love and closeness can be shared by multiple people."

"So you don't see any sort of conflict or incompatibility between what you believe and what you do in the lifestyle?" Leah asked.

"I did at first, certainly," Mary answered. "But I read a lot of scripture, and I prayed and meditated. I studied how the original biblical texts had been translated. And to be honest with you, I feel closer in my walk with God now than ever before. I believe there's a time and place for me to gratify my desires, which I'll tell you, have gotten a lot stronger since I've gotten older. Seems like every year I just get friskier and friskier!"

She laughed, and Leah watched the sunlight streaming through the window across from them dance in her eyes. They were creased with crows' feet, and she had a few age spots near her temples along with wisps of gray hair, but other than that, she had the spirit and countenance of a vibrant, much younger woman.

"Oh, Mary, I can't even tell you how wonderful it is to hear these things. I am so overwhelmed by guilt sometimes. But I want to make Cap happy...and, to be honest, there are so many things I want to try. I hate feeling like I'm a bad Christian or a hypocrite, you know?"

"You love him, don't you?" Mary asked, her gray-blue eyes twinkling as if she could see straight into Leah's soul.

Leah nodded. "I do. It took me awhile to admit it, but I want us to be together, and I think this is part of the package."

"Okay," Mary said in her soft, delicate voice. "Just make sure that you're doing it for yourself too, and not just for him. I know Cap is a good man down deep, but I also know he can be awfully charming and persuasive when it comes to getting what he wants. And I just don't want to see you get hurt."

"Do you think he'd hurt me?" Leah asked, her eyes suddenly wide and trembling with fear at the thought.

"Not intentionally," Mary replied. "I've seen a lot of lifestyle relationships come and go, Leah. I'm not trying to scare you—please don't think that—or dissuade you in any way. Lifestyle relationships take more work, more communication, and two people who are absolutely on the same page. Marriages between swingers are some of the healthiest, strongest marriages I've ever seen, but I've also seen some pretty shaky couples try to use swinging as a way to heal wounds and solve problems. That really won't work, trust me. That's what happened between me and my first husband."

"Oh," Leah sighed. "I'm sorry to hear that."

"Don't be." She laughed. "I always say that when God takes one person out of your life, it's to make room for someone who is better for you. And that was definitely the case for me. I couldn't be happier now. John and I are truly blessed, and I honestly think swinging brought us closer together and forced us to be better communicators and more in tune with each other.

"You know, life is way too short to be unhappy or to stay in unhappy relationships. I tell all the couples I counsel that," she said, her face brightening.

Leah felt like she could see all the way down to Mary's soul, and it was pure. She remembered the definition of pure she'd thought up during her trip to the homeland. Mary was one hundred percent a kind, loving human being; and zero percent anything else: no ulterior motives, no pretense.

"Oh, you do couples counseling?" Leah asked, intrigued. "That's so cool! Lucky couples!"

"Oh, thank you," she replied graciously. "I do, both premarital counseling before I perform a wedding, and I do counseling for couples having issues too."

Leah couldn't help but think that Mary was an angel sent by God to help her work through all the guilt and confusion she was experiencing. Later that afternoon, she told Barry she was going to take a few personal hours, and he gave her his blessing. She ran home and put Glory on her leash, then walked across the street to the beach side of the strip, across the parking lot of the condos and down the sand-covered boardwalk.

The beach was almost deserted under the early May sun, and she could see it stretching for miles and miles north toward Delaware and south toward Virginia. She plopped down on a blanket and staked Glory's leash in the sand. She pulled Mary's thesis and began to read, slowly digesting her words. Eventually she was distracted watching the gulls swoop down onto the shoreline and Glory lurch toward them till her leash jerked her to an abrupt stop.

The shorebirds cried as they took back to the air, soaring high above the waves. She watched a boat way out on the horizon and wondered if it was Cap, who said he was doing an impromptu charter that afternoon. The gentle breezes washed over her and then blew toward the surf.

How can any of this be wrong? she asked God. *I feel so happy and so at peace with Cap. My job is going well, and the future of the club looks bright. After talking to Mary, I feel like the last piece of the puzzle has been set into place.*

●◌●

They were running late for the party. Leah hated being late for anything, and she was feeling flustered and out of sorts. All the peace she felt on the beach after her lunch with Mary the day before had somehow leaked back out again.

She fidgeted in the cab of Cap's truck, trying to adjust the strapless bra she was wearing underneath her nearly backless silk gown. It was an Asian-inspired dress featuring a high neck, accented with frog closures to the side and a narrow slit down the middle offering a peek at her cleavage. The skirt was cut on the bias to skim her hips. In the back, a large keyhole revealed her delicate freckle-kissed shoulder blades. She wore her hair in a sleek French twist held by a black clip with matching jet-black beaded earrings dangling from her earlobes.

"Would you stop it?" Cap chastised her. "You look amazing. Now sit still and enjoy the ride."

It was an important night. Casey and Cap were going to announce their venture to their friends. Casey was bringing a dozen bottles of champagne to toast The Factory. It was their hope the local community would rally behind the entrepreneurial trio by joining the club and providing the base membership.

"I'm trying. I guess I'm just nervous," Leah admitted, not familiar enough with all of Cap and Casey's friends to be able to predict their reaction to the news.

He reached over and squeezed her knee that poked through the slit of the ankle-length gown. "It'll be fine. Everyone's going to be surprised and excited. I can't believe how many times I've overheard folks saying we need a life-style club here in OC."

Cap was right. They made the announcement at 9 PM when most of the fifty anticipated guests had arrived. Casey was hosting the party at her huge eight-bedroom, six-bathroom estate on Fenwick Island. Her kitchen opened to the living room, which was surrounded by windows overlooking a grassy marsh of a front yard and a picturesque dock jutting out into the bay. There were dozens of people gathered around the kitchen island and dozens more congregated on the sofas in the plush living area, all raising their glasses to toast The Factory.

Throughout the night, Leah was pulled in all different directions by people who wanted to give her comments or suggestions regarding the design and functionality of the club. She wished she'd brought her tablet to record the ideas. She wanted to make the club as functional as possible.

Cap was being pulled in different directions too, but nearly always by a woman. Leah tried to keep her eyes on him, but there were times he disappeared from her radar. Panicky blips would start vibrating through her nervous system as she furtively glanced around the room for him.

He made a promise to me, she kept repeating in her mind, forcing herself to take deep breaths and try to soothe her racing heartbeat.

It wasn't that she didn't trust him. She didn't trust some of these women. She'd seen plenty of drama, both at the hotel parties and house parties, and most of the time, it seemed to be caused by a woman.

She saw Cap escape to the deck with Rhonda, and she decided to check in with him. Although Rhonda had made a point to be sugary sweet to her every time she'd seen her since New Year's Eve, Leah still didn't trust her. There was something about the woman that set off Leah's bullshit detector.

She excused herself from her conversation with Jeremy and his new girlfriend, Amanda, and sneaked into the master bedroom on the main floor, which had a terrace that extended off the side of the main deck. She slid the glass door open and tiptoed out, taking care not to get her heels caught between the planks of wood. She braced herself against the stucco exterior of the house and inched her way toward the main deck.

The hazy moonlight drenched the bay with dappled light, and a smattering of stars peeked through the clouds. The water in the bay was calm and still. She could faintly hear frogs croaking and crickets winding up their nocturnal overture.

"Well, I wondered what you saw in her," she heard Rhonda's tinny voice float out toward the bay.

Cap's response was so deep, she couldn't hear it. Then she heard Rhonda laugh. "Oh, I see how it is. Well, good for you, Cap, good for you." Her voice trailed off into the night sky, and then there was silence.

She turned the corner and watched Rhonda pull out of Cap's arms just as the two caught sight of her. Rhonda wore a funny, smirky look on her face and practically ran back into the house. Leah approached Cap cautiously, not sure what to make of the scene she'd just witnessed.

"Spying on me?" he asked with a half-smile, his dimples half-accounted for.

"Yes, I am." Leah smiled back. "Surprised you still have your clothes on, to be honest."

"Me?" Cap feigned surprise. "I can't believe no one has ripped this gorgeous dress off you yet. I, for one, am dying to see what's underneath."

"You already know what's underneath, silly," she retorted.

"That's true, but I'm sure Jeremy and his new girlfriend would like to solve the mystery," Cap suggested with a wink. "I saw you talking to them inside. Isn't Amanda hot?"

Leah bristled. No matter how used to the new mindset she got, she felt like she would always cringe when her boyfriend claimed another woman was hot. *When does that go away? When do I just smile and say, "I get her first?"*

"Oh," Leah said, "I suppose she's hot if you like well-endowed chicks with long dark hair and big brown eyes."

"Well, I don't have a problem with them," Cap announced. "Do you?"

"Not in theory," Leah played along. "And I am almost positive I don't have a problem with hot, sexy teachers like Jeremy."

"Fair enough. Shall we?" He offered his arm.

The moments between sliding the deck door open to re-enter the house and shutting the door of one of the eight lavishly decorated bedrooms were pretty much a blur. Next thing she knew, Cap was lifting the silk dress over her head and revealing her strapless bra and matching thong to a very curious Jeremy and Amanda.

Amanda turned out to be quite forward. "Can I touch you?" she asked assertively as she removed her own white three-tiered skirt and skimpy fuchsia camisole. She was not wearing a bra or panties.

She faced Leah, standing at the edge of the bed, her full, heavy breasts jutting out in front of her, and a thin line of pubic hair trailing down to her sex. She was small-boned and tan-skinned with a beautiful hourglass shape. Leah's eyes traced her delicate collarbones, rounded shoulders and the curve from her waist to her hips. She nodded to Amanda's question and watched the brunette's lush brown hair wave around her shoulders as she crawled across the bed toward her.

Amanda reached behind Leah's back and unhooked her bra with one hand. She tossed it to the floor casually and then went to work sliding Leah's thong down her long, pale legs. The men sat down on the bed, one on each side of the pair of ladies. Amanda only had eyes for Leah, though, as she straddled Leah's bare hips and lifted her chin to touch her lips with her own. The tiniest sigh escaped Leah's lips as Amanda's tongue traced the line between them, signaling for them to part.

Leah couldn't believe how soft Amanda's mouth was

against hers. It was the lightest flutter of her tongue against Leah's that sent chills racing up and down her spine. She shuddered as Amanda gently sucked her lip into her mouth and nibbled it ever so delicately. Leah was used to big, wet lips; rough, callused hands; and bristly facial hair rubbing against her face. She'd never felt such a soft kiss; it was like the caress of an angel's wing.

When Amanda broke away, Leah turned to find Cap's eyes boring into her. "Open the door," Leah begged in a whisper, her voice stolen by desire. "I want to be watched."

Jeremy popped off the bed to honor Leah's request, and as he returned, Leah noticed the bulge that had grown in his pants. Amanda eased herself down Leah's body, tasting her stomach, her hips, her thighs, trailing kisses down the slit between her netherlips until she parted them with the same gentleness she'd used on Leah's mouth.

Jeremy resumed his position on the bed, but this time on his knees facing Leah. She watched him unfasten his pants and release his engorged cock only a foot from her mouth. Looking up at him with desperate eyes, she hoped he would get a sense of how badly she needed him in her mouth.

She gasped as Amanda's tongue found its way to her clitoris, softly encircling it with very light pressure just as Jeremy slid his thick cock past her lips. Cap watched from the other side of the bed, calmly observing his girlfriend immersed in pleasure as a crowd gathered outside the door.

"You can come in and watch," he advised, and then several bodies lined the wall opposite the bed. A chaise lounge was available, along with a bench at the vanity, and a few of the ladies took a seat while the men looked on with raging erections and ravenous eyes.

Leah felt herself surrender to Amanda's ministrations,

not once, not twice, but three times before becoming so sensitive that she needed a reprieve. So satiated and grateful, she felt it was only right to return the favor.

She sat up and patted the bed where she had lain, gesturing for Amanda to take her place. "I've never done this before," she whispered.

Amanda licked Leah's juices off her lips and then pushed the strawberry blonde's head toward her sex, urging her to use her mouth for purposes other than speaking. Cap stroked his fingers through Leah's hair as she tentatively descended upon the dark-haired woman's pussy. "That's it, Sugar, go slow at first, taste how badly she wants you."

The flavor was mild and creamy. It soaked into Leah's tongue as she glided it up Amanda's labia. She absorbed the scent of her desire mixed with jasmine perfume as she teased Amanda's swelling clit with the tip of her tongue. A hand snaked across her ass, and she thought it was Cap preparing to take her, but she quickly realized the hand was smaller and softer. She briefly glanced behind her and saw that Jeremy was rolling a condom onto his cock and rubbing himself against the cleft between her cheeks.

"May I fuck you?" he asked politely and waited for her to nod approval before sinking himself into her. "Oh god," he cried out as he filled her soaking pussy. He tried to find a slow pace, but his grip on her hips kept tightening, and his thrusts came closer and closer together.

Cap had suffered enough in observation mode and removed his clothes in the blink of an eye. He presented his cock to Amanda, who was gasping for air and crying out as Leah began to suck her clit into her mouth. Amanda began to lap greedily at his offering, her tongue running up and down Cap's thick shaft until he'd had enough of that too and forced two-thirds of it down her throat.

She choked and sputtered but became so turned on that she tangled her fingers in Leah's hair and pulled her closer until her face was buried in her juicy mound. She began to wildly buck under Leah's mouth as Cap throat-fucked her. Her muffled screams broke free when Cap pulled out.

Leah felt Amanda explode underneath her. *Holy shit, I just made a woman come with my mouth.*

She gushed her sweet nectar all over Leah's face as her pussy spasmed and contracted against her lips. While that was happening and Amanda was recovering, Jeremy took the opportunity to pull out and drag Leah to the end of the bed. He stood between her thighs and reinserted his cock, grabbing her legs and throwing them up against his shoulders.

The new angle and depth caused Leah to cry out from the relentless stimulation of her G-spot. She began to orgasm not once, not twice, but again in triplicate as Jeremy stuffed her cunt full of his cock over and over again. Finally, he pulled out, stroking his shaft with one hand and pulling the condom off with the other. In only a few seconds, he spurted a huge white load of cum across Leah's stomach.

Amanda promptly scrambled to kneel over Leah and lick it up. She gathered up a mouthful of it and pressed her lips against Leah's, pushing the hot, salty semen into her mouth so they could swirl it back and forth between them.

While the two ladies were snowballing Jeremy's load, Cap ambled over to the space Jeremy had just vacated between Leah's legs. He entered her, pushing her thighs back toward her shoulders. She pulled away from kissing Amanda to make sure it was him, even though the fit of him inside her felt like home.

Jeremy and Amanda both moved back and joined the spectators watching as Cap drilled into her. At least one of the voyeurs had his eyes glued to her while another lady perched on her knees in front of him, sucking his cock for all it was worth. But it was Leah he was watching, Leah that he desired.

Another man sat in the corner with his hand resting on his erection, just slowly stroking it up and down as he viewed the scene on the bed. Knowing she had an audience who was getting off just by watching her made her orgasm again, her pussy spasming so violently that she nearly expelled Cap's massive tool even though he was slamming it into her with impressive vigor.

"Come on, baby, give me that cum!" she yelled through clenched teeth, her body tensing up for another climax to claim her. She grabbed his hips and pushed him harder and deeper into her, wrapping her legs around him to achieve maximum penetration.

It only took those words to elicit the infamous growl, starting deep in his throat and roaring out his mouth. One heartbeat later, he filled her pussy with his load, coating her inside and out with cum. Once he finished and withdrew, she collapsed with her head in Amanda's lap while the two men went to retrieve some towels. Her body felt like a million rubber bands limply coiled in a pile after being relieved of their duty to hold together a skyscraper.

That night when she and Cap left the party, out of the corner of her eye, she saw Rhonda staring at her. And the look on her face was not one of hate or jealousy—or even curiosity. It was one of pity.

She was not expecting any visitors to her office. It was supposed to be a day of reconciling receipts with her budgets. Her head was swimming in numbers when her assistant's voice came through the intercom announcing, "There's someone named Mary here to see you."

Leah sighed. She hated being interrupted when she was in the middle of balancing budgets. The name Mary didn't resonate with her. It could be any number of staff or vendors. *Isn't there a Mary on the night shift cleaning crew?*

She was taken aback to see Mary from Casey's Group appear in her doorway, Mary the ordained minister whom she'd had lunch with the week before. She had her long, gray-streaked brown hair braided down her back and wore a simple denim sundress with Birkenstocks. Although she normally had a sunny smile affixed to her face, today she looked weary and concerned.

Leah stood to greet her, already forgetting her annoyance at being interrupted. "Mary, it's so nice to see you. Is everything okay?" Leah was good at reading people, and it was obvious Mary was upset about something.

"I really need to talk to you," Mary said quietly, taking a seat in one of the chairs across from Leah's desk.

"Of course." Leah sat down and slid her chair back under her desk. "What's up?"

Mary crossed her legs at the ankles, folded her hands in her lap, and leaned in toward Leah's desk. Leah stared at the older woman's hands, the veins protruding through thin, waxy skin, dotted with age spots but topped with delicate fingers and bare but well-manicured nails.

"I don't know where to start exactly," she admitted. "But I really thought you should know what I've heard so you can discuss it with Cap and make sure you're still on the same page."

"What are you talking about?" Even before her mind could process Mary's statement, her heart began pounding against her chest.

"I spoke with Casey this morning. She told me she heard from a reliable source who spoke with Cap at the party the other night..." Her face was etched with worry lines, and her cheeks were sallow. She looked as though it would physically hurt her to speak another word.

Leah was agitated, her nerves buzzing with dread. "Heard what?" she demanded, no longer able to rein in her patience.

Mary hesitated again, but only for a moment. A deep breath later, and she let the information escape like air bursting out of a popped balloon. "Apparently Cap was talking about you and your relationship, and he said that his interest in you was purely professional. That he was grooming you for the lifestyle and for managing the club.

And he claimed he didn't have any romantic feelings toward you."

Leah scanned Mary's eyes for signs of honesty and found them in her trembling gray irises and large inky-black pupils. She reached her arms across the desk to clasp Leah's hands in her own.

Leah's throat swelled shut. She had no words and no tears. Her entire body was gripped with shock. Finally, words made their way from her brain to her mouth, somehow squeezing through the erratic nerve impulses and furiously pumping blood. "Who did he say that to?"

"Casey wouldn't say, just that the source was trustworthy. She called me this morning because she was so upset, and she didn't know what to do. She wanted my guidance. I said you needed to be told, and she didn't think she could do it. She was crying and beside herself. She cares for you a great deal."

Mary patted Leah's clammy hand and then squeezed it. "I'm not sure what this means for the club. I don't know if she can work with Cap after this, but I know she's poured a huge amount of money and energy into it that she'll lose if she pulls out now."

"I need to talk to her." Leah rose from her desk on trembling legs, her heart on the verge of exploding.

"Okay," Mary whispered, choking back the empathetic tears that were forming in the corners of her eyes. "Do you want me to come with you?"

Leah's whole body was shaking as she gathered up her phone and her purse. "No, thank you, though. This is something I need to deal with myself."

On her way out the door, she remembered the one-sided conversation she'd overheard between Cap and Rhonda on the deck at Casey's party. Then the look of pity painted across Rhonda's face as she left the party on Cap's arm flooded back to her.

●○●

Leah was relieved that Casey was in her office, but she was on the phone, so Leah had to wait fifteen minutes to have an audience with her. She sat outside the office staring at the knockdown finish on the walls. It was a bright terracotta color, and all the artwork featured sunsets over the bay or sunrises over the beach, reflecting the same shade as the walls. Leah got so lost in one painting that she nearly jumped out of her skin when Casey came to the door to welcome her.

She started to sit down in the blue chair across from Casey's desk but suddenly forgot why she was there. She stood in the middle of the office, paralyzed. She couldn't remember driving there and had already forgotten the fifteen-minute wait in the hallway outside the office. All she recalled was one picture that captured her attention: a row of houses with black roof lines stacked against the amber clouds that drifted over a dusky violet bay.

Her eyes and mouth were dry. In just the course of a half hour, it seemed like all the moisture had evaporated from her body.

Casey's makeup was smudged around her eyes as if she had been crying. She surveyed Leah's state, then stood up and immediately pulled the younger woman into her arms, pressing her tightly against her bosom and stroking her fingers soothingly down her back. Leah burst into tears in Casey's embrace, the liquid welling up from some reservoir deep within. She was shaking uncontrollably, no words able to break through the shattered glass that was formerly her mind.

"Oh, sweetheart, I have no idea what that bastard is thinking. I tried to call and give him a piece of my mind—to ask him what he has to say for himself, but there was no answer on his cell or at his shop," Casey offered in her calming alto voice.

"He's out in the boat," Leah managed to sob. "He's got two charters today. Some big group of executives who came down from New York. He won't be home till late tonight."

"Okay, okay. Well, what can we do, sweetheart? I want to help." She ushered Leah into the blue chair she'd originally attempted to take and handed her some tissues. Leah began to blot her splotchy face, urging her brain to create speech.

Casey rolled her desk chair around so the pair sat knee-to-knee. "I've cleared all my appointments for the rest of the day, so whatever you need me to do. Just say the word."

"He told me he loved me," was all that came out of Leah's mouth.

Casey's face scrunched up with rage. "That fucking son of a bitch," she seethed, a whole octave lower than her normal voice. Leah was shocked to hear foul language being ejected off her usually eloquent tongue.

"So it was Rhonda, right?" Leah guessed. "She is the one he told."

Casey nodded. "I know she seems abrasive at times, but she has a good heart, and she and Cap go way back. They used to date a long time ago. He and his ex-wife got her involved in the lifestyle, actually. And she and I have been friends forever. I trust her. If it had been anyone else, I'd probably question it."

Leah felt lost. She remembered her apartment was all

packed into boxes. At the end of the month when her lease expired, she was supposed to move in with Cap. She was going to put all of her things in storage. He promised her that once the club took off, Casey would help them find a house to buy with a big yard for Keeper and Glory.

"I just don't understand how this can be," Leah said. "I've lain in his arms. I've looked into his eyes. He promised me he'd be faithful to our agreement, and he'd put swinging on hold till I was ready... He made me trust him."

Those words "promised," "faithful," and "trust" felt hollow and empty now, as if their very meanings had collapsed under the weight of her broken heart. All she could think of was how she'd been betrayed by the other men she'd given a piece of her heart to, Will and Todd. Did she just fall victim again to Cap?

Casey patted her hand in a motherly fashion. "I thought he had changed," she sighed with disappointment. "When I first met him, he was such a schmoozer, a real player. I saw him go through a half-dozen women in a year or two. I think he got bored with them. I also knew what happened with his ex-wife.

"But then I got to know him better, and I learned about his dad's sudden death, and I saw what kind of father he was to his girls, even met them a few times. I knew there was a good man in there after all. One seeking redemption.

"The way he was so taken with you...at least I thought he was... I never thought he'd step back from the lifestyle for any woman, but he did with you." She paused for a moment, her face full of reflection, like she was reviewing all the memories she had stored in her brain involving Cap.

"Thinking about it now, I do remember him calling me up shortly after he met you at that first event last fall. We had already begun looking for a property for the club. I had my eyes on the warehouse, but I was waiting to hear back from the listing agent. He and I shared this dream of opening a club for a long time, and I figured with both of us knowing so many people and being used to dealing with the public, we'd have no problems with the marketing and publicity.

"What we lacked was the know-how for running a business like this, something that's more like an entertainment venue. Yeah, he's a keen businessman, sure. But he knows fishing. And I know real estate. Neither of us has a clue about something like this.

"When he met you, he called me up and said he found our manager. When he said it was you, I was delighted. I connected with you immediately, Leah. I knew you had a good character and a strong work ethic. I knew you were going places and that you were trustworthy. He kept telling me he wanted to wait to tell you about the club, wait till you knew more about the lifestyle, till you understood it. And I agreed.

"But never, ever in my wildest dreams did I think that Cap would seduce you to bring you on board. Hell no, I would have never, *ever* given my consent to that crazy, ridiculous bullshit, Leah. I genuinely thought he was falling for you and you for him. And I was thrilled beyond belief that it was all working out like that!

"I know he told me so many times that he was a confirmed bachelor and had no intention of settling down with another woman – not ever, no way, no how – but I knew you were special. I wasn't surprised that he'd changed his tune! But now...after what Rhonda told me, I have to reconsider all that, examine his motives and his true character..."

"Back up a minute," Leah interrupted her. "What did

you know about Cap's ex-wife? I know about his father already. But what about his ex?"

"Oh, he hasn't told you about Sharon?" she asked, her eyes wide.

"Not much, really, just that he felt like she got pregnant to trap him into marrying her," Leah replied.

"Well, that much may be true," Casey agreed. "But the story was, when his daughters were small and Sharon used to stay home with them, Cap not only had his business up here during the summer, but during the winter he used to go down to Florida and work for a buddy of his to help out with his charter business. And during that time, he had a whole other wife and family."

"What?!" Leah felt anger bubbling up under the surface of her skin like hot magma about to explode from a volcano.

"That's what Sharon told me long ago. They used to swing together, and she and I were friends. She figured it out by some medical bills that got sent to their house here in Ocean City by mistake. He had a winter family and a summer family, apparently. When she found out, she left him."

"I think I'm going to be sick," Leah groaned. She stumbled into the restroom in the hallway and spewed the entire contents of her stomach into the toilet.

Casey was waiting in the hallway when Leah emerged. She had scrubbed her face so vigorously, she thought she might have removed some of her freckles. Upon closer inspection, they remained intact, but her skin was raw and splotchy.

"What are we going to do?" Casey asked her. She put the emphasis on the word "we."

"I'm not sure," Leah admitted, "but I think I am going to go home to bed. At least I know he'll be gone all evening, so

I can get my dog from his house and my things, and I won't have to see him."

"If I pull out of our venture, I'm going to lose all my money," Casey said. It wasn't an argument, a persuasion, or even an excuse. It was just a remark, verbalizing the realization that had broken through her other thoughts.

Then she returned to the subject at hand. "Let me go with you to pick up your dog and get you settled back in your apartment. Or you can come stay with me. I really don't know if you should be alone, Leah. I'm worried about you."

"Casey, I really appreciate everything you've done for me, but I'm a big girl, and I can take care of myself. Just answer one thing, though, okay?" Leah asked bravely, smoothing out her skirt and straightening her blouse.

She was going into crisis management mode now. *Usually when I do this, it's someone else's crisis.*

"Anything you need, sweetheart. You know that."

"You really believe Rhonda? I mean, you really trust her word over Cap's?" Leah felt like her next move completely hinged on Casey's answer.

"I've known them both a really long time," Casey said. "I just can't imagine why Rhonda would lie about it. Why would she come to me with it? What would she get out of it? If she wanted me to dissolve my partnership with Cap, I'd understand, but she's as excited about this club as I am. She wants a job there, actually."

"She does?" Leah questioned. Something about that didn't sit well with her.

"Yes, I think that's why she's been trying so hard to be nice to you," Casey smiled. "Ordinarily, Rhonda is pretty leery of anyone new in the group, male or female. It takes her a while to warm up to people. But once she realized you were involved with the club, and you might even be her boss someday, she totally changed her tune. She's spoken very highly of you, actually."

"I see," was all Leah could reply.

"I know you are a good judge of people," Casey said. "Why don't you talk to Cap and ask him what he said to her? Just outright confront him! I bet you will be able to tell a lot from his reaction."

"Maybe I will," Leah replied. "Not tonight though. For tonight I just want to get my dog and curl up in my own bed."

"Okay, darling," Casey said, giving her a light kiss on the cheek. "Please let me know if there is anything at all I can do."

● ● ●

Thankfully, Cap was still out on the boat when Leah went by his place to retrieve Glory. She tried not to look around the house or interact with Marlina or Keeper. She unceremoniously loaded up Glory and a box of her things, then headed up Coastal Highway toward her apartment, the one she had been visiting once or twice a week, mostly to pack things to put in storage.

She was relieved that all her furniture was still in place, so after taking Glory for a walk, she settled down on the sofa and flipped on her television. *I guess it's a good thing I keep forgetting to cancel the cable.* She put her feet up on the rattan ottoman.

Her stomach still reeled from the nausea she'd experienced in Casey's office. She kept playing her earlier conversations with Mary and Casey over and over again in her mind. It all culminated in one thought: *how could I be so stupid to fall for him when he's completely fake? How did I not see the signs?*

Using me, making me believe that he loved me was one thing, but apparently his deception runs much deeper. He had a whole other family when he was married before? And, of course, he never told me. I wonder if his daughters even know.

She considered calling Aimee and crying on her shoulder for a while, but she was too sick and too embarrassed. A part of her wanted to load up her Jeep with Glory and all of the earthly possessions she could squeeze in and head off for parts unknown.

There were dark, morbid, disturbing thoughts swirling around in her head that night, the kind of thoughts that reminded her how close a normal, seemingly well-adjusted person such as herself could be to falling off the edge of sanity. She wondered at times how it was she hadn't fallen off yet, but then she realized the reason was that she was too paralyzed to move, literally or figuratively.

Every time she received a text or phone call from him, the pain doubled up inside her. The first text came at 8 PM:

Cap: where are you?

Then at 8:30 PM, a phone call. No voicemail.
At 8:45, another text:

Cap: are you ok?

9:05: phone call and voicemail. She couldn't bring herself to listen. Then two more texts at 9:30 and 9:55.

And then her phone was silent.

●　●

The next day, Leah aimed for business as usual. She decided not to tell Aimee, not to return Cap's phone calls, and only to return Casey's text with a brief *I'm fine, thanks*.

She breezed into The Pearl, offering morning greetings to the front desk staff and a few other employees she saw in the hall. She exchanged pleasantries with her assistant and then waved to Barry as she proceeded to her office.

"Well, you're in a good mood today!" Barry observed, poking his head through her open doorway.

"Just happy to be at work!" Leah exclaimed, turning on her computer. "I have those end-of-month reports for you, and I'm all set to interview for the vacant head of house-keeping position."

"You're the best!" Barry winked and headed off to the staff lounge to refill his coffee mug.

Imagine where I'd be if I'd already tendered my resigna-tion like Cap wanted me to. I'd be up shit creek, that's what.

What would become of The Factory? Would Casey pull out of the partnership? Would Cap be left to flounder?

This is where I belong, she resolved, looking around her office. She logged into her computer and began poring over the day's agenda.

It's like I had a momentary lapse in judgment. Well,

momentary as in about six months, but whatever. At least I'm finally coming to.

She shook her head as if she could free herself of the last particles of insanity that had infected her.

At lunchtime, she ran home to walk Glory and bumped into a woman she recognized from Casey's Group, who was also walking her dog. Leah didn't realize they lived in the same complex, probably because she'd hardly been there since she started dating Cap.

"Oh, hey, Leah," the woman said, and Leah was grateful the name "Judy" came to her at the last minute.

"How are you, Judy? Nice day out, huh?" Leah tried to feign cheerfulness.

"I'm good," she replied but couldn't muster a smile. Instead, a look of concern washed over her. "You sure you're okay? I heard what happened with Cap."

Geez. Word travels fast, huh? She bit her lip and then managed a smile. "Oh, yeah, I'm fine," she replied dismissively.

"Cap's a snake," Judy offered. "I dated him a few years ago, and it was all about him. Doesn't surprise me in the least that he was using you. He thinks women are put on this earth to satisfy his every whim. You're better off without him, sweetie, trust me."

Leah was reeling from a mixture of anger, shock and frustration. *Where were all these naysayers when I first started seeing him? Why didn't anyone warn me?* She didn't know whether to thank Judy or smack her across the face.

"I know you probably feel like crap," Judy guessed after Leah failed to respond. "I'm sorry. I'll leave you alone." She began to steer her pug in another direction.

"No, really, I'm fine," Leah insisted. She smiled again and jerked Glory's leash back toward her building.

But when she settled back into her desk chair later that afternoon, a solitary tear rolled down her cheek as the realization that it was over began to sink in. She held her breath for a moment, waiting for the sensations to pass, for the pain to fade again and allow her to get on with her day.

But one question echoed repeatedly through her mind: *was anything we shared real? Was even one single moment genuine?*

●●●

Two days later, during her mother's weekly phone call, Leah confirmed she'd be attending Andrew and Mikayla's wedding alone, no plus one. Her mother complained that she was looking forward to meeting the new boyfriend. Leah simply explained, "We broke up. Don't worry. You wouldn't have liked him anyway." Mrs. Miller had the good sense not to demand elaboration.

That day, Leah also shared the news with Aimee. "Oh, Leah, I'm so very sorry," her best friend said. "Do I need to come down there? I could help you unpack all your things. Natalie could entertain us while we put everything away. She's got a few new tricks since you saw her last."

When Leah heard the concern in her friend's voice, she could contain her sorrow no longer. She sobbed into the phone, "I don't know if I can stay here. I hate being in OC without him."

She realized another dream had died, the dream of a child she and Cap might have someday far in the future. She'd get flashes sometimes when she thought about Aimee and Natalie. She'd let those little glimpses come and go without too much attention or concern. They floated around in her mind, untethered to any specific expectations, but nonetheless nascent.

She could finally admitCap was right when he claimed that someday, when she met the right man, she'd want to have his baby. *In my heart of hearts, I thought he was the one, even though I was too scared to believe it.*

Her admission illuminated the depths of the loss she had suffered. She had downplayed it, sidestepped it, and danced all around it for a few days now, but the simple fact was, another man she loved betrayed her.

And what does that say about me? Is hurting me so inevitable? Do men enjoy it? Do I seem like easy pickings?

"Leah?" Aimee's voice came through the phone line. "Are you still there?"

She realized this had been the longest stretch of time she'd gone without communicating with him in months. And after the other night, he hadn't tried to contact her.

I guess he knows he's guilty and isn't even going to try to redeem himself. I guess that's better than hearing the lies come out of his mouth with my own ears.

"Yes, I'm here," she assured her friend. "I just don't know what to say anymore. I don't even know who I am anymore."

"I know exactly who you are," Aimee answered. "You're Leah Elizabeth Miller, valedictorian of your high school class, 4.0 *summa cum laude* graduate of Cornell, and the youngest assistant general manager of a hotel I've ever heard of. You're the smartest, kindest, most generous person I know. And you're also the most capable. I've never seen you tackle a situation and not arise victoriously. You are one of the strongest and most stubborn people I have ever met, and I know damn well you aren't going to let some redneck fisherman take any of that away from you!"

By the time Aimee finished her speech, Leah's face was drenched with tears. "Thank you," she managed, trying hard to swallow down the rest of the sadness and get herself together. "I really needed to hear that."

"I know you did, and I meant every word. Please let Natalie and I come see you this weekend?" she asked.

"Okay," Leah brightened. "You got it."

That night when Cap finally tried to call again, Leah simply picked up the phone and said, "You're not who I thought you were. Please don't contact me again."

Without saying a word, he ended the call.

THIRTY

It's amazing how the heart handles grief. In the beginning, there's only numbness and denial. You wake up in the morning and wonder if maybe it was all a bad dream. The sun still shines with brilliant, unparalleled joy. *Any world this golden can't be that cruel.*

And then the darkness creeps back in: no, it wasn't a dream. Your heart really did shatter into a million unfixable pieces. The mind is finally able to process what it all means, to accept that those broken pieces will never fit together like they did before.

There is permanent, irrefutable damage. And then the pain comes on with such an excruciating, intolerable force that the human body cannot manufacture enough tears to soak it. Not even the ocean contains enough salt water to wash it away.

Next comes a funny thing called hope. It seeps into all those broken joints and presents a shiny, beautifully wrapped gift. *Maybe, just maybe things might work out after all. Maybe he will call and have all the right answers. Maybe it was all a joke, a misunderstanding, or even a dare.*

But this passes too.

Days turn into weeks, and those into months, and there is a strength that has formed in the scar tissue holding the broken pieces together. There are times when a thought, a memory inflicts a sting, a little welt rises up, but it's quickly covered over.

And then, you realize you've survived a broken heart. You're no longer a victim. You're a survivor.

Leah went through these stages after her relationship with Captain Chris Sheldon fell apart. She couldn't even think of him as Cap anymore. He was some sort of fable, a cautionary tale.

By June, she was headed off to Nebraska for her brother's wedding feeling formidable, a paragon of resilience. She didn't even take Aimee to serve as a buffer. She stood up in the wedding party as a bridesmaid, in her somewhat unflattering peach satin dress, and mingled with family and church-goers at the reception. And she felt strong and healthy doing it.

The day after, her mother pulled her aside and asked if she was okay. "I know you and your boyfriend broke up last month. What happened?"

"He just wasn't who I thought he was," Leah explained, and it was not a lie.

One thing she had decided: she was tired of always erecting an impenetrable façade and trying to meet everyone's expectations. She could only be herself, flawed and imperfect, but genuine. She wouldn't stop trying to please people, for that was her gift, but she would no longer do it at her own expense.

"I'm sorry to hear that." Mrs. Miller pulled her daughter into an embrace. She got a funny, misty-eyed smile across her lips. "Have I told you lately how proud I am of you?"

Leah looked up at her mother with surprise. She hadn't heard her mother say those words in years. She always believed quite the opposite, that her parents were disappointed in her choices. She hadn't followed the path they desired for her, the path her little brother had willingly chosen.

"You know, when I was a little girl, I wanted to be a flight attendant," her mother admitted. "I'd never even been on a plane before, mind you. But I was fascinated with them! I think I saw it in a movie or something. It seemed so romantic, flying in and out of different cities, never knowing who you might meet. Maybe I thought some handsome pilot would sweep me off my feet! Literally, you know?"

Leah was stunned. She'd never heard her mother talk like this, of hopes and dreams that didn't involve marrying her father, having babies, or serving the Lord. She stared at her mother's creased hazel eyes and searched for that little girl she was describing.

She had grown up poring over faded snapshots of her mother and her family pasted into brittle photo albums, always trying to imagine what life was like for young Evangeline Yoder. She always wondered how things were different back then, how they were the same.

She distinctly remembered a Polaroid from Easter, circa 1970. Her mother wore a peasant-style dress with a wide sash tied around her waist. *That little girl, that Evangeline Yoder, who would one day become Mrs. Miller, had wild hopes and dreams*, Leah thought, *just like all little girls do.*

"When I got older, I got scared," Mrs. Miller continued. "I realized how big the world is, and I was so scared to go off into the big, wide world alone. I was petrified to go to college, but my parents pushed me. They knew I needed to get out of the nest. I was so tentative and cautious.

"Then I met your father, and he didn't seem scared of anything. He paraphrased Luke 12:27 for me, 'Consider the lilies and how they grow. If God takes care of them, wouldn't He also take care of you? Why do you have such little faith?' Your father has always been my rock, Leah. I would have followed him to the ends of the earth and trusted him to take care of me.

"But you – you did it all yourself. You went a thousand miles away to school. You got your own car and own place and own job, and you've always been so independent. You don't seem scared of anything, Leah. You always face challenges head on, and I admire you for that so much. I wish I had been like that. You definitely got it from your father, not from me."

Leah was struggling not to cry. Her mother had never paid her a higher compliment.

"Oh, Mom, sometimes I *do* get scared! It's not always easy for me to venture into uncharted territory, but it's always paid off for me. I've always learned so much by risking a little, by challenging myself."

She considered the past year and the new territories she had explored. *It took a lot of courage for me to risk getting hurt when I met Cap. It was a huge risk for me to explore my sexuality and to discover I'm an exhibitionist. It was really difficult for me to reconcile my faith with all the conflicting desires I had. But I did, I did all those things, and I don't regret it.*

She appreciated that she was stronger as a result, and, just like Mary said, once she'd put all the scriptures into context and prayed about her feelings and desires, she realized she was closer in her walk with God than ever before.

Her mother's words were still with her a few days later when she boarded the plane back to Maryland. She had collected so many happy memories during her visit home; her mind was full of images of her brother with his new wife, her cousins and their babies, her youngest brother's slick dance moves at the reception, stories her Grandma Yoder shared about when she was little, and her mother and father sharing a sweet embrace, still so in love after nearly thirty years of marriage.

She knew how lucky she was to come from a good family who loved each other. Even though she felt so far removed from that life, from that world, she was still proud it was her heritage.

She was lost in memories when the pilot's deep, smooth voice came across the plane's audio system. "This is Captain Robert Goodson again, folks, sorry for the interruption. I just wanted to let you know that we've identified a slight mechanical issue with the plane, and we'll be making an emergency landing in Chicago. Don't worry, it's nothing dangerous or life-threatening," he clarified as a loud murmur rose up from the cabin of the plane. "We just want to err on the conservative side. Naturally, the safety of our passengers is our primary concern."

Hearing the title "Captain" momentarily sent Leah's heart into a tailspin, but she made a fast recovery. She sighed and gulped down the remainder of the soda she'd been served by the flight attendant. For a second, she tried to picture her mother in the flight attendant's place.

Nope, that just isn't happening. My mom was meant to be a music teacher in tiny Wahoo, Nebraska. There's no doubt about it.

About fifteen minutes later, Leah felt the plane descend into Chicago. She hadn't been to O'Hare for a very long time, but she'd always enjoyed visiting the Metropolis of the Midwest. She wondered if she'd have any issues getting a connecting flight back to Philadelphia or Charlotte, the two hubs that served the regional airport in Salisbury, Maryland, or if they'd just give them a new plane, and they'd be on their way to Philadelphia again.

Ordinarily, she would be flustered by having plans deviate from her agenda, but a peace enveloped her. *What doesn't kill me makes me stronger,* she repeated, a mantra that had served her well in the past few weeks.

●○◦

An hour later, Leah finally found herself next in line at the airline counter. The staff member wore a navy cardigan and a red and navy-striped ascot at her neck. Her hair was pulled back into a severe bun, and her glossy red nails sounded like machine gunfire as they punched away at the keyboard searching for flights. She kept scrunching up her nose as if a foul odor had permeated the space around the counter.

Finally, she stopped typing and looked up to address Leah. "Well, I can't get you into Philly or Charlotte today, but I can tomorrow. Since it was a mechanical problem with the plane, we will put you up in a hotel tonight."

As tempting as it sounded to have a free night in Chicago, Leah knew she needed to get back to The Pearl for an important meeting in the morning with the contractors who would be redesigning their lobby area that winter. "There's nothing available at all today to get me into Salisbury?"

"Not into Salisbury," the lady responded and resumed her furious typing. After a moment, she smiled as if she'd just found the key to a locked door. "I can get you into Baltimore late this afternoon, though. Is that close enough?"

"BWI?" Leah asked. The lady nodded.

I could rent a car and drive to Ocean City, I guess. "Okay," she agreed, deciding quickly. "That will work."

She headed toward the gate to board the flight to Baltimore, feeling relieved that everything was going to work out. *See, things are fine after all!* A man passing her in the corridor thought her smile was intended for him and smiled back.

Leah's cheeks flushed a little with embarrassment once she processed how handsome the passerby was. She remembered promising her mother that she would join the Christian dating site where her friend Janet's son met his wife. *I guess I have nothing to lose.*

She had a little time before her flight, so she opened up her laptop, connected to the wi-fi and pulled up the dating site. She quickly scanned the homepage, then created a minimal profile. *I'll upload pictures later.*

She bought herself a coffee from a nearby stand and did a little mental toast. *Here's to getting back out there,* she sighed.

Soon she was boarding the plane with Zone 4 and stuffing her carry-on luggage in the nearest overhead compartment. She identified her seat and noticed there was a woman in it. "Oh, I think that's my seat," she said apologetically.

"Oh," the woman replied, glancing down at her boarding pass. "I thought I had the window seat this time." She studied the pass again. "Yeah, you're right. I'll trade you. I'm sorry."

"You can stay by the window; it's no problem. I'll just take the aisle seat."

"Are you sure?" the woman asked. She had short blonde highlighted hair, tan skin and brown eyes popping out from heavy black eyeliner. She wore jeans, a black shirt and black high-heeled boots that came up to her knees.

It's a little warm for those boots, Leah thought, taking her seat. They reminded her of her own tall black leather boots that seemed to be part of the requisite swinger uniform. Almost every woman she knew in the lifestyle owned a pair. It made her wonder if the woman who took the window seat was also a swinger.

"Do you live in Baltimore?" the lady struck up a conversation with her while the flight attendant was going through the safety instructions.

"No, I live out on the Eastern Shore, in Ocean City," Leah answered. "How about yourself?"

"I live in Frederick; it's about an hour west of the city. You know, I used to live in Ocean City. My ex still lives there, in fact," she revealed.

"Oh," Leah answered. "Did you like it out there?"

The lady nodded. "Yeah, I miss the beach sometimes. I'm from Pennsylvania originally."

"You and half the population of the Eastern Shore!" Leah laughed. "I'm from Nebraska myself. Gosh, I don't hardly know anyone who is *actually* from OC."

Except for Cap, she thought, though she didn't want to.

"My ex was from there originally. He comes from a long line of fishermen," she shared.

Leah had to forcibly pry her heart from her throat, and she couldn't control the way her mouth gaped open at her seatmate's revelation. She breathed deeply just as the lady was beginning to look concerned about Leah's mental faculties.

There are lots of fishermen in Ocean City, she reminded herself.

"Yeah, my younger daughter keeps telling me when she

graduates from college she wants to go live with her dad at the beach. She spends quite a bit of time there in the summer, but I remind her all the time, 'Now, Emma, you know it's a ghost town in the winter. You'd be bored and miserable!'"

Cap's younger daughter is named Emma, her brain screamed at her. She really could not formulate any words.

"So what do you do out there?" the woman asked.

By this time, they were airborne, ascending to their cruising altitude. Leah felt like her heart was beating as fast as the plane was flying.

"I work at a hotel," she managed. She gulped another huge breath of air into her lungs and remembered what her mother said about her facing challenges head on. "Um, this is going to sound really strange, but is your name Sharon, by any chance?"

The woman's heavily-lined eyes grew into wide circles. "How did you know that?"

"I know your ex-husband. Chris Sheldon, right?" Leah asked. *What the heck are the chances that this could be happening right now? And now that I've opened this can of worms, what do I do?*

"Well, well, well. Small world, isn't it?" She smiled.

Now the swinger boots totally make sense, Leah thought. She had been part of the lifestyle with Cap years ago. Maybe she was still involved.

"Do you know him well?" she asked after a moment of silence had forged an awkward space between them.

"Pretty well," Leah answered vaguely.

"Emma is there with him right now. Have you met her?"

Leah nodded. "I met her and Ashton both a few months

ago. Really lovely young women. A credit to you both as parents."

"That's sweet, thank you," Sharon replied. "Emma says Cap has been really busy with charters, and she's hardly seen him. She's been a little worried about him, though. She said he's depressed because his girlfriend left him."

And now, now her nerves were like miniature bombs detonating inside her body. "I'm sorry to hear that," Leah replied, trying to maintain her neutral appearance but fighting every single synapse's urge to bellow out she was the girlfriend.

"Did you know his girlfriend too?" Sharon inquired. "How do you know him?"

Ordinarily, Leah appreciated people who cut to the chase. It was one of the qualities she loved most about Aimee. But to hear it from a complete stranger in such a delicate situation was intensely overwhelming. And, naturally, it happened to be a complete stranger who was her ex-boyfriend's ex-wife—someone she was trapped next to on a plane for at least the next hour and a half.

"I'm the ex-girlfriend," Leah revealed solemnly, wincing from the pain it caused her to admit it. She remembered her earlier promise to herself, to quit trying to be someone she wasn't just to make people happy. In the past, she might have lied about her identity to spare the feelings of this complete stranger. She hated to make people uncomfortable.

"Wow, well, I don't even know what to say." Sharon laughed. "Emma didn't know why you two broke up. Cap wouldn't tell her, apparently."

Leah took a deep breath. "It's a pretty long story," she said dismissively, as though it was completely uninteresting.

"Well, we have a pretty long flight ahead of us," Sharon

replied, looking eager to devour some juicy gossip. "My daughter was pretty bummed about the breakup too, for the record. She said you were pretty and nice, and she thought you were good for her dad."

Leah hesitated. *Why in the world would I share details of my personal life with his ex-wife, let alone a complete stranger?*

But part of her, the less mature part that would have been really thrilled to feel just an ounce of vindication, pressed onward.

"Well," she began, "I found out not too long ago that Cap was just using me for the business he and his friend were starting."

"Oh, you mean Casey?" Sharon asked, clearly much more aware of her ex-husband's life than Leah expected.

She nodded, still stunned that this conversation was actually happening. "Casey's friend Rhonda spoke with Cap at a party we all attended a while back, and he told her he wanted to get me interested in and comfortable with the lifestyle so I'd agree to manage the club they were opening."

Whoa, did that just come out of my mouth? She wished she could shove all the words she'd just spewed back down her throat.

"Casey told me she really believes Rhonda is telling the truth. Then she told me some pretty horrible stuff that Cap did to you," Leah finished.

"Like what?" Sharon asked, intrigued. She seemed personally removed from the situation, as if she were watching a soap opera drama unfold, and she was anxious to see how it would end.

Leah stared at her for a moment. *She has to know what I'm talking about. Maybe she just wants to hear me say it, to prove that I know.*

"Well," Leah cleared her throat as if that would help her choose her words more carefully, "Casey told me that when your daughters were little, Cap used to work in Florida during the winter, and he had another family down there."

She never expected Sharon to burst into laughter. "Casey told you that?" Her body was shaking with amusement. "That's not what happened at all," she finally said.

"It's not?" Leah asked. "What do you mean? Casey told me you told her yourself."

"I thought that was what was going on for a while. I found some bills that came to our home in OC. I did some investigating, and I did learn that Cap had a family living with him, a young Cuban woman named Maria and her little boy. I thought it was his kid. He kept denying it, said it was his friend's housekeeper's daughter and her son that he was helping out, letting them live with him, and he was providing for them. He promised me he wasn't sleeping with her, but, of course, I didn't believe it."

"I still don't get it. You divorced him anyway?" Leah asked.

"The truth was, when he was away in Florida, I was having my own affair with a man in Baltimore. He'd come over to OC every weekend because he had a beach house there. And once I thought Cap was cheating, it was an easy way to divorce him, and I wouldn't have to be the bad guy. I know, stupid and immature, but I was like, what, your age when that happened? What did I know?" She shrugged nonchalantly.

"So when did you find out that he was telling the truth?" The bombs exploding inside her were getting bigger, more destructive.

"A couple of months before the divorce was final. I'd already moved to Baltimore, but I'd taken the girls over to

OC to see their dad one weekend. His buddy from Florida was up visiting, and he told me himself. Said the girl had since gotten married to some guy she met. Cap was still sending her money for her son, though."

"Wow," was all Leah could manage to respond. "Casey was so sure that was what had happened. She'd barely forgiven him herself!"

"I had lost touch with Casey and all our other lifestyle friends on the Eastern Shore by then. And I wasn't really a fan of admitting I was wrong so...I never set the record straight," Sharon explained. "I guess I figured, after so long, it didn't really matter anymore."

And it doesn't change what Cap did to me.

"Well, in any case, he was still using me for his business. Rhonda told Casey everything," Leah shared. She almost felt like she had known Sharon forever by this point. Their conversation seemed like the most natural, ordinary thing in the world.

"Rhonda? Oh god, she's a bitch, Leah. A royal bitch. Trust me on this," Sharon claimed. "Look, the whole time Cap and I were in the lifestyle together, Rhonda did everything in her power to stir up drama and try to tear us apart. She always wanted Cap for herself. You shouldn't believe a goddamn word that cunt says."

Leah's eyes bugged out at the C word, which most women only reserved for the lowest of the low. She gave her heart a moment to stop galloping in her chest and her mind a moment to lay out all of the new information, reconciling it with the old.

"So, what you're saying is, there's a chance he was honest with me the whole time?"

Sharon shrugged. "It's possible. You never know what's going on behind those vicious dimples and big blue eyes," she laughed, "but I can definitely dispel what Casey told you, and I can certainly advise you not to trust anything that comes out of that bitch Rhonda's mouth."

Leah's brain was working so hard at processing everything that she could barely get her legs to function when it came time to walk to the rental counter and request a car to drive to Ocean City. She said goodbye to Sharon at the gate and thanked her for their serendipitous meeting.

Her father always told her that God brought the right people into your life when they were needed. She had a feeling there was a divine hand in so much of what had just transpired, from the mechanical failure of the plane and emergency landing in Chicago, to there not being any flights to Philly or Charlotte, to the seat assignment next to Sharon, to every strand of conversation that led up to the discovery of their mutual interest in Chris Sheldon.

If one thing had happened differently, she realized, *the truth may have never come out. The Lord works in funny ways. Funny, crazy, miraculous, completely unbelievable ways.*

THIRTY-ONE

The drive down the peninsula on Route 50 that late Tuesday summer afternoon was pleasant and green with neat rows of corn rising up from the fields, and yellow and fuchsia wildflowers dotting the embankments along the way. Leah used the two-hour drive to think about how she should handle what she had learned about Cap.

Leah was glad to make it back to Ocean City before the boarder closed up for the night. She couldn't imagine any creature more excited to see her than Glory. Her tail was wagging so wildly, Leah thought it might propel the little dog into the air. Her white muzzle looked like it was stretching her mouth into a huge grin. And then there was her tongue, floppy and wet, coating every reachable inch of Leah's skin with slobbery welcome home kisses.

"Alright, girl, alright. Yes, I'm happy to see you too! Let's go home!"

She unpacked and cleaned out the rental car so she could return it in the morning. When she looked up the return location, she realized it was next to Casey's real estate office.

I guess I could drop in and see if Casey's around. Maybe she would drive me back to work. She had barely spoken to Casey since everything had happened with Cap.

The next morning she drove the rental car across town. She parked, dropped off the keys and came out of the building, spying Casey's car in the lot outside her office.

She poked her head in, and the receptionist said Casey was in her office preparing to leave for a showing. Leah made her way down the hallway, remembering the last time she'd been there and the nausea she'd lost a battle to in the women's restroom.

"Leah!" Casey exclaimed as soon as she saw her cross the threshold. "It's so good to see you, darling!" She rose and embraced her, patting her back vigorously.

"What brings you up this way?" Although it was hot outside, Casey looked as cool as a cucumber in a striped sundress and matching cardigan the color of a honeydew. Her copper-colored hair was swept up into a tortoiseshell clip.

"I had to return my rental car next door, and I'm looking for a ride back to The Pearl. I know you have a showing, just wondered if it would be too much trouble to drop me off on your way?" Leah asked.

"Oh, of course! I am headed to Ocean Pines, actually, but I have enough time to drop you off if we leave right now." She grabbed her fashionable salmon-colored clutch and plastic clipboard off her desk, then ushered Leah back down the hallway and out into the parking lot.

"So why the rental car?" she asked as they climbed into her sleek black sedan. "Something happen to your Jeep?"

"No, not at all. I was in Nebraska for my brother's

wedding, and my flights got all screwed up. I had to fly into BWI and drive over to the shore yesterday afternoon," Leah explained, her heart thumping with the looming decision of whether or not to tell Casey about meeting Sharon.

"Well, I'm certainly sorry to hear that, but I'm glad you made it back in one piece." Casey pulled out onto Coastal Highway and headed south toward The Pearl.

"I need to tell you something," Leah advised after they'd passed through one intersection.

"What's that?" Casey's eyes never left the road.

"I met Cap's ex-wife on the plane yesterday," Leah shared.

Casey slammed on the brakes and came to a screeching halt at the next stoplight. "Are you kidding me?"

"Um, no," Leah replied. "I wouldn't kid about something like this. It was definitely a surreal experience. I was sitting next to her, and we started chatting, and it became clear once she mentioned her ex-husband was from the OC area and was a fisherman, and they have a daughter named Emma. I was absolutely floored."

"That's completely crazy!" Casey cried, shaking her head in disbelief.

"Yeah, and Casey," her voice quieted, "she told me she was wrong about Cap and the other family thing."

"What do you mean? She told me she saw the bills, and he confessed to having a woman and child living with him. She said the child was his."

"Apparently it was a woman and her son, and he was helping them get on their feet. They weren't together, and the kid wasn't his. Sharon found out a few months before the divorce was final, but by that time, they'd both moved on. She'd was already living in Baltimore and lost touch with most of her friends in OC. She never told anyone what really happened," Leah explained.

"Well, I don't even know what to say," Casey gasped.

"There's more," Leah continued.

By this time Casey had pulled into the parking lot of The Pearl. She shifted into park and turned to Leah, giving her full attention with wide, anxious eyes.

Leah took a breath before sharing the last juicy tidbit. "Sharon told me not to trust anything that Rhonda says. She said Rhonda made every attempt to cause drama and break them up way back in the day, and she was positive nothing has changed."

"I don't understand why she would make up what Cap said, though," Casey answered, shaking her head in bewilderment.

"I'm sure she prefers that Cap stays single," Leah conjectured. "I took him out of the lifestyle. She can't sleep with him anymore. I think that's motive, don't you?"

"But she wanted to work for you," Casey argued. "I just don't get it."

Leah stared at the entrance to the lobby, knowing she only had a few minutes to get to her meeting. Her brain hurt from trying to unravel all the truth from the lies, to understand the motives behind what was said and done. "Maybe she wants to work for you and Cap, not for me."

"Well, I'm afraid it's a moot point now," Casey sighed.

"What do you mean?"

"Cap is selling the warehouse. He goes to sign all the papers tomorrow," she stated.

"What? Why would he do that?" Leah's nerves became agitated by the adrenaline that instantly shot through her body upon hearing the news. "Why would you let him do that? This was his dream. It was your dream!"

She was stunned that he would give up The Factory just because she'd walked away. *There are other people who could do that job. I'm not irreplaceable.*

Casey shook her head again, but this time with regret. "We got into a pretty big fight after everything went down last month. He insisted Rhonda made it all up, and Rhonda called him a liar to his face. I was there for the whole thing. It wasn't pretty. And I just assumed because he didn't go after you...I assumed there must be something to what Rhonda claimed."

"So let me get this straight," Leah said. "This whole deal blew up because of me? Who cares about me? Anyone could run that place with a little experience or training. You two shouldn't destroy your dream just because of me. It's *really* not necessary."

In her mind, Casey's observation about Cap not chasing after her stung, sending a stabbing pain through the old wounds she thought had scabbed over.

Casey's face was gripped by sadness and confusion. "I don't know what to say. I'm pretty disappointed that everything blew up, but I think Cap has made up his mind. Honestly, I think he could only imagine you running the club, and if you're not going to, he doesn't want to do it anymore."

"Why didn't you tell me this was happening?" Leah questioned, wondering if all the misunderstandings could have been prevented.

"I didn't think you wanted to be involved. I thought you wanted to move on. That day you walked out of my office you acted like you needed to be alone, to put all this behind you. You barely answered my texts, and to tell you the truth, I didn't even know if I would see you again. I thought you were done with me too," Casey admitted. "I wanted to help you, Leah. I have always admired you so much and considered you a friend, even more than a business associate."

Leah knew she was running late for her meeting now, but she couldn't bring herself to get out of Casey's car. Her entire world had just been turned upside down. Again. As much as everything had been jumbled and broken a month ago when Mary showed up in her office, now things were just as chaotic and confusing.

"I'm sorry, Casey. I never meant to hurt your feelings or reject your friendship. I just needed to step away from Cap and everything that reminded me of the world I'd shared with him. You were part of that world too. But you're right, you have always been a wonderful friend to me, and I would like to think our friendship transcends all of that other stuff."

"It makes me really happy to hear you say that!" Casey gushed, throwing her arms around Leah even in the cramped cabin of the car. When she pulled away, she looked solemn again. "But what are we going to do about Cap?"

"What do you mean? There's nothing I can do about him now." She shrugged and began to open the car door.

"I think you may be right about Rhonda," Casey offered. "And if what you said Sharon told you is true, then don't you think you should talk to him? Tell him what you heard was wrong? And maybe you should tell him he shouldn't sell the warehouse?"

"I told him not to contact me again. I really doubt he wants to hear from me." She imagined seeing Cap so hurt and angry that his eyes looked like ice and his dimples stayed hidden. She didn't know if she could handle seeing him like that.

What if he's been the innocent victim in this all along?

He won't want to take me back. And if I caused all this just because some stupid bitch tried to stir up drama, I don't deserve him, anyway.

"I think you should at least try, Leah. He's going to regret giving up the club, and I don't think he'd listen to me if I told him not to go through with it. But he would listen to you. And I'm not just saying that because it's in my best interests to open the club. I just think there's still a chance for a happy ending for all of us," Casey beamed through leftover tears.

Leah shook her head. "I don't think there's any chance of us repairing our relationship. The best we can hope for is forgiveness and closure at this point. But, okay, I'll try. If he really didn't say what Rhonda claimed, then I do owe him an apology. I'll text him later today. I'm sure he's out on the water right now, anyway."

"True, it's sort of hard to catch him right now. From what I understand, he's been doing three charters a day. He's barely been home at all," Casey said.

"I'll try. There's no guarantee he'll even talk to me."

"Trying is all I'm asking for," Casey assured her. She gave Leah another hug and watched her walk through the lobby of The Pearl.

●●●

I t took Leah a while to catch Aimee up on everything that had happened during the last twenty-four hours since leaving Nebraska. "So I'm going to text him this afternoon," Leah confessed. "I can't believe I'm the one who's going to contact him. I always thought it would be the other way around—if it happened at all."

Leah could hear Natalie babbling in the background.

It's hard to believe such a tiny human can create so much noise.

She looked at the clock. *Almost noon. Cap will be coming in from his morning charter, dropping off one crew and picking up the next for the afternoon trip. He'll probably check his phone.*

Her whole body was buzzing with a mixture of anticipation, anxiousness and dread. "I'm afraid he won't text me back. And even if he does, I really need to talk to him in person. He's not going to have time to see me before he goes to sign the papers tomorrow."

"Is his evening charter full?" Aimee questioned.

"What difference does that make?" Leah asked.

"I have an idea!" Aimee explained. "A perfect idea!"

●·●

When Leah called to reserve her space, she asked if anyone else was signed up for the charter. The teenage girl on the other end of the phone flipped some pages in a book and then put Leah on hold.

Oh, great. I hope she doesn't put him on the phone!

She heard the phone line come alive again. She was relieved to hear the girly, high-pitched voice say, "We did have four others, but they actually just called a few minutes ago and rescheduled for tomorrow. There's a storm coming, and Captain Sheldon doesn't know if he'll get the whole trip in tonight."

"Oh," Leah said, happy to hear there was no one else but not that a storm might mess up her surprise. "So what do I do?"

"Well, come on down to the shop about fifteen minutes before departure, and we'll check the radar. If it looks bad, we can reschedule, just do a shorter trip, or whatever you prefer, depending on the weather," she advised.

"Okay, that sounds reasonable. Thanks a lot. Oh! One more question. Can I bring my dog?"

"Since no one else is going tonight, that should be okay. Captain Sheldon usually takes his dog on the smaller charters, though, so if your dog might have an issue with that, you probably want to leave him at home."

"Oh, I think she'll be just fine with his dog!" Leah laughed. She thanked the girl again and hung up.

Everything's falling into place. Who would have thought I'd be thinking that? Maybe this is more divine intervention, just like yesterday.

The clock crawled like a turtle as the hour hand approached 5 PM. Leah had abandoned any hope of concentrating on work. She'd updated Aimee via text several times, and she'd also given Casey a heads-up. Casey's excitement was evident in her response: *YOU GO GIRL!!!*

Finally, it came time to shut down her computer, lock her office door and head down to the lobby. She would have to walk to her apartment to get Glory and her Jeep since she had returned the rental car that morning.

The sun was starting to make its descent toward the west, but low on the horizon was a dark mass of clouds. She wondered if that was the impending storm and if it would ruin her plans. *Really, God?* she asked incredulously, looking at the sky. *Surely You didn't bring me this far just to have everything fall apart again. I don't know how much more emotional turmoil my heart can take!*

She nearly jogged the three blocks to her apartment, hooked Glory to her leash and rushed to the Jeep. As she zoomed down Coastal Highway, her body began to throb with nervousness. Down at the southern end of the strip, the sun was still bright in the sky, and she could smell the salt water as soon as she climbed out of the Jeep.

She walked up the wooden steps to Cap's shop and immediately heard Keeper let out a single, ear-piercing bark. She wasn't surprised that the chocolate Lab was standing just inside the door, recognizing the approaching scent and poised to maul Glory with affection for old time's sake.

Glory was just as excited to see her old friend, and the two spent a moment celebrating their reunion by wagging their tails and sniffing each other's behinds. Leah let Glory off her leash and passed down an aisle full of artificial lures and hooks toward the office at the back.

The teenage girl at the counter was none other than Emma, Cap's daughter, who recognized Leah immediately. Leah put her fingertip to her lips and whispered, "Shhh!" before Emma could react. The young lady's face exploded with color and hope. "I want it to be a surprise," Leah explained softly.

Meanwhile, she had lost track of Glory. She and Keeper had wandered down an aisle with sunscreen, hats and gloves, and snacks, then turned up the back wall toward Cap's office. Leah heard Cap's deep baritone voice pierce the silence with a whoop and then a holler: "Glory, glory, hallelujah, how the hell are you, girl?!!"

As soon as it sank in that Glory meant Leah too, he came rushing out of his office toward the counter. Leah watched him, his skin so tan that his eyes glowed like blue flames. His hair was bleached out, his beard trimmed down low and nearly white from the sun. The dimples were so deep and pronounced, his cheeks looked like they had two holes punched on either side of his huge grin.

He stared at her for a moment, saying nothing, basking in awe that she was standing there in his shop. He glanced at Emma, who smiled shyly and excused herself to the back room to give her father some privacy.

"I really hope we can catch up," he finally said, seeming as if he still didn't quite know how to react. "But I have a charter leaving in a few minutes. I know there's a storm coming, but I think if we take off on time, we'll be able to get an hour or two out on the water."

"I'm the charter, Cap," Leah revealed with a soft giggle. "It's me." She smiled and waited for his reaction.

"Oh!" he exclaimed, obviously surprised. "I...I don't even know what to say." He raked his fingers through his wind-ravaged hair. "I can't believe you're standing here in my shop."

His eyes washed over her, from her honey-colored ponytail to her crisp white sleeveless blouse to the pink and white gingham capri pants hugging her curves. "You look really good, Leah."

"We need to talk, Cap," she said soberly, not wanting him to get ahead of himself. And not wanting to get ahead of herself either. She was surprised he was happy to see her. There was no trace of bitterness in his voice or across his face, just slight bewilderment.

"So you want to go out on the boat...or not?" he asked, still unsure what her agenda might be.

"I do," Leah answered. "To talk. Not to fish." She cleared her throat, trying to muster up the strength to say what she wanted to say.

Ten minutes later they were loading the dogs onto Cap's boat and drifting out into the bay. The late afternoon sun sparkled on the water like diamonds, even though to the south, a thick band of dark clouds approached.

"Are we going to be okay weather-wise?"

Cap looked toward the south, then the west, and nodded. "The radar indicates it'll go about twenty miles south of us. Water's gonna be choppy, though, so we aren't going too far out."

As many times as she'd tried to imagine Cap in his natural environment or accompanying him out on the boat, she would have never guessed it would happen under these circumstances.

When they were several hundred yards out from shore, he turned around from his captain's chair and simply asked, "What's up?" as if he couldn't stand the suspense any longer.

"You're not really selling the warehouse tomorrow, are you?" were the words she chose to open with.

He didn't seem surprised that she knew. *Small town and all that.*

"That's the plan," he answered without hesitation. "Don't see any reason not to, and I'm getting a pretty fair price considering that it's half remodeled for a swing club." There was no resentment in his response. He smiled as if he had long since severed his ties with his former dream.

"I don't understand why you changed your mind," Leah admitted. "I hope it's not because of me."

Cap stood up and moved toward her. The dogs sat up at the bow of the boat peering over the edge. He saw her watching Glory with concern. "Don't worry, Keeper never jumps in. They'll be okay."

She stood and called Glory back to her side anyway. The beagle looked disappointed but obeyed. "You didn't answer my question," she protested, looking back into his eyes.

"You didn't ask one," he retorted, looking back at the water, avoiding her eyes.

"So we can't talk about this?" Frustration was starting to warm her cheeks.

Maybe this is a mistake, me coming here and blindsiding him like this. Maybe he doesn't want to rehash the past. He's over it.

"I can't for the life of me understand why you believed what Rhonda and Casey said about me." He shrugged as if it had long since stopped hurting, then he turned back to the wheel. He steered them toward a little island perched in the bay with low scraggly shrubs and orange-tinted sand.

Leah's throat closed up, preventing any sound from escaping. Cap continued to steer with his back toward her.

"And you didn't even ask me what really happened," he continued. "You've never trusted me, Leah."

"You didn't come after me," she finally said, the wounds breaking open, oozing fresh blood.

"I tried to contact you," he argued. "You wouldn't talk to me. You told me not to call anymore."

"When you didn't show up at my doorstep, like you had every other time we'd had a disagreement, I thought it was because you knew I'd found out you were using me all along. And you weren't denying it."

Those words sent him flying off the chair and to her side, suddenly enraged. Even in the dimming light, she saw the veins popping out in his neck and temple. It was taking every ounce of restraint he had not to yell at her.

Instead of screaming, his voice came out a hoarse whisper, as if it was the only compromise he could make. "How do you think I could lie next to you every night for months, plan our future together, ask you to move in with me, give up the lifestyle I loved, totally devote myself to you...if I didn't love you, Leah? Do you really think I'm that great of an actor? Do you really think I can fake my attraction to you, my connection with you, my desire to make you happy in every single goddamn thing I do?"

Besides being dumb, she was also frozen. He stared at her, his face gripped with the pain they thought they'd both conquered, piercing into him with a brand-new blade. He stared at her expectantly as his wounded heart bled, daring her to answer the questions he'd posed through clenched teeth.

She felt his passion and fire evaporating from his body. And she knew beyond a shadow of a doubt it was not something that could be fabricated. Her heart pounded irrationally, distracting her mind from being able to verbalize her thoughts.

I have to say something. I have to make him believe that I trust him.

But she couldn't make her vocal cords work. All the emotion inside her welled up like a fountain and sent her sprawling forward into his arms. She slammed against his chest, her cheeks absorbing his sweat, the musky scent of him filling her nose. Her body convulsed with the onslaught of tears, weeping like a thunderstorm in his arms that slowly encircled her.

His lips brushed against her forehead, and his entire body softened with relief. She felt it too, the sudden feeling that she was home, where she belonged. Her larynx began to vibrate, signaling she was finally capable of producing sound. She pulled back to see the tears clinging to his cheeks.

"Oh, Cap, I'm so sorry; I'm so very sorry. I should have trusted you... I should have trusted this." She squeezed his arms as all the thoughts she'd stored away began to tumble out uncontrollably.

"I've been so confused the last few months, not knowing how I feel about the whole swinging thing, not really understanding what you see in me. Not knowing if God was going to strike me down, not knowing if my parents would ever forgive me if they found out. Not knowing if I was going to lose my job, not knowing what the future held for me.

"But there was one thing I thought I *did* know, one thing I thought I was absolutely certain of: that I loved you. When Mary came to tell me what Casey said and what Rhonda said, all of those unknowns just blew up in my face. The one sure thing I thought made up for all the unknowns suddenly didn't matter anymore if it was built on false pretenses.

"When I talked to Casey, she truly thought you might be capable of using me. She still believed you had a second family all those years ago in Florida, which, by the way, I got the story straight on that. It's a wild, completely crazy thing, but we'll talk about that later.

"I've always looked up to Casey and thought she was so wise. And with everything so uncertain for me, and all the fears about what I'd learned about myself, I thought maybe I'd just been suckered in, that I'd felt something that was never there. And then when you didn't rush in and save me; you didn't even try to convince me that your feelings were genuine, I thought Casey was right and I'd just been a naïve, lovesick fool."

"Me too," Cap interrupted. "I thought I'd been a fool to trust Rhonda, Casey, and yes, even you. I was sure there was some sort of conspiracy against me being happy, against me achieving my dreams. I always felt like you were too good to be true, Leah. And I convinced myself you were."

"So what now?" Leah asked. "What happens next?"

He looked out across the bay as the sun descended closer and closer to the water. The threatening clouds to the south had blown away, and the sky was warming up as if preparing to put on a glorious show. The dogs had moved onto the vinyl-covered benches flanking the sides of the boat. They seemed happy to be reunited and were sprawled out, gazing at each other through heavy-lidded eyes.

He pulled her back into his arms. "I love you," Cap breathed against her cheek. "I want to be with you, Leah. I'll give up swinging, and I'll give up the club. I don't care about that stuff. I just want us to be together."

She pulled back from him and studied his gleaming blue eyes. All she saw was love. Nothing more, nothing less.

If he was willing to give up swinging and the club to be with her, she knew his motives were pure. And there was that word again. *Pure: 100% one thing and 0% anything else.*

She couldn't prevent a huge grin from spanning her face, stretching her cheeks so wide they ached with joy. Seeing her smile set off a chain reaction, and soon Cap was displaying his dimples for all they were worth as he took her into his arms and held her close to his chest.

The sun had gradually melted into a fiery crimson band highlighted by streaks of orange and gold. The clouds had gathered in the eastern skies, waltzing across the Atlantic in rosy ballgowns trimmed with lavender ruffles. In between the clouds and the sinking sun, golden beams shone down glazing the gentle rolling waves of the bay with a gilded brush.

Leah imagined what she and Cap might look like from a passing boat, silhouetted against the sky's surreal canvas, lovers intertwined, the distinct boundaries of their bodies lost against the setting sun.

"You don't have to give up anything for me," Leah finally whispered into his ear. "I love you too. And I want what you want. I want to make you happy."

"You already do." He smiled, looking over her shoulder to scan the horizon. "Look at us, sailing off into the sunset. If that's not a fairytale ending, I don't know what is."

"It's a little cliché," Leah admitted, "but I'll take it."

She watched him turn the boat toward the shore, and with the movement, the dogs perked up their ears and ran to the bow again, feeling the bay breezes blow against their wet black noses.

"So you're sure you're okay with me being some old fisherman and not a fairytale prince?" he joked.

She slung her arms around his neck and leaned down, her chin perched on his shoulder. "You may not be a prince, but at least you're a captain."

"I'll take it, Sugar," he said, his dimples showing. "I'll take it."

EPILOGUE

Leah didn't deny being nervous. Six long months of work and The Factory was finally opening its doors. Everything was in place: the bar was tended, the dance floor was waxed, the lights were adjusted, and the private rooms were comfortable and ready for play. The security guards had been well trained and were at their stations. She and Casey had generated as much buzz as possible about the grand opening over the past few weeks. Now she and Cap were just waiting in the office until the doors opened at 7 PM on the nose.

"It's nice that we have a few moments alone before it gets crazy in here," she commented, scooting her desk chair back and moving to where Cap stood fidgeting with something in his pocket. "Are you okay? Did we forget something?"

He glanced down at her and smiled, giving her a brief flash of the legendary dimples. "I think this is the most well-planned grand opening in the history of swing clubs." He laughed and stroked a finger down her cheek. "I can't imagine that we forgot even one trivial detail."

"Good!" Leah exclaimed. "I want it to be perfect."

Suddenly, he fell to one knee. At first she was concerned. *Is he hurt? Did he drop something?*

And then the realization of what was happening washed over her. Her body began to tremble before even one word passed his lips.

"You, my dear, are perfect. From the moment I met you, I have wanted more and more of you. When I thought I lost you, I was devastated. I had lost a treasure. I believe God brought us back together; how else could everything have fallen into place like it did? And you know what? Even after a year, I still want more of you. I want you to be my wife. Leah Elizabeth Miller, will you marry me?"

She didn't want to mess her eye makeup with tears, but the more he said, the less of a choice she had. Looking down at him on one knee, opening a small hinged box that held a huge diamond perched on top of a platinum ring, she could do nothing but nod and cry.

He plucked the ring from its velvet nest and slipped it onto her finger, then jumped to his feet. He threw his arms around her, picked her up and swirled her around in a circle, her heel-clad feet flying off the ground. He set her back down on the floor, and she witnessed a wave of confusion crash onto his face.

"What's wrong now?" she asked, only half-exasperated.

"So that was a yes, right?" he clarified.

"Oh my gosh!" The tears were already drying on her cheeks, which were spread into a wide grin. "Of course! YES! YES! YES!"

The door burst open, and camera flashes began blinding them. He pulled her into an embrace and pressed his lips against hers. When he finally released her, he spun her toward the door, and there was Aimee and Anthony, Casey,

Mary and her husband, Cap's daughters Emma and Ashton (who were only slightly freaked out when they were told about the club), and all of their lifestyle friends with cameras and champagne. Noticeably absent was Rhonda, who had been effectively banished by the group once word circulated about the havoc she had wreaked.

"We open in an hour," Casey announced. "But first, we celebrate an engagement!"

There was a collective whoop that arose from the crowd. Leah stumbled into the hallway, where she was kissed and hugged by dozens of people. She was completely overwhelmed by the outpouring of love and joy, not to mention shock that someone had actually managed to surprise her.

She worked her way through the crowd and toward the bar, where a huge sheet cake took up a significant area. The sides were embellished with beautiful marzipan starfish and shells, and on top was written in flowing script: "Congratulations Cap & Leah!" There was a tiny couple in a tiny boat sailing off into a frosted sunset.

After the crowd began to disperse and mingle as Casey served up the cake, Cap pulled Leah into the little hallway on the other side of the bar and pushed her up against the wall, pressing his large frame into her body. The lighting was too dim to make out his facial expressions, but it heightened all of her other senses. She smelled his familiar, musky cologne and heard his breaths falling against her face and chest as he trailed his fingers down her cheek.

"I know you hate surprises," he apologized.

She clasped her hands around his neck and felt the new sensation of the hard, cool diamond pressing into her skin. "I do hate surprises," she agreed. "I'm sorry I'm not very good at this fairy tale stuff sometimes."

"That's okay. I'm pretty sure there aren't any fairy tales about swinger clubs, anyway," Cap observed.

She giggled. "Maybe there should be!" He couldn't see in the low lighting, but her eyes were glinting like gemstones.

"Well, there's a swing club in ours!" He grinned. "And I'm pretty sure lots of dreams are gonna come true in this place."

She pulled him in close to her again. Just before she pressed her lips against his, she hesitated for a moment, long enough to whisper, "I know *my* dream has come true."

"Mine too, Sugar," he agreed, claiming her lips with his own. "Mine too."

THE END

The Eastern Shore Swingers series continues in Book 2, books2read.com/TheCatchESS2 where we meet new characters Paisley Parker and Calvin Mitchell.

Join Phoebe's newsletter here:
bit.ly/PhoebeAlexanderNews
Join her Facebook reader group here: www.facebook.com/groups/PhoebesAngels

ABOUT THE AUTHOR

USA Today Bestselling Author Phoebe Alexander writes romance about characters like her: with extra curves and life experience. Her stories often include themes of ethical nomonogamy, such as polyamory. She believes love is love, and everyone deserves a happily ever after, no matter your size, shape, age, or color.

Phoebe lives near the beach on the East Coast with her husband and multiple fur babies. When she's not writing, she works as an editor and consultant for indie authors. She also volunteers to run a 6000-member indie author support group.

Phoebe enjoys hanging out with her three adult sons, as well as travel, Broadway musicals, dark chocolate, swimming, hiking, college basketball, and making Seinfeld references whenever possible, especially in her books. Her single greatest fantasy is just having some free time. Join her newsletter for bodypositive memes and plenty of dog pics!

facebook.com/phoebealexanderauthor

instagram.com/authorphoebealexander

bookbub.com/authors/phoebe-alexander

tiktok.com/@authorphoebealexander

threads.net/@authorphoebealexander

amazon.com/stores/author/B00ANN43WK

Mountains Trilogy

Mountains Wanted

Mountains Climbed

Mountains Loved

Christmas in the Mountains

The Navigator

The Explorer

The Adventurer

Mountains Transcended

Eastern Shore Swingers Series

Fisher of Men

The Catch

Siren Call

Sailors Knot

Turning the Tide

Spicetopia Series

Sugar & Spice

Virtue & Vice

Fire & Ice

Naughty & Nice

Dares & Dice

Loyalty & Lies (crossover with Eastern Shore Swingers Series)

Penny & Pryce

Alpha Bet Guys Series

A Hole

The Big O

Need the D

Hard F

Ride the C

Spice Up Our Marriage Series

The Playground

Project Paradise

Rule Breaker

Keeping Secrets

Polyam Fam Series

The Scottish Play

Break a Leg

Stealing the Show

Standalones

Authority Issues

Clean Grammar for Dirty Minds